Readers love
J.S. COOK

Come to Dust

"If you have not been following this excellent series, then what are you waiting for? Go on a quest to find the first ones. You will not be disappointed."

—Sensual Reads

"…if your game is sleuthing like Sherlock in dark and sinister Victorian London, then you're gonna love this book… A real treat."

—Sinfully… Addicted to All Male Romance

The Quality of Mercy

"A great little story, packed with great reading, I highly recommend."

—MM Good Book Reviews

"A recommended period story of atonement, hurt/comfort and renewed hope, which left me with a big smile on my face."

—It's About The Book

By J.S. COOK

But Not For Me
Come to Dust
As JoAnne Soper-Cook: The Eye of Heaven
Famous Last Words
A Little Night Murder
The Lovely Beast
Oasis of Night
The Quality of Mercy
Sixteen Songs About Regret
Skid Row Serenade
The Stranger at My Door
Valley of the Dead
The Winter Dark

Published by DREAMSPINNER PRESS
http://www.dreamspinnerpress.com

SKID ROW SERENADE

J.S. COOK

Published by
DREAMSPINNER PRESS

5032 Capital Circle SW, Suite 2, PMB# 279, Tallahassee, FL 32305-7886 USA
http://www.dreamspinnerpress.com/

This is a work of fiction. Names, characters, places, and incidents either are the product of author imagination or are used fictitiously, and any resemblance to actual persons, living or dead, business establishments, events, or locales is entirely coincidental.

ISBN: 978-1-63476-098-0
Digital ISBN: 978-1-63476-099-7
Library of Congress Control Number: 2015906573
First Edition August 2015

Printed in the United States of America
∞
This paper meets the requirements of
ANSI/NISO Z39.48-1992 (Permanence of Paper).

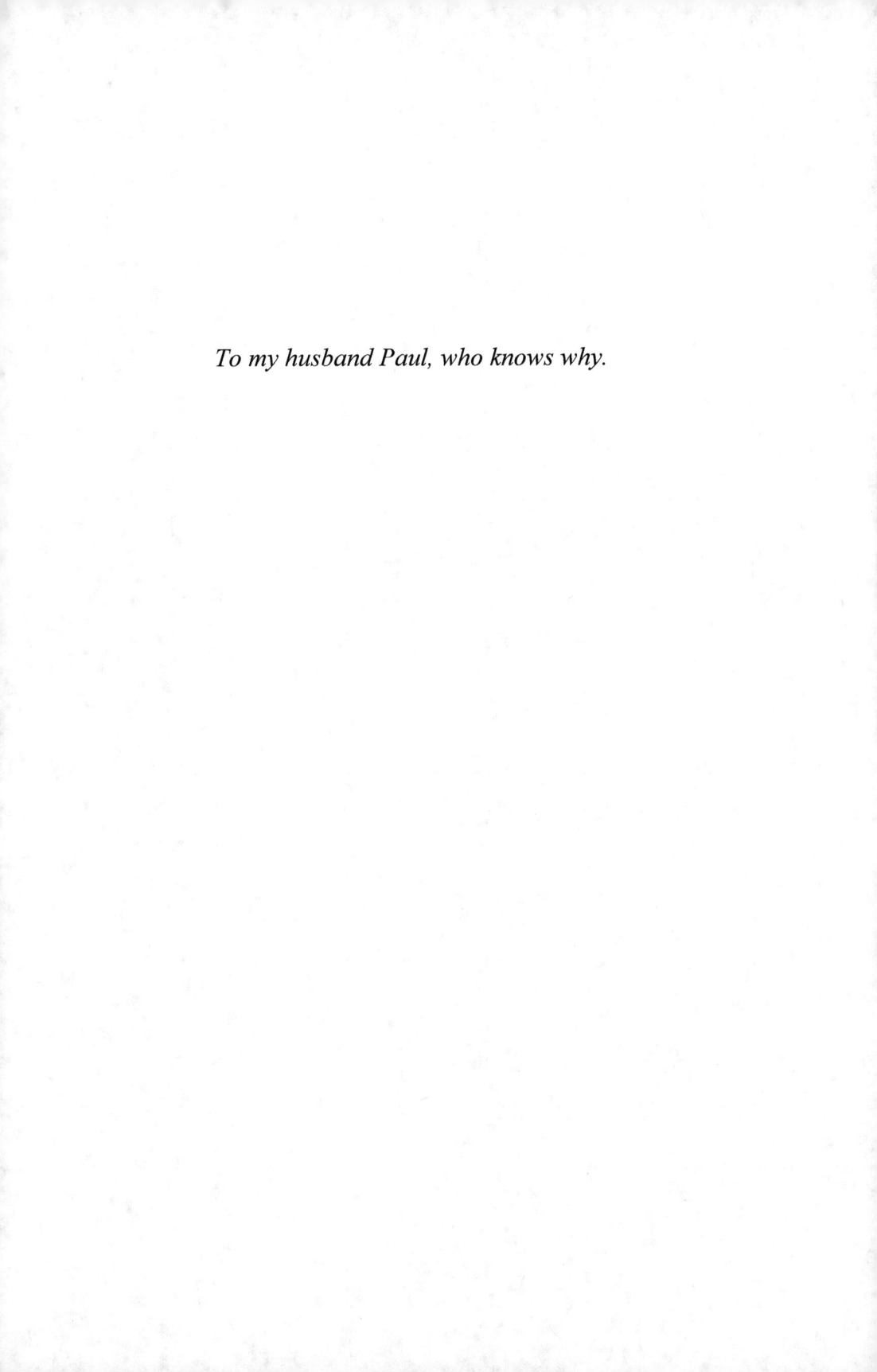

To my husband Paul, who knows why.

Acknowledgments

I would like to thank Elizabeth North, who liked this book in manuscript and said yes to it. Without Tricia Kristufek, Kelly, Lee, Victoria, Yv, and artist Aaron Anderson, there wouldn't be a book. They worked long and diligently to make this novel the best it could be. I'd be absolutely nowhere without them. Thanks to everyone at Dreamspinner Press, for everything you do. You guys are amazing.

Special thanks to Lola, who listened.

To say goodbye is to die a little.
    (Raymond Chandler, *The Long Goodbye*)

Chapter One

California: 1947

THE FIRST time I laid eyes on Ed Malory, he was being rolled by three drunks in the chapel of the seaman's mission on Fromsett Street. The first and tallest of the three held him against the wall while the other two, their hands surprisingly deft—considering—delved into his pockets and relieved him of his valuables. When they were done with him, they let go, and I watched as he slid gently down the wall. He didn't make a sound.

"Are you drunk?" Since I'd noticed all of this, the least I could do was speak to the poor bastard. "Mind you, I'm not judging if you are. I just thought you might need some help." He seemed young—I saw that immediately—almost ridiculously young and tender-looking, until you saw his eyes. Those eyes had seen plenty. I reached out a hand to help him up, and he accepted. "In a pretty bad way, aren't you?"

He sneered. "Really? What gave it away?" He was dressed in the most astonishing assortment of cast-offs—baggy tweed trousers and a pinstriped coat, a ragged shirt that had been white once, and a pair of scuffed brown wingtips. "I don't need your help." He reminded me, even then, of a medieval knight errant: bereft of luck and a long way from home, his armor much dented by the vagaries of life.

"Oh, I beg your pardon." I made a show of dusting my hands. "Happy landings, old chap. See you around." And I turned on my heel.

"Wait."

I turned back. "Yes?"

"This is a mission for drunks." He nodded at the sign over the makeshift altar at the front of the room. "What are you doing here?"

I smiled. I couldn't help it. "Surely a clever chap like you can put it all together."

He squinted at me, the sort of look I knew he'd been practicing in the mirror. "You?"

1

"Two very nice policemen brought me in after I'd fallen off a streetcar. Landed quite literally in the gutter." It was my standard line, the one I used on everybody, mostly because it worked. "But stick around. They serve a cracking good Sunday dinner here." I stuck my hand out, but he didn't take it. "Tony Leonard. Some people call me Tony Lionheart," I said, and hastened to add, "It's a joke."

He'd been sleeping rough and he smelled like it, so as soon as possible, I got us both away from there and home to my apartment. The fact that I lived in a posh flat over in Westwood amused him. He roamed about the place in his fumbling, drunken way, commenting on things and touching them, lingering jealously (I thought) in front of my books. "I thought you were a drunk."

"You thought correctly." I gave him one of my thick bathrobes and sent him to the shower. While he was gone, I kindled a fire in the fireplace and burned the clothes he'd been wearing. We weren't exactly the same size, but something of mine would do until other arrangements might be made. I found a suit of clothes, a shirt, and socks and underwear I'd bought but never worn. I laid all these out in the spare bedroom, and while I waited, I mixed a couple of martinis: three shots each of Tanqueray, a dash of bitters, the obligatory (well, from my end) sprig of rosemary because I'm so bloody superstitious and no Englishman would dream of leaving the rosemary out of a martini. I'm not exactly an Englishman, but still. I shook the whole thing over ice and was just distilling it into glasses when my knight appeared, wrapped in my white bathrobe and a becoming cloud of steam. I handed him the drink and steered him to the sofa. "Just a snifter, old thing, to keep you from falling to pieces." I raised my glass and winked at him over the rim. "Cheers."

He quaffed most of it at one go, clearly experienced in the bibulous arts, and held his glass out for another, which I readily supplied. I had no real idea why I was doing this—any of it—except he seemed to need me, or need somebody. My thoughts must have showed on my face, because he asked, "Why am I here?"

By now I'd moved back into the kitchenette and was busy shaking Tanqueray and bitters into a second drink. "Don't you remember?"

"Yes." His voice was suddenly behind me, and I turned, startled. He took the drink I handed to him. "Not what I meant, though." He sipped the martini and made some small noises of satisfaction. "I'm nothing to you. You don't even know me." He took a deeper swallow, the tightness in his face loosening its hold. "You do this sort of thing all the time?"

2

"Not usually," I lied. I tried to keep my voice level, my tone pleasant, but I could feel my control slipping. They aren't supposed to ask *why*. They're never supposed to ask why. The fact that I do it ought to be enough. *Be their savior, Tony. Be the one who drags them out of the same gutter you've been rolling in. See if that stink will wash off.* "You impressed me as a special case." I suddenly wanted him out of my apartment. This had been a mistake. *Wonderful technique you've got there, Tony,* I chided myself. *Brilliant way to go about a seduction. Is this what you've been doing all these long months, rescuing drunks until you find one good enough to fuck?*

"Why me?" He laid the empty glass down on the counter. His eyes were very, very blue—big eyes, wide and long-lashed, the kind of eyes that Innocence would have in some allegorical French painting. He wasn't as young as I'd initially suspected. He'd have to be at least thirty-five, perhaps even forty—closer to my age. "I mean, a guy your age—" He must have seen my expression, for he stopped abruptly. "That's not what I meant."

"My hair, you mean." I started to touch it but let my hand drop halfway there. "Because…. Of course. It's a natural assumption." I was losing him. I was going to lose him because I hadn't explained myself appropriately. "I… had an accident."

"Car crash?"

"Something like that." Not exactly true, not even close to it, but he didn't need to know. "Immediately afterwards it started to grow out like that." I laughed, albeit not very convincingly. "The doctors couldn't quite explain it."

I mixed another round, and we talked in a desultory fashion about everything and nothing. By that time the drinks were done. The sun was coming up over the hills, and the big, angry city stirred itself to life again. I walked him to the curb to wait.

"Have you got a name?"

He blinked. The dawn was rose and gold, tinted a darker pink at the horizon. The hills appeared purple against it, like a row of empty houses left standing in a vacant street after some catastrophe had passed. "Ed Malory." He did shake my hand then.

He left in a taxi. I imagined I would never see him again.

Chapter Two

I DIDN'T see him for rather a long time, and I assumed he'd gone his own way. Most people, if given half a chance, will discover their own path to Perdition regardless of outside help—or outside interference.

It was a month or so before Christmas, and I had just come out of a bookstore on the Boulevard, the small one with the cardboard cutout of James Joyce in the window. I saw something shuffling its way along the opposite side of the street, something that might at one time have been a man. It stopped in front of a cigar store, leaning for a moment against a convenient wooden Indian.

It was Ed Malory. Even from here, I could see he was absolutely stinking drunk. He was still wearing the clothes I'd given him that first night, but now they would have looked at home on a scarecrow. His shirttails were hanging outside the waistband of his trousers, and one shoulder of his overcoat was torn; he wore no tie, and his feet had been shoved bare into his decrepit shoes. But his clothes weren't the worst of it. His expression—that is to say, his entire demeanor—was that of a man utterly defeated. Ed Malory had come to the end of his tether.

I went quickly across to him and took hold of his arm. "Straighten up and walk," I said, perhaps a little too brusquely. "The cops around here like to collect drunks. I believe they can claim a set of silver-plated spoons once they get so many."

"Tony Lionheart." He clutched at me like a drowning man. "You came. I wished for you and here you are." His eyes were red-rimmed, and he had a cough that sounded like galloping consumption. There was an awful flu going round that year, I remember, that had half the city in its evil grip. Perhaps that was what was wrong with him.

"Come on, now." I held him up and propelled him forward. I told myself that we looked like two chaps out for an afternoon stroll. "Off we go."

"Oh, I'm not drunk," he said. "Just a little hungry."

"Hungry or drunk," I said through gritted teeth, "you'd best straighten up."

"You got it."

He let me walk him to the corner, where I hailed a cab and stuffed him in the backseat. I got in after him.

"No problem, bub," the driver said, "but it's your ass if he throws up in my cab."

I had the driver take us to my place, and I tipped him extra for his patience. I thought Malory might have trouble navigating the stairs—my apartment is a walk-up, and there are three flights—but he surprised me. I let both of us in, and he sat wearily on the sofa.

"Go ahead and say it." He fumbled with a pack of cigarettes, managed to get one out and lit, then tossed the pack on the coffee table. "You might as well."

I was in the kitchen, setting the coffee pot to heat on a high flame. "What is it I'm supposed to be saying?"

"You're supposed to be saying 'I told you so.'" He rubbed both hands over his face. "Look, why don't you just drive me back downtown and drop me off?"

"Nothing doing." I went into the living room and picked up the phone. "Formal or informal? I could go for a sandwich at the Nickel Diner, if you like."

"What? I need a shower. And a shave."

"Food. What do you want to eat? There's nowhere in this town you can get in without a reservation." He hesitated. I could see his pride warring with his hunger. In a minute pride would win, and I couldn't have that. "Look," I said, "I'm starving, so make up your bloody mind already." I laid the receiver back in the cradle. "Munro's does a marvelous porterhouse steak. Why don't we go out?" I moved into the kitchenette and took the coffee pot off the flame. "You can have a quick shower, and then we'll get going. What do you say?"

"Tony, look… it's nice that you found me and I'm grateful—"

"Please." *Not gratitude*, I thought. *Anything but that.* "I don't cook, and even if I did, there's nothing here to eat. I'm not interested in starving. Are you?"

He glanced down at his torn and stained clothing, indicating by a gesture that he was hardly fit for polite company.

I didn't mind. I've been there more times than I can count. "I'll loan you something of mine," I said. "We're about the same size." I deliberately didn't mention the last "loan" of clothing I'd given him. No need to bring that up. "Come on. Won't you join me?"

Half an hour later, showered and shaved and wearing one of my suits, he was fit for company. No, scratch that. He was goddamn stunning. He'd scraped the side of his neck—most likely with my unfamiliar razor—and I found myself drawn irresistibly to that tiny wound. I wanted to trace its ragged contours. I wanted to taste it and then to consign that momentary bliss to the darkest vaults of memory. I didn't expect anything from him. This wasn't about payment due or having him feel he owed me something. If I couldn't have him on his own terms, I didn't want him at all. I do have my pride.

"That suit quite does you justice," I said when he appeared. "You're the sort of chap whose pyjamas are probably tailored, or ought to be." The dark coat contrasted beautifully with the vivid blue of his eyes, and the crisp white shirt lay against his skin like a caress. His hands—lean, long-fingered, beautiful—were manicured and had recently been clean. Whoever he was, and however he'd come to be in the mission on Fromsett Street, he wasn't a habitual drunk, nor was he a down-and-outer. Believe me, I know them all, at least around here. I'd have noticed him long before now. He's the type you can't possibly overlook.

BERNARD GREETED us at the door—Munro's was absolutely packed, but then, it usually was—and ushered us to a private table near the windows. He isn't quite a friend, Bernard, but he is everything a maître d' should be, and I suppose that's good enough. "Bottle of wine, Mr. Leonard?" He pointed the wine list at me. It was at least as long as his forearm. "We have a nice beaujolais. Very light and saucy, the perfect thing for an evening meal."

"Sparkling vouvray," I said. I didn't need to look at the list. If there was a wine on it that I'd not heard about, I'd eat my handkerchief.

"A sparkling wine, Mr. Leonard?" His expression said I was an idiot. Nobody drank sparkling vouvray with a meal, not nowadays.

"A sparkling wine, Bernard." I watched him go, then turned back to Ed. "Amazing we can still get vouvray, considering the state of things in France. I suppose it's a bottle they've had in storage." I turned the water glass around and around. Its bottom made a soft dent in the white tablecloth. "I do so hate wine snobs."

Ed laughed. It was the first genuine laugh I'd ever heard from him. I liked it. "Will you tell me now?" His gaze caught and held me. "The truth. Why you keep rescuing me. Why you keep turning up when I need you." He grinned. "Who the hell you are, for starters. I've been up and down the city records, and I can find no trace of you. You're not listed in the city directory. You aren't in the phone book. I've searched the newspaper morgue going back twenty years, and you aren't anywhere in there either." He produced a packet of cigarettes and shook one out. I reached across to light it for him. "As far as I can tell, you don't exist." He blew a series of smoke rings. "The boys on the street say you're some kind of do-gooder who goes around to the drunk tanks and the missions, looking for someone to save." His dazzling blue eyes made it hard to lie to him, or even to prevaricate, and I've had plenty of practice. "Why?" he asked. "What makes you do it?"

Why *do* I do it? Especially in the afternoon around three, when the guilt and the trembling and the shakes are strongest. That's when I go out looking for them. I find the really desperate ones and I bring them home. I feed them and stand them to a good, hot shower and a change of clothes, if we're near enough in stature. I have literally dozens of tailored suits, each one a gift from my estranged wife. She was equally generous with shoes, with overcoats and hats and gloves made of the finest Italian leather, butter-soft. She was a generous sort of girl, lavish with her gifts and with herself. She believed absolutely in that old saw about giving first of all to others.

"I like to help people," I said at last. "I've recently come through a bad time. Helping others… well, it takes my mind off things."

If I can drink enough—and quickly enough—I can almost forget, at least some of it. The days and nights alone in a hole in the ground; the torture when they came to take me out. A year and twenty-seven days of it, if you must know. I kept a very careful tally of my time in hell.

"Thorough type, aren't you?" I lit a cigarette of my own. "One would think you were a detective out of some pulp novel."

His eyebrows rose. He was laughing again. "You catch on quick."

I took the small card he passed me: ED J. MALORY, PRIVATE INVESTIGATOR. "Oh, for Christ's sake!" It amused me that he really was a detective. I've always had a weak spot for the clever ones. I wanted to ask what he'd been doing down on Fromsett, consorting with drunks and ne'er-do-wells, but I didn't really know him.

We ordered oysters as a starter, followed by steak with *frites*, and thus passed an amiable meal together. Ed was a charming interlocutor, very much interested in my stories and interested, too, by what I did for a living.

"I'm a writer. Novels, mostly, although I've been known to make the odd foray into short fiction. I write under a pen name, though, so don't bother looking. You've never heard of me."

"Forgive me, but it looks like you make a decent living." He glanced up at me from under his brows. We were drinking coffee now, with a soupçon of brandy in it. "I mean, your apartment, your car...."

I was driving an Aston Martin in those days, a gorgeous little convertible coupe with all the trimmings. My wife's father had it shipped over from England because I'd let it slip one afternoon during cocktails that it was my favorite car. He's the sort of man who throws money at a problem.

"My apartment isn't quite as grand as you make out," I said, "and the car was a gift from my wife, courtesy of her old man's money. So I suppose it's really a gift from him."

"Wife." It was as if I'd thrown a bucket of ice water over him. "You're married?"

I didn't really care to discuss Janet but, having mentioned her, I had no choice. "Yes and no."

"Which is it?" His warm blue eyes were suddenly flinty, and his voice had steel in it. He was nobody's fool, this Ed Malory. "Yes or no?"

I signaled the waiter for the check. "This isn't the most conducive atmosphere for a serious discussion. Will you take a drive with me?"

We got my car from the valet and headed up Mulholland, away from the city. The road winds for some distance, climbing higher and higher into the hills, affording an absolutely beautiful view of the city lights below. I thought we might stop somewhere along the way for refreshments or, better yet, buy our own and find a secluded spot on some hard-to-get-to beach. There are drinks and *drinks*—and some of the most enjoyable have been quaffed on a moonlit stretch of sand, in the presence of a friend. Or someone one wishes was a friend.

About half an hour outside the city, I found a little roadside store, still open. I parked the car and went inside. The shop's interior was like something out of Norman Rockwell, all wide board floors and tall wooden shelves. "Have you got wine?" I asked.

An old man sat on a high stool behind the counter, peeling oranges. He did this very slowly and methodically, working from the top and unraveling the peel in one long, unbroken strip. "Got wine." He nodded toward a glassed-in cooler at the back of the store. "None of that imported crap."

I selected a bottle of muscatel—horrible stuff, but there wasn't much choice—and brought it up to the counter. "This will do."

He raised one hoary eyebrow. "You old enough to buy this stuff?"

"Absolutely," I said. I wasn't quite smirking. "I dress myself and everything now." I paid him, telling him to keep the change.

When I went back outside, Ed was standing by the car, smoking a cigarette and looking at the view. "It's always so beautiful," he said. He turned slowly to look at me, like a man dragging himself back from some pleasant, private reverie. "All the lights, down there."

What are you doing in LA, I wondered. *You don't belong here.*

We drove north along Mulholland Highway with the top down, reveling in the warm night winds and listening to the hypnotic murmur of tires on asphalt. He didn't talk like some people do, merely to fill the silence. He only spoke when he had something to say.

"You've been living in San Francisco," I said after a while. "You used to work with Charlie Blackwell until he threw in the towel." I glanced across at him. "I heard he went into treatment somewhere back East."

"Been doing your homework, have you?" He grinned. God, I loved looking at him.

"Maybe."

Eventually I pulled off the road to one side of a beach I knew to be deserted. It was located on private property, the estate of a friend who was seldom home but who had given me permission to wander when I felt like it. The tide was high, and even from the road, we could hear the roar and crash of waves against the cliffs below. I nodded to Malory. "Follow me down. There are steps but be careful. They can be kind of hard to see in the dark."

Sober, he was nimble, and we descended to the sand with very little trouble.

For a long time, perhaps an hour, we strolled quietly along the beach, regarded only by the moon. I wanted to say something profound, something not usual. I wanted to quote poetry to him, but I was afraid of seeming ridiculous.

"Really a lovely night," he said. "If you like that sort of thing."

"Why are you pretending to be a drunk?" I asked a little later. We were sitting on the sand somewhere north of the city, him and me. We'd taken off our shoes and socks, jettisoning a sense of propriety. He'd suggested we wade in the water, like little children do. The notion was oddly appealing. "Is it for your work?"

"I've been here in LA since I was old enough to drive. I was on Fromsett Street because my client needed me to be there."

"To investigate drunks?" I asked. It was very late; there was no one about. Now and then the lights of a passing car would spill an uncertain illumination on us, discovering us in our sheltered little cove, but no one ever stopped and no one came near.

"One drunk in particular." He reached behind us to pull the bottle out of the cold pit we'd dug in the sand.

It occurred to me what he meant. "To investigate me, you mean." He didn't deny it, but he didn't acknowledge it either. That made me vastly uneasy. "Her father hired you, didn't he?"

"I go where I'm sent," he said quietly.

"You take your work very seriously." I tried to keep the bitterness out of my voice. "I've never heard of anyone becoming a drunk on purpose. You're a real pragmatist."

"Am I?" The moonlight cast half his face in shadow and picked out hidden strands of silver in his hair. "My bank account refuses to let me by with anything else." He sighed. "Anyway, I can't tell you. I have a strict nondisclosure policy with my clients." He dug his hand into the ground, letting the cool, damp sand trickle through his fingers.

"Oh, for Christ's sake! You're in Los Angeles pretending to be a drunk so you can investigate me—even if you won't say so." Obviously the reports of my personal dissolution had been wildly exaggerated. "Janet's father probably hired you. He thinks I've suddenly made a million and I'm living it up, the successful novelist and his life of ease. He wants to find out why I'm still sponging off his daughter, my wife." I laughed, even though it made my chest hurt. "My estranged wife, rather. That's why he's sent you here, so he can familiarize himself with my habits. He probably thinks I'm drinking Janet's fortune."

He touched my cheek, the bad one, and traced the shallow groove running from my temple down to my jaw. It surprised me. I'd begun to think he wasn't the type, that I'd got him wrong. "I really can't talk about it." He sighed. "Not even to you." I wasn't sure if this last was intended to flatter me, to prevent me from asking further questions, or both.

Malory has never allowed a great deal of his inner self to surface. Even with a friend—I assumed I was a friend—he always held back, kept some part of himself in reserve. Can't say as I blame him.

"Maybe she thinks someone might be trying to kill her." My fists clenched involuntarily. "Maybe she thinks it might be me. Or an old boyfriend. God knows, she has quite a list of conquests."

"Tony. Let's just—" He looked at me, then leaned in so close that his features blurred. His mouth was hot, wet. His hands closed on my shoulders, gently squeezing. He kissed as earnestly as he did everything else; it was over too soon. My body was beating with a dozen discrete pulses: in my ears, my throat, my hands and fingertips, my cock. I cradled the back of his head and pulled him in again, licking at his mouth, sucking his tongue and lips, siphoning the taste of him.

"Tell me something," he said after a while. The pale moonlight glanced off his forehead, the strong column of his throat. "Something true, something about yourself."

I was shuddering with my need to touch him, to caress his body with my mouth and hands. "What sort of thing would you like?"

"Tell me something about you." He paused, and I sensed he was gauging me, sounding my depths as it were. "The truth."

"The truth." I took a pull off the bottle. It must have looked like I was thinking—I wasn't. "I'm dying." There was the usual shocked silence that almost always follows that pronouncement. "Oh, not right away… and not all at once." He'd asked me for the truth, but I feared I'd been a little too dramatic. "But eventually."

"When?"

I let out the breath I'd been holding. "Five years, maybe. Perhaps more. Perhaps less." His expression bothered me. He looked as if he didn't—couldn't—believe me. "I don't think about it every minute… sometimes not even every day."

"What is it?" he asked, and I told him. "Huh." He was searching for something to say, for the right thing to say. People usually did. Nobody wants to pile pain on top of more pain, except sometimes it's inevitable. It can't be helped.

"Janet and I were happy once… for about five minutes." Somewhere out there, over that expanse of black ocean, there was… what? Mexico?

Or was I pointed in the wrong direction? "We go our own ways. Janet has a taste for beautiful young men. Beautiful young men have a taste for Janet. There's a guesthouse on her father's property. It's where she takes them when she wishes to... entertain."

"This is fine by you?"

"No, Ed. It isn't. But I can hardly chain her to the wall. It's been a long time since I had that sort of claim on her." I made a show of looking at my watch. "It's getting late. I'd best get you home. Your old man will come after me with the shotgun." I grinned. "Is he the shotgun type, your dad?"

He stood up, dusting sand off his clothes. "My parents are dead," he said quietly.

It was one of those moments when you wished like hell you could unsay what you just said. "I'm sorry."

"I grew up in an orphanage." He shrugged into his suit coat. "North of here, in Santa Rosa."

I wanted to ask questions: *How old were you when they died?* and *Was there no one in your family, a relative, who could have taken you in?* and *What was it like?*—except I already knew how such things went. Les Petites Soeurs de Notre Dame, in the oldest part of Montreal. I was five. "Jesus, Ed. I didn't mean—"

But he was already moving up the slope to where we'd parked the car, and anything I'd thought to say was irretrievably lost.

We drove back to LA in comparative silence. I dropped him at his door. "When can I see you again?"

"I'll call you," he said. He didn't invite me in.

I DIDN'T go home right away, but drove around for a while. I like the noises of the city at night, the rhythm of the traffic. When I'm driving, I can kid myself that I'm actually going somewhere, that I'm not just drifting aimlessly.

I found a dive off Hollywood Boulevard and went in for a nightcap, but the place was full of people I didn't know, so I took a seat at the bar. It was late, but nobody seemed inclined to leave, or maybe the booze was really that good. I ordered a gimlet and lit a cigarette with a matchbook someone had left on the bar, but when the drink arrived, it was a sad arrangement of lemon juice and sugar and some inferior brand of gin, so I left. I toyed briefly with the idea of stopping in at Nero's, a Turkish bath near Wilshire, but I didn't have the energy, and anyway, I wasn't sure I had the stamina for pretty boys. Instead, I drove to Janet's house and parked my car at the bottom of the long, winding drive.

Janet's father was one of the richest men in the northern hemisphere. I don't know how he made his money, but I do know he's got it, and he's not the type to spare expense. If one of his children—Janet or her equally spoiled-rotten sister, Deborah—wanted something, they got it, no questions asked. When Janet asked her father for a separate guesthouse on his property—some place where she could entertain a dozen of her closest friends one at a time—he had it built immediately, nothing but the best. I know. I've been inside.

The guesthouse was near the end of the long, majestic drive leading to the main house and screened by an arrangement of ornamental shrubs and small trees. Janet decorated it herself, and believe me when I tell you it's lavish. It had its own swimming pool, but that's not the main attraction. The house was mostly bedroom and the furnishings were mostly bed: a huge, Edwardian-type thing you almost need a ladder to get into. Because of the climate, it's dressed in light silks, but there's a small fireplace to one side, should madam feel the need. The whole thing was in that colonial style you see in the French Quarter of New Orleans—lots of louvers on the windows and the doors, and giant yucca plants in pots along the walkway. It also had a somewhat hidden entrance, if madam's closest friends preferred not to announce their presence, and it could also be accessed from the pool. I daresay that's convenient for those late night parties where everyone was swimming naked and soused to the gills.

I was thinking about Ed while I walked, the things I'd said to him. Back there on the beach, alone with each other and the constant moon, it sounded fine. Now I wasn't too sure.

Tell me something... about yourself.

I'm dying.

Why was that the first thing that came to me? Why was death—of all things—so ever-present in my mind? That kiss hadn't been nearly enough, dammit. I wanted more from him. I wanted all of him.

"Janet?" It was well after 1:00 a.m. by my watch, and from outside it looked as if just one light had been left burning in the guesthouse. If she was with someone, I'd sooner not interrupt them. Of course, if she was with someone, I'd have heard her long before now. Janet was always the vocal sort. "Are you in here?" I tapped again. "Look, if you don't say anything, I'm going to come in. Is that all right?" I waited, listening, but I couldn't hear anything much. She liked to listen to the radio, and I fancied I could hear music playing quietly somewhere inside the house. I put my fingertips against the door and pushed. It swung open easily. "Janet? Did you hear what I said?"

The first three steps took me into the bedroom, and I stood there for a while, unsure of what I was seeing. The high bed was bare of sheets or other coverings, and the mattress lay askew the frame, as if it had been pushed or dragged there. A spreading red stain, vaguely circular, had soaked into the mattress and run down onto the floor.

She was completely nude, lying on her side facing the room, with one arm flung over her face and the other somewhat parallel to her body. A rope had been fastened to her wrists and ankles and looped around her neck, the frayed ends behind her head. A hard wooden knob, maybe two inches long and approximately the size of my thumb, protruded from the nape of her neck. Was this part of the game, I wondered, more bondage gear? A pair of pale pink knickers was tossed over the back of a chair, and a stocking lay discarded nearby. A single high-heeled shoe—black, with an ankle strap and what looked like dark mud on the heel—had been tossed onto the floor.

I didn't want to touch her—knew I really shouldn't touch her—but I had to know if she was alive or dead. "Janet?" I pressed two fingers into the shoulder nearest me and slowly, grotesquely, she rolled onto her back.

Her face and head had been beaten to a bloody pulp.

I lurched outside just in time to empty my stomach over the side of the patio. I heaved until there was absolutely nothing left inside me, and then I wiped my mouth with the back of my hand and tried to breathe. My watch said it was a quarter to two.

I went down the drive, got back into my car, and pushed the starter with shaking fingers. I couldn't think. I had to think. I had to go. Somewhere. Vaguely I realized I was talking to myself, aloud, a low hum of sounds that might be words or might be something else. I reversed onto a manicured patch of lawn, then pointed the car back the way I'd come. I couldn't stay there. I had to get away. When the cops discovered Janet's body, the first person they'd come looking for was me.

Chapter Three

I LEANED on the doorbell, holding it flush against the frame with my thumb. There were no lights on inside, probably because it was four thirty in the morning. I didn't know what I was going to say to him, only that I had to say something, and the plainer, the better.

I heard footsteps, the inner door swung back, and Ed Malory was there, peering at me through the screen. He was wearing boxer shorts and his hair looked like the back end of a cat.

"I expect you've been sleeping," I said. "Dreadful time of the morning for me to come calling, I know."

"Tony." He opened the screen door and took hold of my arm. "For God's sake, you look terrible. What's wrong?"

"Ed, I'm in bad trouble."

He drew me inside and walked me over to the couch. "Sit here. I'll make some coffee." He disappeared into another room and reappeared wearing a robe. His hair was neat, and obviously he'd combed it. "What time is it?" he asked, squinting at a clock on the wall. "Christ. I should kill you for coming here at this hour."

I couldn't smile back. My face felt frozen, like it had after my captivity, when I woke up in the American field hospital and tried to talk but couldn't. *You have sustained some serious damage, young man.* The doctor was absurdly tall and thin, with small round glasses. He was familiar, and angry. He spoke to me like what had happened was all my fault. *We will do what we can, but I make no promises.*

"She's dead. Janet's dead. He beat her head in." I was going to be sick again. I tried to breathe slowly. "I went over there, after I'd dropped you here. The door was open and I went in." The enormous bed, the spreading pool of blood, the pale pink knickers, the stocking, and the high-heeled shoe. "There was a handle, a wooden handle coming out the nape of her neck. I know I shouldn't touch her. They always tell you not to touch them."

"Icepick," Ed murmured. "That's a professional job."

"No," I said, "it was sloppy… there was so much blood."

15

He knelt in front of me, took hold of my hands, and turned them palms up. They were clean. "You didn't touch her?" He was infinitely gentle.

"Her shoulder. With two fingers. She rolled onto her back." I shuddered. I'd see those images for the rest of my days.

"Who killed her?" He watched me carefully, as if afraid I'd bolt. "Someone must have gone down to the guesthouse with her. She didn't beat her own head in."

"I don't know." It was all swirling together in my mind, and I couldn't keep any of it straight. "I don't know. He was gone when I got there, whoever he was."

"Did you notice any footprints?"

"It's all grass. Just mowed yesterday. There's an irrigation thing that keeps it watered. I think it comes on at night."

"What about inside the house?" Ed asked. "Blood on his shoes, maybe?"

"No. There was a lot of blood on the bed, but not on the floor."

"So she was killed on the bed," he murmured. "Tony, listen very carefully." He held my hands gently but firmly. "This is extremely important." His gaze was sympathetic, and his eyes were very, very blue. "If you have committed any crime in connection with this—I mean anything, even a speeding ticket—you can't tell me about it."

"That's right." My voice sounded blurred, as if I were speaking under water. "You could lose your license."

He stroked my cheek, the damaged one, tracing the ragged landscape of my scars with his thumb. He was so close I could feel his warm breath on my face. The thumb smoothed small circles on my skin, drifted to caress my lower lip, and I shuddered deep inside my belly.

"I need to get to Tijuana."

"We'll figure something out."

HE STOOD on the tarmac as I walked aboard the plane. There were only six of us, and everyone else had already boarded. At the top of the steps, I stopped and turned around, but I didn't dare wave. He was still watching, but he was wearing dark glasses, and at this distance, I couldn't tell what he was feeling, if indeed he was feeling anything at all.

"Thanks," I murmured, hardly loud enough for anyone to hear. "Thank you." Then I went inside and took my seat.

He watched as we taxied down the runway. He watched as we turned, and as the motors powered up and began to roar, and he was still watching when we left the ground and lifted into the naked air. I won't say I missed him, because that would be presumptuous. I hardly knew him. What I felt was much more powerful, and much more painful—the dark sense that I had lost something inestimably precious.

The little plane turned south, heading for Mexico and my relative freedom. I'd never gone this route before, but I'd never been fleeing the police before. At least, I supposed that's what it was. I kept seeing Janet's bedroom, her lifeless body lying crumpled on the bed. I couldn't imagine who would do such things to her... probably because I didn't know who'd hated her that much. Had she died from asphyxiation, with those ropes tied around her neck? Had she been stabbed—there had been an awful lot of blood. Maybe the beating had killed her, except he'd only bothered with her head. Could a person die from that?

The droning of the engines acted on me like a soporific, or maybe it was the previous night's strain. I took my coat off, rolled it into some semblance of a pillow, and pressed it against the bulkhead. I thought to sleep most of the way, but no matter how hard I tried, I couldn't relax. My body was full of strange little tics and twitches, and every time I closed my eyes, I saw Ed. There was so much I needed to say to him, so much I didn't get to say. *I'm sorry*, I thought. *I never meant to involve you, but I didn't know where else to go.* How do you tell someone like Malory that you've got no friends, that you never made any because, at bottom, you're just no good? You're no good.

Janet and I had been married for nearly a year and a half when she brought home her first conquest. He was young, blond, and very fit—an athlete in the Hollywood mold who'd very nearly made the Olympic diving team. Fittingly, for one who so fully embodied the primeval ideal, his name was Adam. I found them in our bed, both naked as a peeled apple and going at it like demented rabbits.

He approached me at a cocktail party some weeks later and attempted what was either an apology or a seduction. My own proclivities I already knew, but how he'd guessed, I'd no idea. Of course I was perfectly polite, pouring him drinks and offering to light his cigarette. I think it was this attitude that invited Janet's scorn: she believed in the cuckold's righteous anger and expected I would slap her around a bit, perhaps blacken both her eyes.

At the time, we were living with her father (her mother had died of cancer when Janet and her sister were both at boarding school) in a mansion not quite as large as an airplane hangar, and with more bedrooms than the palace at Versailles. I rarely saw her, and she had long since stopped offering herself for sex, preferring instead an endless parade of stout young swains eager to fuck her brains out.

Well, they were out now.

Jesus, Tony, I thought. *Not quite so grim, if you don't mind.*

I drifted into something that was not quite sleep, and when I woke, we were dropping down onto the little airfield at Mazatlán. I couldn't see very much—there wasn't much to see—except a flat expanse of parched-looking ground dotted with what I assumed were fruit trees and a handful of scabby palms. The airport building was small but very well kept, with a door on each side and a sort of hallway or porte cochère where travelers were obliged to present themselves with proper documents in hand.

This last made me rather nervous. Of course I had a passport, and I'd obtained a visa for Mexico earlier. I planned to write a book partly set in Mexico, and having a visa readily at hand would save me a lot of trouble at the border. If the police in LA were looking for me, they'd have almost certainly sent a wire south of the border, which would mean I'd probably be spending the night in a cozy Mexican jail. But the customs people didn't so much as look sideways at me, except to direct me to the men's room after I'd asked for one.

I wasn't staying in Tijuana. I wasn't staying in Mazatlán, either, on the second leg of the trip. As soon as possible, I found space on a flight to Torreón, from where I'd fly to Ixtagapa, a tiny town in the middle of absolutely nowhere. While I was waiting to board, I ducked into the bathroom. The mirror showed me a man with dark circles under his eyes, a man haunted by the knowledge that something awful was waiting for him, and this waiting thing was patient, as patient as death itself. I took off the shirt I was wearing, rolled it into a ball, and shoved it in the trash.

There hadn't been much time to pack, but Ed had provided me the bare necessities—razor, pyjamas, shaving cream, toothbrush—and I'd stopped at Schwab's for cigarettes, chewing gum, pancake makeup, and a tin of shoe polish, to hide the color of my hair. It was absolutely vile stuff—a viscous dark-brown paste that stained my scalp and the palms of my hands. With the razor I destroyed my stylish short-back-and-sides haircut, hacking the top very close and trimming my sideburns so the skin showed. My face I couldn't do much about, the scars being what they were, but I smeared some of the pancake makeup on so it looked like I had a tan. With a straw hat to keep the sun off and my own dark glasses, I looked like a disreputable used car salesman and as nasty as a nun's cold breakfast. With the addition of a dirty, ill-fitting shirt (the charity bin outside of Schwab's had been a godsend) and a pair of scuffed, cheap shoes, the disguise was complete—and since this was merely a regional flight, nobody would bother asking for my papers.

I only hoped my Spanish was good enough.

IT WAS hot as hell when we landed on a narrow dirt road just outside the town of Ixtagapa, a miniscule town on the edge of the Gulf of Mexico. The charter pilot made it a point to tell me how great the fishing was, how big and tasty the fish were, and how his cousin Hector would be happy to take me out in his boat early the next morning. His cousin Hector also ran a taxi service, and would I like Hector to take me to my hotel?

I would.

The hotel was small, just two floors, and built in the colonial style, with bright, vibrant colors and decorative elements straight out of an alcoholic hallucination. I checked in as Señor Guerrero, on holiday from Mazatlán and wanting very much to relax and unwind from his busy life, and was shown to a tidy little room on the second floor. I handed the *mozo* a few centavos and locked the door behind him.

Despite the heat, I was shivering, so I stripped naked and stood under the hot shower for a long time. The hotel shampoo washed most of the shoe polish out of my hair, taking the pancake makeup with it. The sideburns and my improvised haircut I couldn't do anything about, but I took out the razor Ed had given me and shaved. Afterward I pulled the blinds and hung the *FAVOR DE NO MOLESTAR* sign on the outside of my door. Then I lay down on the bed and fell willingly into a deep well of blessed unconsciousness.

It was dark when I awoke, and for a moment or two, I didn't remember where I was. The sound of voices filtered up to me from the street below, but the room was very quiet. The room was very quiet and the door was ajar, and a tall man was standing over my bed, looking down at me.

"Señor Guerrero," he said. "Welcome to Ixtagapa."

Chapter Four

I STARTED to sit up, but he put out a hand to indicate I'd be better off right where I was.

"Don't trouble yourself, señor. I can take care of things."

"What things are you taking care of?" It occurred to me that they'd caught up with me, the police or whoever they were, and it was all over now. I'd be taken back to California in handcuffs, and that would be that.

"Such things as required." He moved to each of the windows in turn, opening the blinds. "Things that you might want for later."

He was carrying an armload of towels and several bars of those tiny little hotel soaps. He went into the bathroom, set the towels on the shelf, and replaced the soap. Then he emptied the trash into a wheeled trolley just outside the door. *For Christ's sake, Tony. He's the janitor or something.* I didn't really believe it. Maybe he'd been sent here to do away with me. Maybe he had a gun somewhere on his little trolley, underneath all the neatly folded towels and the tiny bars of soap.

"I had the sign out," I said. "On the door."

He examined the outside of the door and then the inside. "No, señor. There is nothing—" He bent swiftly and I tensed. The bastard was going for his gun, and now he'd shoot me, and this was how my life was going to end, in an anonymous Mexican holiday hotel with a goddamn sombrero on the door. He came up with something in his hand, brandishing it at me. It was the DO NOT DISTURB sign. "Forgive me, señor. It was here, on the floor. It must have fallen down."

I drew a slow, deep breath. "Right. Of course."

He handed it across and I laid it on the bedside table. "Is there anything else?"

I started laughing. I couldn't help it. It was the sort of laughter that usually occurs when you've just had the narrowest escape of your life—or think you have. "Yes, call my wife and tell her where I am."

"Your wife?"

"Never mind." I sat up, found my cigarettes, and shook one out. "I only married her for her money."

"Of course, señor." He grasped the handle of his trolley almost desperately. The poor bugger couldn't wait to get away from the madman in room 204. He moved on to the next room. I heard him muttering something about *Americano loco*.

"You don't know the half of it," I whispered, but I didn't think he heard me.

The cigarette was just fine, but by now I was absolutely dying for a drink. There was a bar downstairs, but it probably wasn't entirely wise to sit down there nursing a whisky sour in full view of whatever law enforcement might wander by, at least not yet. I didn't know this place. Maybe they had a fantastically efficient police force that could spot an errant cockroach at a hundred paces.

I had about made up my mind to crack open the complimentary bottle of Listerine in the bathroom when I remembered something else Ed had packed in my suitcase: a very nice bottle of scotch. I fetched a water glass and downed a couple of hefty shots, one after the other. That put paid to the headache starting at the back of my neck and the feeling of not-so-vague queasiness washing over me in ever-larger waves. It's true what they say about the so-called "hair of the dog": nothing banishes an incipient bout of alcoholic withdrawal like a shot of the same poison. I remembered the last time I'd had a drink with Ed, sitting on the beach under the patient moon and hoping I could somehow maneuver him around to kiss me. No maneuvering was necessary—he'd kissed me anyway. If I never saw him again, I'd remember those kisses till the end of my days.

I couldn't stand not knowing what was going on back in LA. I decided to take the risk and go down to the *zócalo*—the town square—and see if I could find some American newspapers. Surely by now someone had discovered her body, which meant the police would have given a statement to the press. If they were coming after me, it was probably better that I know about it, and I couldn't stand another minute in this room.

I pulled on a pair of light tan pants and a loose cotton shirt and shoved my bare feet into the scuffed shoes I'd brought. The hat I left, and if I wore the sunglasses now, in the dark, I'd stick out like someone else's shadow. As far as disguises went, it wasn't very effective but the best I could do under the circumstances. I'd find a *farmacia* in the morning and

21

get some more shoe polish for my hair. I stuffed my visa and passport under the mattress and hid the bottle of scotch under the bed, then went down the main stairs to the lobby.

A short, dark-skinned girl with a long braid was behind the desk, sorting some papers. "I beg your pardon," I said. "I wonder if you might have a map?"

She grinned, making dimples in her plump cheeks. She was a pretty little thing. "Of course, señor. Of the town?"

"Please."

She spread it out on the counter, and we looked at it together. "See, here is the zócalo. The shops and everything are there."

"Open late?" I checked my watch; it was after seven.

"*Sí*. And the restaurants serve Picante, the local beer. It's very good."

"Mmm." It was probably horse piss with an egg in it. "I'll bear that in mind. Thank you."

There were maybe half a dozen people in the lobby, most of them Mexicans. One man was standing in the open doorway smoking a cigarette while his wife talked on the payphone. His expression said that for five centavos he'd sell her to the next person who happened by. Two young girls in flower-print dresses lingered near a display of tourist brochures advertising the delights of southern Mexico in winter. An old woman napped next to a large potted palm, her sagging cheeks moving in and out with the rhythm of her breath.

"If I might interrupt, señor." A hand landed on my shoulder, squeezing gently, and I froze. The hand fell away as I turned to look at him. He was about my height, young, and very beautiful, but not in a soft way, not in a feminine way. "You are the American in 204?"

"If you like."

"I have something you will want very much." He nodded toward the open door. "Will you walk with me?" His gaze traveled the length of me, and he smiled. "Such a fine gentleman will no doubt want company in a strange country, no?"

"Thank you, but I'm not interested." I'd heard of this, and I wanted no part of it. This gorgeous little *hijo de puta* would seduce me with promises of bed-breaking sex—*Ir a desgastar el petate*—in return for my watch and the contents of my wallet. He'd come around the next night and try to sell me his sister. "*No follarme*."

He gazed at me for a long moment, then laughed. "You mistake me greatly. I come with a message for you." His eyes were the dark green of summer leaves, and his short dark hair was streaked with blond where the sun had touched it. "From a friend."

I'd heard of this one too. "Look, thank you, but I really am not interested. Now, if you'll excuse me...." I started for the door, but he followed and caught my arm just above the elbow.

"You are American, and yet you speak like an Englishman." He grinned. "Very interesting."

"Please. I haven't any money to give you."

"You know they're looking for you?" He swayed close to me. His scent and the heat of his body were hypnotic, intoxicating. It had been a very long time, and I'm only human. I do get lonely. "The cops from Los Angeles were here." He nodded toward the door. "Two of them came asking about you, señor."

I yanked my arm out of his grip. "I don't believe you." My heartbeat galloped in my chest like the hooves of a runaway racehorse. My palms were slick with sweat. "You don't know what you're talking about."

"It's true." He winked, the kind of wink a pimp gives when he directs the most beautiful of all his girls to capture your attention. "The husband of the American woman. Ah, she is a *puta magnifica*, that one." He pulled a packet of cigarettes out of his pocket, shook one loose, and lit it. The smell of Turkish tobacco—pungent and very expensive—tickled my nostrils like a memory. "Beautiful woman, while she still had a face."

"*Vete a la chingada*," I hissed. "Go to hell." I turned and headed for the door. I didn't look back. I walked until I saw the lights of the zócalo. The town square was all lit up with colored lights strung on poles. I stopped at a stall with an old man sitting on a stool in front of a selection of newspapers and asked him in my rusty Spanish if he had any papers from Los Angeles.

"Sure, I got whatever you want," he said. He indicated a tottering pile held in place by a sizeable rock. I bought one of each and scanned the front pages quickly. The headlines were all variations on the same theme: HEIRESS MURDERED, HUSBAND SOUGHT. *FBI seeking fugitive husband of heiress Janet Leonard in Mexico.* And WOMAN KILLED ON GROUNDS OF GRAND ESTATE. That one took a let's-hate-the-rich theme; the accompanying story suggested Janet had brought it on herself by dint of Daddy's money and her own profligate lifestyle. The third paper down was something different, and it was that one that caught my attention: DETECTIVE QUESTIONED IN LEONARD MURDER. Just below the headline was a photo of Ed Malory. My heart started pounding like a trip hammer.

Private detective Ed Malory today admitted that he knew Tony Leonard, the estranged husband of murdered heiress Janet Leonard, but declined to elaborate further. LA area homicide detectives detained Malory in anticipation of his testimony at the coroner's inquest.... Lieutenant Bridger of the LA police department indicated Malory had been questioned—

Questioned. I knew what that meant. I had personal experience of it. The best-case scenario? He'd been slapped around for a while and then shoved in a cell. The worst? They'd beaten the hell out of him. For Christ's sake, it was practically a code of conduct with the LA police. Some of those bastards should have been working in the goddamn stockyards.

Thinking about it gave me a sick feeling. Oh, Ed seemed plenty tough, and he was definitely big enough to take care of himself. He'd probably handled scores of thugs in his time. But this, I knew, would have been different—like three-on-one different. Maybe one guy to hold him and the other two to do the talking with their fists. Maybe they wouldn't actually kill him, but they'd probably come close. The idea that he'd gone through that for me made me ashamed and a little bit sick to my stomach.

I walked around the zócalo and, wonder of wonders, found an open farmacia, where I bought shoe polish and cigarettes and, on impulse, a packet of those fake mustaches they make for children playing dress-up. At the far end of the square, I found a bench and sat, out of the main flow of pedestrian traffic and closer to the quiet of the twilight town. If I shut my eyes, closed out the incessant flow of Spanish, and ignored the very salient fact that I was essentially a fugitive—

No. It was nothing like being back in LA. Not even close.

I RETRIEVED my room key from the desk clerk and went wearily up the stairs to the second floor. I was debating with myself whether I should use the shoe polish to dye my hair again, in case I needed to light out of here quickly, or if it were better to sit on the terrace in the dark and finish off that bottle of very nice scotch.

When I went to put the key in the door, it was already open. I stepped in and reached for the light switch, then stopped.

"Don't turn on the light."

If he's in my bed, I thought, *I'll bloody well kill him myself.* "How did you get in here?"

"The same way everybody gets in here. Through the door." He chuckled. "I told you before, I have help for you. Help and information, from a friend."

"Can't I turn on a lamp?" I shuffled forward cautiously, afraid of barking my shins on some errant piece of furniture. "It's a bit awkward, chatting with someone you can't see."

"Allow me." He was sitting in one of the two wicker chairs at the far end of the room. The window was open, letting in the warm night breeze. He was still wearing his white linen suit, but his shirt was open at the neck. The little fucker was unbelievably gorgeous, even in the dark. "I have come to help you... if you want my help."

"Help me do what?"

"Escape. Make things right." He waved a hand, an expansive gesture. "Go home, eventually."

"I'm listening." I retrieved the bottle from under the bed and took it over to the bureau. "Drink?"

"Of course."

I splashed two fingers of scotch into a couple glasses and handed him one. "Perhaps you tell me who you are... who this friend of yours is." I took a sip of my drink, enjoying the pleasant burn it made. "After all, you can't expect me to simply take things on faith." I sat on the side of the bed.

He sipped his drink and nodded. "You may call me Seeker. It is a variation of my given name. My friend is someone who can greatly help your dilemma." He tilted his head on one side, considering me. "Someone who has a unique solution to your problem." At my raised eyebrow, he reached into his pocket and brought out a small brown envelope, which he held between two fingers, gently, as one might hold an expensive item of jewelry. "Watch closely." He opened the envelope, dipped into it, and sprinkled some fine white powder onto his hand. Then he held it out toward me. "Not too close, and don't breathe on it." He spread the powder around on his palm. "If I had any small cuts in my skin, I couldn't do this."

"What is it?" I asked.

"*Muerto viviente*," he said. "The living dead." He dropped the powder into an envelope he took from his pocket and tucked it away.

My entire body went cold. I'd heard of this. I just hadn't believed it really existed.

"You see, Señor Leonard, one cannot be tried or convicted of a crime if one is dead." He smiled—a slow, sinister smile that set my teeth on edge. "If one is dead...." He shrugged. "The case against you will instantly dissolve. No one—not the *Federales*, not even the FBI—can prosecute a dead man."

"And you know this how?" I asked. If he expected me to take his story purely on faith, he was out of his mind.

"I am not unfamiliar with the processes of law." He reached into his pocket and pulled out a suspiciously bulky leather wallet, which, when flipped open, displayed a police badge: POLICÍA FEDERAL. It looked genuine, as far as I could tell.

"You knew I was here." My heart pounded frantically in my throat. "You were waiting for me."

"In a manner of speaking. The news of your wife's death reached us almost immediately—through official channels, you understand." He put the badge away. "Please accept my condolences," he said offhandedly, "but you can be very useful to us, if you are willing."

"Oh?" I didn't like the way it sounded. "In what way?"

"The woman's death, tragic though it is, provides an opportunity to reopen an investigation. Since the end of the war, many American businessmen are suddenly interested in Mexico. Operations that have been suspended for the past few years are suddenly viable again. Some of these operations are not exactly legal." He drew out a pack of cigarettes and lit one. "Some of them are very dangerous." He took a drag off the cigarette and regarded me through a rising arc of smoke. "The cost in lost revenue is considerable. The cost in human lives is even greater."

I still didn't understand and told him so. "American businessmen like Linton Stirling?" I couldn't believe I'd uttered the name of Janet's notorious father out loud. It was like invoking the Devil, or something.

He didn't even hesitate. "Yes."

I hadn't expected that.

"We suspect—" He grinned. "Even given the wartime boom, Linton Stirling's fortune has been growing ever larger. A good Mexican friend of his in Sinaloa helped Mr. Stirling improve his export business. The *narcos*—you know this word?—harvest their crops of opium and other narcotics and send them north, where buyers like Mr. Stirling are waiting.

Sometimes this Mr. Stirling, he doesn't even wait, but sends his private airplane south to pick up the product and bring it back to the United States. Since the war...." He shrugged. "With industries powering down and manufacturing returning to peacetime levels, Mr. Stirling and his friends find they must look elsewhere for profitable business.

"Certain parties in the United States insist that you are the first and only suspect in the lady's death, this Linton Stirling's daughter. Her death has made things... inconvenient for her father. His business requires quiet, and suddenly his entire family is the subject of much speculation in the press. The police are looking everywhere for someone to blame. They cannot allow a murderer to go free. The quicker a suitable candidate is found and dealt with, the better. Mr. Stirling and his associates can go back to doing whatever they were doing." He leaned forward and picked a particle of lint off the knee of his trousers. "They need a fall guy for this murder. I believe in your country such a person is called a 'patsy.'"

"You mean me."

He nodded. "Once you have been taken care of, they will cease to be careful and will reveal themselves."

"Ah."

He smiled. Christ, he was beautiful. "You say 'ah' like you understand, Señor Leonard, but I don't believe you do. This woman's death has focused a great deal of attention not only on Señor Stirling but also other prominent American families, people we know are involved in the suddenly copious flow of narcotics from north of our border." He lifted his shoulders and let them fall. "Thinking we are busy with you, they will perhaps relax a little bit... go back to taking risks for the sake of their business."

"So you want to use me to force them out into the open." It sounded ridiculous. "I don't understand how."

"We will make it known that we have arrested you and that you are being tried for the crime of narcotic trafficking. A small envelope of drugs will be found among your belongings. You are suspected of working for these certain prominent families. Because of this, and because you are suspected of killing your wife, we are prepared to extradite you to the United States for trial. Before this can occur, you kill yourself. Our suspects relax, and their shipments of illegal drugs resume."

"Because they'll think it's safe," I said. "You caught me."

"Once we have made this business public—once your suicide is a matter of public record—then you are free to go wherever you wish. Disappear. Begin a new life. Be somebody else."

LATE AT night or very early in the morning, the town of Ixtagapa became still and utterly silent, as though in expectation. It was long past four, perhaps, or drawing close to five, and I ought to have been in bed, but I couldn't sleep, or didn't want to. I felt a sense of quickening, an excitement coursing through my veins like adrenaline, like the lover waiting for his beloved. When had I last taken the kind of risk Seeker was asking me to take? When had I taken any risk at all, for that matter? And if what Seeker had planned was a setup, bound to fail, what did it matter? It wasn't the first time I'd looked Death in the face. If this failed, I would probably die. If I died, I would never see Ed Malory again. I'd never get to take him to my bed and make love to him and whisper sweet dirty things in his oh-so-willing ears. There was that to consider, after all.

"*Sueña conmigo....*" Dream with me: something to be said upon arrival in the bedchamber, whispered as the layers of restraint are shed along with the clothes. Then to lie together, hands and mouths and bodies straining toward the other in the dark. Christ, I wanted to feel him under me, wanted to wrap myself around him and stay with him forever, my detective. I wanted to roam the lurid California night with him and drink horrible wine on a deserted beach with him and make love until the early hours with him. I was reasonably certain he would want that too.

At some point I had decided, even if I didn't remember, that I would do it. It was utter madness, but I was beyond all caring. But first there was this, and this had to be done.

Acting upon the instructions left me by Seeker, I took a clean sheet of writing paper and a pen out of the desk in my hotel room. This sort of thing is my business, so you think I'd know where to begin—but all my literary hubris seemed to have left me.

> *Dear Ed. By now you will have figured out where I've gone, more or less. If you say "Nowhere, Mexico," you win a prize. I'm not altogether sure what that prize might be, but you'll have plenty of time to come here and collect it. I'll*

leave it with the woman at the desk. Her name is Angela. You'll like her.

I've been following the papers from Los Angeles, so there's no point in trying to keep things from me. I know everything that's happened, and I am heartsick that you had to go through that because of me. Believe me, my dear friend, when I tell you I never wanted any of this.

No doubt your instincts have led you to draw certain conclusions about me and about this entire situation. Whatever you've guessed is probably right, but I only ever had the best of intentions.

I didn't kill Janet. I know you believe that. Maybe if I had, all this would make a hell of a lot more sense than it does.

Please don't blame me. They say a brave man never runs, but I did the only thing I could think of.

Fondly, Tony

When I had written it, I lay down on the bed and smoked a cigarette and listened to the rising chorus of birdcalls that heralded the dawn.

I MUST have slept, because it was full daylight when I next awoke, and I could hear the clatter of breakfast being served in the hotel restaurant below. My usual amnesia upon waking—a souvenir of the war—was curiously absent. I knew precisely where I was. I knew, too, that Seeker would be coming back later today and I would be paying him some money. I'd already counted it—just about everything I had—and sealed it in an envelope. Beyond that, there was nothing much to do. My clothes and personal effects I'd leave in the hotel room, along with my passport and visa, so they could identify me. That part was necessary. If nobody knew who I was, then the whole thing would have been for naught. Seeker would have wasted his time and I would have wasted my money. Linton Stirling would continue to peddle drugs across the border, adding to his already immeasurable wealth. Janet's death would count for nothing.

After a little while, I washed and shaved and changed clothes. I went down to the restaurant and took an outside table, and when the *mesera* came, I ordered a big breakfast. She was young, pretty (as so many of the girls there are), and awfully friendly. When I'd finished, I gave her a large tip, then walked down to the zócalo and bought a copy of the LA *Times*.

Janet's murder was still big news, largely because of her family's prominence and wealth, something that must have irritated her father to no end. He had a morbid fear of the public gaze. He would have immediately charged out and hired the best cadre of ambulance chasers money could buy. He'd want it kept out of the newspapers as much as possible, so he'd be willing to invest extra to keep things hush-hush. If I'd gone to Mexico, that was one thing. If I went to Mexico and killed myself, that was even better. The main suspect bumps himself off and the entire case dissolves.

Oh, the police would try to follow the threads of it, but certain threads would disappear and others would seem as if they'd never existed at all. Linton Stirling would make sure of it by burying the story in the back pages of every newspaper he owned, and guaranteeing the same thing happened in the ones he didn't. The fact that the case was still front-page news must have had him madder than a wet hen. None of *his* papers were reporting on the story, but there were still one or two rogue journalists who hadn't lost their balls, who recognized a complicated story when they saw it. Not being able to control what they wrote about his daughter's murder would eat away at him like a cancer. Not being able to find her murderer—or a reasonable facsimile—would be a perennial thorn in his side.

I couldn't say I felt entirely sorry for the old bastard.

The *Times* said there'd been no new leads, but Janet's father would have private police scouring the country, men who'd have carte blanche to pry wherever they wanted. They wouldn't be too particular about which apple carts they happened to upset along the way. They would hunt the man who'd done it, find him, and dispatch him quickly, with about the same degree of sentiment one feels when squashing a bug.

The Los Angeles police, on the other hand, were constrained—more or less—by their profession, and while they might suspect Ed Malory knew more than he was telling, there wasn't too much they could do about it. Having nothing to charge him with, they had let Ed go. California law frowned upon detaining people more than forty-eight hours, especially when no criminal charges had been laid. I wondered how much he'd told them, if anything. Good Christ, they'd held the man on the off chance he knew more than he was telling. God only knows what they'd done to try to get it out of him.

The thing with Seeker, this ruse we'd planned, touched the case of Janet's murder in several key places, but it only really bothered me on one small point: if, as Seeker had said, the case against me would dissolve, where did that leave Janet? Quite apart from old man Stirling's filthy business deals, somewhere out there was the person who'd killed her. With their prime suspect—me—gone, would suspicion fall on some other poor bastard? The only one who'd hated her enough to kill her (as far as I knew) was Janet's sister, Deborah—rich, much-married, beautiful, and as spoiled rotten as Janet. But she lived in Switzerland with her surgeon husband—the same one, incidentally, who'd operated on me after the war. He ran a small clinic near Bern, the sort of place where all the really chichi people go to have their wrinkles smoothed out and their ears put back where they'd been twenty years ago.

No, Janet's murderer couldn't have been Deborah and certainly not their father, who wouldn't risk dirtying his hands. No, he'd be more likely to put his energies into something guaranteed to make money. Janet's mother had been dead for years. No particular suspect.

For Christ's sake, Tony, you're a goddamn mystery writer. Stop trying to play detective.

If this were a mystery story, one I was writing, I'd make the murderer someone who'd been close to the dead woman but who had no particular love for her. I'd make him the least likely person, someone peripheral, the sort of man you'd never in a million years suspect. Perhaps he'd be retained for that very purpose, and once he'd dispatched her properly, he'd be able to hide, disappear back into his regular life with no one the wiser. The very best assassins are the ones no one ever suspects.

In the zócalo they were hanging decorations: sugar skulls and paper devils, simple chains of bright crepe paper, and the more complex tissue flowers that every little girl is taught to make in Mexico. It would be beautiful later in the evening, when the stars came out and all the hundreds of little lights came on and the air was heavy with the scent of flowers. Already the zócalo smelled of incense and ripe fruit, the resinous overburden of the precious copal used to appease visiting spirits and chase away any lingering evil. We were coming up on that most garish and spectacular of Mexican holidays: *Día de los Muertos*, the Day of the Dead. The cemeteries would be filled with mourners, assembled to dress the graves of their beloved dead with fruit and flowers and small remembrances made of clay or paper. Candles would be lit on and around the tombs, and loved ones would sit up all night long, waiting, for this was one night of the year when the partition between the worlds of the living and the worlds of the dead was thin and easily penetrated.

I wondered if anyone would light candles on Janet's grave.

I SPENT the rest of the day in my room, reading the papers and napping, occasionally starting out of my light sleep at the slightest sound. My nerves, never particularly steady to begin with, twanged like overstretched guitar strings. I turned on the bedside radio, but there was only an exhaustively lengthy *corrido* about a man's love for his rifle, interspersed with violent bursts of static.

It was two o'clock in Los Angeles. I sent down to the desk for the afternoon papers, but there was nothing much of interest. Time passed at an excruciating pace while I lay on my bed and watched the slow blades of the ceiling fan stirring the tepid air.

EVENTUALLY I got up and went to the hotel restaurant, which served late-afternoon tea and sandwiches and little cakes done up in paper doilies, all quite civilized. Something niggled insistently at the back of my mind, told me it wasn't safe to be in plain view like this, that the authorities were hardly stupid and someone was bound to recognize me sooner or later. The entire ruse would collapse if I decided to parade around in public.

I took a table in back and waited in heart-pounding anticipation while the mozo brought the tea. The sandwiches were good and the tea was hot and strong, but I could scarcely taste it.

About twenty minutes into my mistaken sojourn, two men appeared in the restaurant entrance, which was partitioned off from the rest of the hotel by an ornate screen door. My stomach gave one of those little jumps like when something dangerous and horrible is about to happen. I got up as quietly as I could and slid out from behind the table. There was no other exit, and no back way, so I'd have to go out the door I'd come in.

I'd almost made it when the taller of the two grabbed my elbow. His eyes were a pale green, almost colorless, and his nose was thin at the tip, pinched-looking. He didn't seem to be someone who derived a great deal of enjoyment out of life. His fingers dug into my flesh like steel pins. "Tony Leonard?"

"*No entiendo.*" *I don't understand.* "*Lo siento,*" I said. *I'm sorry.*

The second man, standing directly behind him, was reaching for his inside pocket. I wrenched my arm free and pushed the first one, catching him by surprise. He stumbled backward into his companion, knocking him down, and while the two of them struggled, I leaped for the door.

I ran out of sheer, animal terror and had no idea where I was going, but an adjoining alley beckoned. I followed it to its terminus, where it joined another, similar passageway running behind the back of a shop. I slid past a bundle of clothes that might or might not have been a dead man, and hastily dodged the trajectory of a slop bucket. By now I was running full out, something I hadn't done since my brief rugby tenure when I was at university, and my lungs felt close to bursting. I ducked into the doorway of a liquor store and waited, listening for shouts or running footsteps, but there was nothing. Not wanting to tempt fate, I slipped behind a row of shops on the west side of the zócalo and stayed there until sunset.

THE DAY of the Dead, they call it—*Día de los Muertos*—and the air was full of music, shouts, shrieks of delighted laughter and mock fear. Barely dusk, and the street outside my hotel was lined with revelers, many of them dressed in fearsome masks, while others gamboled and caroused as *catrinas*, because for some, Death is a beautiful woman and She can neither be appeased nor satisfied. Children were running wild, darting in and out of the crowds of people who had come to Ixtagapa for the celebration. Small, dust-colored dogs wandered the length of the main street, leaping and barking, hoping for a tidbit, while old women swayed in and out of doorways, not quite drunk on mescal, their withered necks hung with garlands of marigolds. Later, the parade would draw them out into the streets to dance with Death or any of his similarly garbed cousins—some in traditional dress, some in more formal top hat and tails. The *Día de los Muertos* is a time when the usual observances are suspended and chaos reigns.

It's rather like Los Angeles in a way.

The zócalo was teeming when I got there, many of the local people crowded around a temporary stage that had been erected in front of the post office. A group of musicians, some in traditional garb and others in costume, played mariachi and *banda*, and a small group of young people jigged about energetically in front of the platform. Someone made up as Death went by on improbably high stilts, dressed in layers of brightly colored tulle like a flamenco dancer, and with long strings of colored flowers around his or her neck. Someone called out, *"Los muertos vivientes!"* The flamenco-dancing Death performed a quick little two-step, then bowed to the crowd.

A young man who'd been standing by me ran up to the figure and removed a string of flowers, capering and blowing kisses to the crowd. He rubbed the flowers over his face and neck and pretended to swoon, then popped back up to full standing position again, grinning madly. The fingers of his right hand made a gesture against the evil eye, and he pranced through the crowd toward me. Plucking a flower from the necklace, he presented it to me, still grinning. His teeth were very white, and his eyes shone with something other than an innate joie de vivre. I suspected he'd been smoking a brand of cigarette they don't advertise. *"Los muertos vivientes,"* he murmured. He stuck the flower in the pocket of my shirt and disappeared into the crowd.

I bought a glass of beer from one of the stalls and made my way to a bench in front of a statue erected to commemorate some 18th century politician. His elaborate moustache sat on his face like the handlebars of a bicycle, and his broad shoulders were dappled with pigeon shit. His expression said that a brave man endures all things, even centuries of being shat on; I found that an admirable sentiment, and so I toasted him with my upraised glass.

An arm insinuated itself around my waist. "They say, like God, he watches everyone." The voice was a mere flutter of sound against my ear. "So you have decided?" One hand squeezed my shoulder companionably. "Come with me. It's not safe to talk here."

I followed him down a narrow alleyway and into a small courtyard with a fountain. He bolted the gate behind us and led me by the hand to a sheltered alcove. I expected he would tell me the whole business was off, that his friend had decided the risk was too great, or that he didn't trust me to follow through. "So?" I asked. "Have you got it?"

He lit a cigarette and waved the spent match out with a flourish. "Have you?"

I produced the envelope from my inside pocket and handed it to him. He opened the envelope and counted the bills, his lips moving silently. He grinned. "This is the correct amount. You understand I must have something to give him. But I can't give you the powder."

The hair on the back of my neck rose, and I was flooded with an intense, unreasoning anger. "What the devil do you mean? You bastard, I've just paid you—"

He laid his fingers over his lips, a shushing gesture. "It must be administered by someone who knows what he is doing. I would not take the risk." We would go to my hotel room, he said, and the man who had given him the powder would do the rest.

We threaded our way through the festival crowds and back to my hotel. An extravagant altar to the dead had been set up in the lobby, with candles and marigolds and photographs of various beloved deceased. "You know about the Day of the Dead?" Seeker asked. He touched the altar lightly, with just the tips of his fingers. "My mother and grandmother used to start building the altar many weeks before the festival. We could look at it, but we weren't allowed to touch it. My mother put photographs of my brother and my father side by side, so they wouldn't be lonely on their long journey from the afterlife." He touched the framed photographs one by one. "I wonder what that journey is like," he said, and I knew he wasn't talking to me.

I waited for him to finish his contemplation, meditation—whatever it was. He saw me looking and smiled. The hotel was, in all likelihood, being watched, and I had no desire to linger in the lobby.

"You are in a hurry. What kind of man rushes to embrace death?" He genuflected to a framed painting of the Virgin Mary and nodded toward the stairs. "It's time," he said, and he grinned, a flash of white in his tanned face. "I hope everything is right with your soul."

I WAS never certain, afterward, if the single candle placed upon the table was for atmosphere or to prevent me from seeing what they were doing. I felt distinctly ridiculous, shirtless and lying flat on my back with my hands folded across my abdomen, a garland of marigolds around my neck. The room was dark, the blinds drawn against the waxing moon and the twinkling festival lights. Seeker and an unnamed man who smelled—not unpleasantly—of aniseed had arranged my belongings so the scene would point to suicide. The letter I'd written to Ed but had not yet sent lay on the bureau, pinned down with my watch. I wasn't sure leaving it in plain sight was a good idea, but Seeker assured me it was necessary.

"How are they going to make certain connections, señor, unless things are appropriately evident? They will need to contact him, your friend, and also the police and other officials in Los Angeles." He pronounced it the old way, with a hard "g," the proper Spanish way, and not the bastardized version favored by the gringos. "Are you all right?" He sat on the side of the bed and leaned over me, his young face appearing quite serious in the candlelight. "At any time until he gives you the powder, you can say no. After that…." He shrugged, that expansive gesture of the arms and shoulders that can mean anything, or nothing at all.

"Right." I forced myself to breathe. After all, I reasoned, it might be the last time. It occurred to me that this was absolutely mad, and no one in his right mind would ever consider doing something so foolhardy. It also occurred to me that I wasn't in my right mind. "Off we go, then."

The other man appeared out of the gloom, his features somber. "You are a brave man, señor." He waved Seeker back. "Here is what will happen: I administer the powder. You will feel a growing stiffness over your entire body. For some, this begins in the chest, but for others, the feet are the first to go. At the same time, your senses as you know them will begin to shut down, starting with your vision, which will grow dark around the edges and then fade entirely. Sounds will seem to come from far away. Your ability to speak—and to swallow—will be taken from you. Your lungs will fail to draw your breath. Then, there is a space of darkness."

"Right, I understand that, but how long a space?" I tried to laugh, but it came out sounding like a croak. "I've things to do, you understand."

"You are frightened." Seeker appeared out of the gloom and laid a hand on my shoulder. "It's hard to trust. But you are in the very best hands." He turned to pour a glass of water from the jug on the bureau, and as he did so, his jacket fell open. He was wearing a shoulder holster. What sort of man brings a gun to an occasion like this?

"I'm assuming you've done this before." I was suddenly— ferociously—thirsty. I gulped down the water he gave me and gestured for more. "With other people, I mean." The tiny little voice in the back of my head—the same one that screamed out bits of wise advice at the most inopportune times—shrieked, *For God's sake, Tony. Think what you're doing.*

"Papa Loi trained with the very best bokor in Port-au-Prince," Seeker told me. I knew instinctively that his name wasn't really "Papa Loi." I also knew he'd been in Port-au-Prince around about the time I was cutting my third set of teeth. "Shall we begin?"

36

I was going to die; I had already handed myself over. Even if I wanted to stop, I doubted they would let me. It was a done thing. "And I will wake up." I swallowed back a rising wave of panic. "Afterwards."

Seeker reached for my hand and held it in his. "I promise." He suddenly drew my arm out straight, and then Papa Loi was leaning over me, his expressionless face coming closer. His teeth closed on the tender flesh of my upper arm, a lancing pain that grew until it towered over me like a living thing.

"The left arm." Papa Loi drew back, his teeth and lips wet with my blood. "Closer to the heart."

I felt the powder falling on my skin like tender satin needles. My body was on fire from the inside out. It happened a lot faster than I'd expected. There was a roaring noise, like a hurricane wind, and the room was full of sounds. I tasted salt on my lips and something else, something dark and bitter that seemed to swell the back of my throat. My heart began beating faster and faster, thrumming so violently that it seemed it would split my ribs. I tried to breathe, but there was no air—*You have to stop it.* My throat was paralyzed. I couldn't speak. *I've changed my mind.*

A moving wedge of darkness drew down over me with an appalling inevitability; the room was going away. The darkness was pressing down, and there was nothing I could do about it, there was nothing—

Chapter Five

THE MORNING sun was hot where it came streaming through the gap in my bedroom curtains. I turned onto my side and drifted, smiling. I was in bed with Ed, our bodies pressed together from shoulder to hip, our legs entwined. He was sleepy-eyed, a little grumpy, endearingly rumpled, and utterly desirable.

"Don't be an idiot," he murmured. "She wasn't really dead. It was a joke. A ruse."

"Some ruse." I smoothed my palms down his chest, a possessive gesture. *Mine. This man is mine.* "What does she do for an encore?" But my caresses had successfully diverted his attention.

He rolled me onto my back and pressed himself into me, his erection throbbing against my belly. "Nice house." He whispered it into my open mouth. "I bet you can't even hear the screams."

I opened my eyes. I was flat on my back in a strange bed, in an unfamiliar room. A large ginger cat was lying on my abdomen, purring with a noise like rain falling on corrugated tin. He regarded me with his bright yellow eyes, unimpressed. "Were you in the dream?" I asked. I scratched him under his chin. "If that's what this is."

The door flew open and three small children—I couldn't tell if they were boys or girls—pushed into the room, dislodging the cat, who streaked away for parts unknown.

"Good morning," I said. This sent them into a flurry of giggles. "That one really worked," I mused aloud. "Must write that into my next book. Ah, is your mother about?" Blank looks. "Mother. *Madre*?" I sat up and was just about to push away the blankets when I realized I was completely naked. Not only that, but my dream had left a souvenir behind, as stiff as a winter lawn chair. Goddamn the male anatomy, anyway. "Look, why don't you go and find your mother." I made shooing motions. "Give a chap a chance to get decent. Off you go."

They barged out of the room, slamming the door as they went.

I slipped out of bed and examined myself in a full-length mirror that was propped against the opposite wall. I looked the same as always—perhaps better-rested—and except for a small, dark bruise on my arm where Papa Loi had bitten me, I hadn't been injured. His sharp teeth had punctured the soft tissue to a depth of perhaps half an inch, creating a tattoo-like wound that vaguely resembled Morse code.

I found a robe lying across a chair, put it on, and double-tied the belt. It was of good quality silk and smelled faintly of sandalwood. The room was painted in shades of red, which was curiously soothing. A window opened onto a sheltered courtyard with a fountain and a scattering of fancy chickens pecking about in the dust. One very large rooster with a magnificent plumage strutted up and down, inspecting his harem. Now and then he would puff out his chest and crow, setting the lady birds all aflutter.

On the opposite wall, there was a wash basin and jug set on a wooden bureau. When I peered into the mirror mounted just above it, I was pleased to see my own familiar face and my hair with its wide streaks of gray. There were no marks that I could see, and except for the dark circles under my eyes, I might have been on holiday. I drenched my face and patted it dry, and found a new toothbrush still in its wrapper and some toothpaste. I wasn't sure how long I'd been unconscious, but each one of my teeth had its own tiny little fur coat.

I was just pondering what to do for a shave when a tentative knock sounded on the door. I imagined the children had come back, so I called out for them to come in now that I was decent.

"You must forgive my nieces and nephews. We don't get many visitors to our home." Seeker was wearing rumpled chinos and a short-sleeved shirt, open at the neck. In the wan autumn sunshine, his eyes looked almost golden. "How do you feel?" he asked. He moved to straighten the lapels of my robe. "I trust you have found everything satisfactory?"

"Seeker, I'll confess I haven't a clue what's going on." I gestured at the room and its contents. "This is very comfortable and I've had a fabulous sleep, but beyond that, I'm lost." I drew a slow breath in an effort to calm myself. "Where am I?"

He grinned, all white teeth and dimples. Christ, he was beautiful. "Rest easy, Señor Leonard. You're at my mother's house in Xalapa. You are quite safe. The situation went very well."

"Then I... died?" I'd no memory of it. I'd no memory of anything after that night in the hotel.

"Indeed." He inclined his head. "There are some clothes in the bureau for you. Also shoes. I wasn't entirely sure of your size, so forgive me if they don't quite fit. I was forced to estimate."

I smirked. "I'd think a young man of your talents would immediately know my size."

He laughed, but for the first time, there was something desperate in it. "Please, don't torment me. You are a very handsome man." He bit his lip. "When you are dressed, come down to the kitchen to eat. We still have to make plans."

I did as he asked, dressing quickly in the clothes he'd left, which fit very well.

"IT WORKS like this." Seeker took one hand off the wheel long enough to light a cigarette. "The police, they have already been to Ixtagapa. The doctor in the town made out your death certificate, and a copy has been sent to Los Angeles. The police there have also been notified." He glanced across at me. "You follow?"

Following the instructions of the Ixtagapa police, I was buried in the cemetery at Xalapa. Being a foreigner, not much was made of my funeral, although some of the ladies did put flowers on the grave. I wondered aloud how they had managed to bribe the town doctor to sign off on a death certificate.

"There was no bribery required," Seeker said. "The powder rendered you quite insensible, a sleep so close to death that no heartbeat could be detected. And, of course, you were cold by the time he arrived." At my inquiring look, he continued. "We packed you in ice." He laughed at my incredulous expression. "And buried a coffin full of stones. A good plan, don't you think?"

"There was a letter...." My scalp prickled. "I left it on the bureau in the hotel. I'd written it to my friend—"

"It has been sent to him," he assured me. "News of your death will also be published in the newspapers."

"Of course." It was necessary, but I didn't care for it. No, I didn't care for it at all. In the final analysis, I was letting a friend—perhaps my only friend—believe I was dead. It didn't sit well with me.

It was a beautiful warm day, and we were driving up into the mountains, passing small towns and villages and being treated to occasional glimpses of the vast cloud forest that hung over the distant hills. The air smelled of flowers, various scents I didn't recognize, lush and intoxicating. To a casual observer, we might be two friends traveling to a secret picnic spot... or two lovers hurrying to a dangerous and clandestine assignation. "And now?"

"Now I am driving you to the airfield at Xocchel, where a ticket has been reserved for you." He grinned. "First class, to take you to Mérida, on the Yucatán peninsula. She said it is where you want to go."

"I'm impressed," I said. "I'm not sure I can afford first class." The implication clicked inside my head like tumblers turning in a lock. "Wait a minute. Why would I want to go to Mérida?"

"The woman said she'd spoken with you on the telephone." He glanced at me, his smooth brow creased in consternation. "She said you'd decided to stay away for the time being, and Mérida is farther away, in case they happen to come looking. She brought the money for your living expenses. For twenty thousand American dollars, you can afford a great deal."

If my stare could have stopped the car, it would have. "But everybody thinks I'm dead." A throb of panic climbed the taut ladder of my throat. "How could anyone know? I'm supposed to be dead. How the hell did anybody find out?" It had all been for nothing. I'd gone through this entire goddamn charade for nothing.

He glanced at me quickly, then back at the road. "The money was in an envelope. She brought it with her when she came to Ixtagapa." His brow furrowed, and I saw his hands tighten on the steering wheel. "She showed me your signature on the envelope. She said the money was to make sure things progressed in the right way." He huffed out a breath, clearly confused. "Your sister. She said you wouldn't want to go back to America, and the money was to see you safely to the Yucatán."

"My sister? I haven't got a sister. What did she look like?"

"Tall, elegant, rich. She was blonde, and she carried an expensive handbag. The money was in one-hundred-dollar bills."

The only tall, rich blonde I knew was Deborah, and I doubted she'd give me the time of day, never mind thousands of dollars. "She said the money was for me... she said that, exactly?"

41

He drew a slow breath. "She said—this didn't make any sense to me—she needed every assurance things would be taken care of. *Todo var a ser atendido*, that's what she said. 'It will all be taken care of.'"

So old man Stirling had sent his dutiful daughter down Mexico way with a purse full of money to make sure I stayed put and didn't get any ideas about coming back to California. Unlike Janet, Deborah did everything the old man told her to. If what Seeker said was true, both the FBI and the Federales would be looking to talk with Stirling soon enough. The last thing he needed was me, fresh from my Mexican exile, to stir things up.

To hell with the old bastard, anyway.

"I'm not going to Mérida. I'm going back to Los Angeles. I don't care who doesn't like it."

THERE WERE no elegant, Spanish-speaking blondes waiting when I disembarked at Los Angeles Airport. It was late afternoon on a gray day, with heavy clouds hanging over the city and the occasional rumble of thunder in the distance. My only baggage was a small portmanteau I'd carried on with me, containing a change of clothes and a rosary Seeker had given me. I had a little over a hundred dollars in my wallet and a handful of centavos in my trouser pocket. That was it.

I caught a cab to my apartment in Westwood, half expecting God knows what disaster, but when I put my key in the door, it was exactly the same as always. The davenport was over by the window, with its little tables keeping it company on either side; the cocktail table I'd had shipped directly to Los Angeles from Ceylon—bought with Janet's money—was still holding court in the middle of the room, still decorated with my typewriter and a dusty sheaf of white bond paper. My new book was to be called *A Sad Farewell*, a provisional title until the publicity department came up with something better. I'd left off in the middle of a scene where the hero and the femme fatale were drinking coffee and talking about her estranged husband in a very civilized manner. There was nothing at all sordid in it. I suspected that was the problem.

In the kitchen, the window was open a tiny crack, letting in the breeze. The air smelled of ozone. A newspaper I didn't remember reading was lying on the kitchen table, turned up to the crossword puzzle. A ballpoint pen lay near it, and an empty coffee cup with a brown stickiness crusted inside. A clean plate and a drinking glass sat in the dish drainer.

I followed the corridor to the bedroom and then to the bathroom, the way you do after you've been away a while, but nothing seemed out of place. It just didn't feel like it was *mine*. Even the copy of *L'île au Trésor—Treasure Island*, the French translation, the one thing left from my childhood in Montreal—felt alien, strange, a set piece. I picked it up and opened the cover, waiting for the familiar scent of old paper to comfort me as it usually did. Even the book didn't smell the same.

I moved quickly around the apartment, opening windows as I went. I couldn't shake the feeling that someone had been there while I'd been away, someone who'd gone through my things, touching them, leaving their traces behind. Maybe there'd been something in that dust they'd given me, or maybe something had gone wrong.

Jesus Christ, Tony, you let some Mexican witch doctor give you zombie powder.

If I'd written it, my publishers would have rejected it. Mexican exile, zombie powder, faking one's own death—it was the stuff of a bad radio serial, for Christ's sake.

I caught the phone on the first ring, hoping it was Ed. "Hello?"

"What the devil are you doing back here?" The voice was barely a snarl, crackling with rage.

"You sound disappointed, Mr. Stirling. Did you expect me to stay hidden down there in Mexico?" How the hell he knew I was back was a mystery to me. He must have had a tail on me since Janet's death. As far as he was concerned, Deborah had gone to Ixtagapa to buy my continued absence—an extended vacation on the Yucatán, courtesy of Papa Stirling. My being back in LA meant Deborah had failed. No wonder he sounded like he'd been chewing nails. "There are some things even money can't buy, and I've never been fond of the Yucatán. Better luck next time."

"I half expected you to show up at your own funeral." He laughed nastily. "Not much of a Mexican exile."

I squeezed the receiver so hard it creaked ominously. "I didn't kill her."

"Yet you turned tail and ran." Janet's father exhaled noisily. "So tell me, Tony, how much would it take to get rid of you for good?"

At first I didn't believe he'd said what he did. I leaned back against the radio cabinet and fumbled for a cigarette. The radio was on, playing something by one of the Dorsey brothers, but I couldn't tell which one. I didn't remember turning the radio on either. "Get rid of me?" I found a cigarette and lit it. "I'm dead, remember? Dead and buried in a tiny little Mexican town that nobody would ever think to visit." My turning up had probably put a crimp in his plans, but Linton Stirling, a Vanderbilt on his mother's side, never let a little thing like failure stop him.

"Don't dodge the question." There was a pause, and his voice went away and then came back again. "I've got my checkbook here in front of me—"

"Haven't you always?"

"Don't be impertinent. I'm willing to write you a check right now for any amount you desire."

"Go to hell." My fingers tightened their grip on my cigarette, crushing it.

"We could make it a donation to charity if you prefer. That orphanage in Montreal, what's it called?" A rustling noise, the sound of paper. "Any amount, Tony. You could guarantee that no other little boy has to grow up in poverty like you did."

If I closed my eyes I could hear them, little boys singing folksongs, me among them. My French pronunciation was atrocious, even then. The rooms were always damp, always cold, and even in the height of summer, the building felt like a tomb. The interior was all dark wood, richly patterned wallpaper in drab colors, slippery walnut floors. It wasn't institutional, not at all; it was more like an eccentric grandmother's house, where there are evil things in the attic and everyone knows terrible secrets. When it rained, the walls creaked and groaned, and wind made the ceilings howl—an eldritch, unearthly sound. I was never afraid there. What I felt most of all was loneliness. I hadn't asked to be an orphan, but nobody ever does. I was asleep in my bed the night the fire burned our house to the ground and killed my parents and Eustache, our much-loved cat. How did I survive? I've no idea. How does anybody survive anything, at all?

"I didn't kill Janet. And I'm not interested in your money." I was about to hang up when something occurred to me. "There wasn't much about it in the papers." Even the LA press, notoriously fond of scandal, had only made a few perfunctory jabs at the story before it sank without trace. "I'd have thought—"

"Thought what?" His voice snapped like laundry on a taut clothesline.

"How did you manage it?" *Sur le Pont d'Avignon…* another old favorite that every French-speaking child anywhere in the world knows; I can probably sing it in my sleep. I was never mistreated at Les Petites Soeurs de Notre Dame. In many ways my childhood was idyllic, and I was exquisitely cared for. I never went hungry and I was never beaten. I had my own little bed in which to sleep at night, and my sheets were always clean. I had toys, and a few books of my own, and a teddy bear I'd named Monsieur Gros. "Apart from the initial frisson, it hardly made a ripple in the newspapers."

"That's because I own most of them," he said. "Good-bye, Tony." And I was listening to dial tone.

He knew. The old bastard knew more than he was telling, and he was keeping it close to his vest. Obviously he'd counted on my staying in Mexico—staying dead. He assumed I'd be too scared or too guilty to come back to a city where I was the number one suspect in my wife's brutal murder. He was counting on the guilt and fear keeping me south of the border. I brooded on this while I made some coffee and drank it, sitting in the living room and looking out my great big windows at my great big view: trees, buildings, the distant skyline. After a while, it started to get dark, and I thought perhaps I could go out somewhere, only the notion didn't have much appeal, and besides, I was deathly tired. This disease slowly saps the life from you, or so they say. Mostly I feel as if I've been fed upon by starving vampire bats and drained to the point of exhaustion. Sleep is no longer a necessary habit but a hobby.

I sat by the windows for a long time, looking out, and I knew if I got in my car and drove for a little ways, I could see the San Fernando Valley, and if I drove a little farther, I could be in the mountains before tomorrow. I could go to Vegas and gamble some of Janet's money on the chance of winning big. I could show them how an Englishman plays baccarat, even though I'm not an Englishman, not really. I wasn't born there. Immediately after the war, I lived there for a while, but London, like most of Europe, had been devastated by the Blitz and the ruins simply made me sad. I remember walking down what remained of Oxford Street, picking my way through broken glass and fallen masonry. The street was empty of all life, the shops and businesses with boarded-up windows and doors, and mannequins that reminded me unpleasantly of corpses heaped up in great piles. London is a collection of sad memories to me.

I could get in my car and drive away from all of this, but no matter how far I drove, it would never be far enough to leave any of it behind. I didn't kill Janet, and I didn't know who had, but I couldn't simply let things lie.

I knew what I had to do. I didn't want to do it.

Chapter Six

IT WAS after midnight, and close enough to the time of my original visit that the coincidence made me a little ill. The door wasn't locked—there was no need—and someone had taken away the stained, battered mattress, the ropes, and all the rest of it. I went in through the poolside entrance, walking quietly and carefully. I needn't have bothered: Linton Vanderbilt Stirling had gone to his Long Island residence, grieving the death of his beloved daughter, Janet. It's amazing what a society reporter will say, given editorial latitude and sufficient column inches, to adequately follow orders. The entire estate was quiet, with no lights showing in the windows of the main house, and no servants or other functionaries to question my being there. In the gardens of the adjacent mansion, a servant drove around and around on a little tractor, dragging up the rubbish and fallen leaves, but if he saw me, he didn't seem to care... or perhaps he cared, but hadn't seen me. Who the hell mowed the lawn in the middle of the night?

We'd been intending to catch a Cunard liner to France for our honeymoon, but mechanical difficulties led to a postponement, and we were advised the ship would sail the next evening. The guesthouse—built when Janet was still a wild young woman—seemed a reasonable alternative. We raided her father's liquor cabinet for some liquid refreshment and went down to the guesthouse, where we fucked like minks until dawn. Janet's extreme avidity was unusual to me, since all the women I'd been involved with in the past parted their legs only under a cloak of maidenly modesty, *Oh dear me, what are you doing? No, I couldn't possibly do that. Whatever do you mean?* Janet's forthright attitude to sex was rather refreshing, and I, newly married and utterly besotted, assumed her eagerness was all for me.

I searched the guesthouse on hands and knees, combing the expensive Turkish carpet for anything I thought might be a clue. I wasn't stupid enough to assume my tenure writing detective novels in any way qualified me to investigate a crime. I didn't even know what I was looking for. I found a hairpin and the button off a man's coat, the latter probably ripped off in the heat of passion, which could have occurred at just about any time. I put both of them in my trouser pocket. The hairpin I knew was most likely Janet's, even though I'd never seen her wear them, but the button could have come from any number of men. Janet was quite omnivorous when it came to bed partners.

The bureau, like the clothes closet, was empty. Likewise for a small table that had once sat beside the bed. There was nothing in it except a length of ribbon and a scattering of lint. I ran my fingers over the tops of all the moldings and the skirting boards and under the rug, but there was nothing else. I lit a cigarette and sat on the doorstep, wishing I had a drink. I was hardly going to paw through old man Stirling's liquor cabinet, no matter how far away he was.

Liquor bottles. Something about liquor bottles niggled at the underside of my mind. Janet and I had taken champagne from the cabinet at the main house on our wedding night, but there'd been no bucket and no ice. Liquor bottles. No bucket. No ice. How in God's name had we kept the champagne cold? Who'd bother drinking warm champagne?

I went into the bathroom. It was the usual arrangement of tub, toilet, and sink, but instead of a vanity cabinet there was a tiny little fridge Janet had insisted her father have installed for her. It was larger than it seemed, with enough room for three or four bottles, but that was plenty. Way in the back there was half a bottle of decent scotch, and quite old enough, according to the label, to leave its mother. I decided to introduce it to my palate, so I twisted the top off with gleeful abandon and took a long swallow.

I nearly choked. I coughed until I thought my lungs would burst and managed to expel something onto the palm of my hand. It was a small, hard object, quite possibly metal, and had been wrapped in cellophane by someone entirely too meticulous for his own good. I managed to get the wrapping off. It was a ring—a man's ring, not a woman's—with an odd sigil I'd never seen before. It looked like a child's drawing of a flower, with five rudimentary petals clumsily arranged around a central circle. I'd never seen Janet wearing anything like this, and it was much too vulgar for old Linton Stirling to bother with. One of her men friends, perhaps?

But why bother concealing it in a bottle of scotch? Janet was hardly a blushing virgin, and her taste for handsome young men wasn't exactly a family secret. Someone had gone to a lot of trouble to wrap the thing in cellophane and seal it with tape against the possibility of it coming undone. Things like this occurred in my novels: so-called evidence, deliberately planted, intended to throw whoever investigated the murder off the scent... or to implicate someone previously considered blameless. Somehow the police hadn't found it. Maybe they were in old man Stirling's pay too.

"I can't figure this one out," I said aloud. "I need help."

I knew just whose help I needed.

I CIRCLED the block three or four times, trying to work up the courage to go and knock on his door. His house was at the top of a flight of stairs so long the mailbox was located at the bottom. Even the mailman wouldn't bother to climb that far. I knew he was awake because there was a light on, and now and then a shadow passed behind the drawn blinds. He was pacing.

I parked too close to a hydrant and walked up, taking the stairs slowly, one at a time. What would I say to him? "Sorry I let you think I was dead. Couldn't be helped." What I wanted to say was "I can explain."

What I actually said was his name. "Hello, Ed."

He stood in the open doorway for a minute, just looking at me. He didn't seem surprised to see me. When he was finished looking, he stepped back and, holding the door open, gestured me in.

"I need your help." I couldn't look at him, so I examined the floor instead. "It's about Janet."

He took two glasses off the sideboard and produced a bottle of bourbon from under the sink. "Want a drink?"

"You know I do."

He splashed a goodly amount into both glasses and handed one to me. "So what brings you by at this hour?"

"You're talking to me as if I were one of your clients."

He sipped his drink, his expression inscrutable. "Aren't you?"

"I see." I moved to lay my glass on the kitchen counter. "My coming here was a mistake. I've no real right to ask you anything. I see that now." I was almost to the door when his hand on my arm stopped me. I didn't turn around.

"Why did you do it?" His voice was very quiet. I don't think I'd ever heard him speak so quietly, or with such profound hurt. "The plan was for you to go to Mexico and lay low for a while."

"I know." I was horribly, abominably ashamed of myself. This man had taken a horrific beating rather than tell the police what he knew about me. I didn't know there were still people in the world who did that sort of thing. "The papers said the police… had you. They held you for a while, it said."

"Yeah. They picked me up downtown, near Fromsett Street. I'd gone back there to question some of the men, thinking somebody might know something. They said they hadn't seen you. Then McAvity showed up, from Central Homicide. They told him to bring me in, and make it rough."

I exhaled a breath that felt an awful lot like a sob. "How rough?"

"Bruises. I was ugly for a couple of weeks," he said. "Some sadistic bastard threw hot coffee in my face."

Those sons of bitches. "I'm always amazed by what passes for police work in America."

"They sent me a letter, from Mexico. They said you wrote it." His grip on my arm tightened, tugging me around to face him. There was something taut and desperate in his face. "I'm not the kind of guy who manages to collect a lot of friends along the way, and I thought—" He drained his glass and slammed it down on the countertop. "McAvity gave me the letter. He said some FBI liaison, working in Mexico, gave it to him. Some kind of joint investigation, them and the Mexicans." He turned to look out the kitchen window, his back to me, his shoulders tensed.

I went to him slowly and laid my hand on his back, my touch butterfly-light. "I'm sorry, Ed."

"Guys like you are always sorry," he said bitterly.

I slid my hand up to his shoulder and squeezed gently. "I missed you." It came out a tortured whisper, and I felt sick to my stomach. "You know what I'm like. I've got no guts." I could see us both reflected in the kitchen window: my face looked more serene than it had a right to. He looked haunted, a man worn thin by impossible emotions. "I should go."

He turned and looked at me, his gaze playing over my face, moving everywhere but alighting nowhere. "I don't want you to go." He swallowed hard. "I want you to stay."

We'd kissed before, so it was nothing new, but the taste of him was a remembered bliss. I held his face in my hands as we kissed—slowly, deeply, each caress a palpable ache—and I felt as if I were flying to pieces.

Naked, he was beautiful—a long column of tense muscle and pale skin untouched by the California sun. He shuddered when I touched him, holding himself a little apart as if afraid of his own arousal. That first kiss blurred into a dozen as our bodies found each other on the taut white sheets, arms and hands and legs tangling eagerly together. He cursed me quietly, his hips and belly grinding furiously into mine as our skins, slick with sweat, slid us over some invisible edge into an ecstatic darkness.

"WHAT'S THIS from?" He dipped two fingers into an indentation just below my collarbone on the right side.

"Mmm, I don't remember." I thought for a moment. "Fell down the stairs. I was an inordinately clumsy child."

"You grew up in Montreal," he said.

"Yes." It didn't surprise me that he knew. I'd have been more surprised if he didn't. "The orphanage was called Les Petites Soeurs de Notre Dame. In Ville-Marie, in the old part of the city. Quite beautiful, really."

"We're both orphans," he pointed out.

"I don't think anything is coincidence," I said. "I think life has its own ideas of how the thing should go."

He reached across me for his cigarettes, shook one out, and lit it. "Why did you come back?" I started to say something, and he narrowed his eyes at me. "Don't say you came back for me. I won't believe you."

"I didn't kill Janet—"

"I know you didn't." He drew on his cigarette and blew smoke toward the ceiling.

"I had to come back. Ed, I can't just let it alone. Somebody killed my wife." I'd never get that image out of my mind. "We didn't love each other, and we weren't even living together when she died, but she was still my wife."

He nodded. "You think Stirling was involved?"

"You know damn well he was. He practically admitted he'd covered the whole thing up." I'd told him about Stirling's telephone call the day I got back from Mexico. "It was quite convenient that I got the blame. A dead man is the best patsy in the world. He can't talk back." I got out of bed, found my trousers on the floor, and dug out the ring I'd found in Janet's guest house. "There you go." I handed it to him. "Found that in a bottle of scotch." I climbed back into bed beside him. "A bottle of very good scotch, mind."

He sat up and snuffed his cigarette in a nearby ashtray. "Ugly. Whoever bought it probably had to club it over the head to get it out of the store." He turned it around, examining it in the pale light from the bedroom window.

"Hard to see it in the dark," I commented. "Have you any idea what it is?"

He reached to turn on a lamp. "It's a man's ring, definitely. Any dame with fingers as big as this would have to be a lady wrestler." He thought for a moment. "You say you found it in the guesthouse. In a bottle of scotch?"

"Wrapped in cellophane."

He nodded. "So somebody went to a lot of trouble to plant it where it would eventually be found." He spent a few minutes turning it over in his hands, his long, slim fingers caressing the crude design. I could practically hear the wheels clacking in his brain. I knew what he was going to ask before he asked it. "Who'd have cause to be at the guesthouse? Besides Janet, I mean."

"She doesn't keep any staff." I thought back to our wedding night. "If she wanted anything from the main house, she'd have to go get it herself." We'd finished both bottles of champagne that night and dressed ourselves hastily to go fetch more. "That late, there'd be no servants about except Pepe. He's the Chilean houseboy." All the lights were out except for the kitchen, where Pepe was smoking a cigarette. "He was flicking the ashes into the sink and looking out the window."

"Looking at what?"

"I don't know. It seemed an odd thing for him to do. All the servants were free to smoke in their rooms, or anywhere they wished, really." The more I thought about it, the odder it seemed, and that was saying something. Nothing about Linton Stirling's family life got within shouting distance of normal. "I don't know. Was he looking for something? I don't want to jump to unwarranted conclusions."

"Not even to tie up the end of a novel?" He smirked. "Yes, I've read them. Of course I have."

"Please." I held up a hand. "Spare me your layman's review."

He leaned close and kissed me, very gently and very tenderly. "You're a damn good writer, Tony."

"Mmm." I was still tingling from that kiss. "And an even better drunk."

"Maybe your Chilean houseboy was waiting." Ed squeezed the ring in his fist. "Watching out the window and waiting for something."

"I don't know." The more I thought about it, the stranger Pepe's behavior seemed—but mere strangeness wasn't quite enough to convict a man. Maybe he smoked in the kitchen every night, looking out the window. "What would Pepe be doing with ropes and such? I hardly think Janet would let anyone tie her up, which is something else I don't understand. What sort of person does such things?" Ed was looking at me carefully and smiling the broad, ingenuous smile of a used car salesman. "Oh no, you don't," I said. "You can forget it right now."

He drew his hand down my chest and belly—a slow, sensuous touch that made my toes curl. "It's all right." He grinned. "You can trust me."

"TOO TIGHT?" Ed gave the silk necktie a gentle tug and leaned down to smile at me.

"Oh, not at all," I said. "I'll make a pretty picture when the neighbors discover my bloated corpse." He'd tied me—a little too expertly for comfort—spread-eagled on his bed, my ankles fastened to the footboard, my wrists tethered to the headboard with a seaman's knot.

"Still feel your hands?"

"Barely," I grumbled. "When were you planning on killing me?" I didn't like being tied up but I didn't want him to know that.

"Quit complaining," he said. "This is educational." He moved to lie between my parted legs and slowly drew the very tip of his tongue up the inside of my left thigh. My cock liked this. It liked it very much. He repeated the same action on the other leg. My cock liked that even better. "People who enjoy these sorts of games know not to take unnecessary chances," he said. He leaned closer, his open mouth hovering over my cock but not touching. He breathed on me, very gently, like someone snuffing a match, and something deep inside my belly throbbed and twisted. "There's always a word, a phrase, or even a gesture—" He licked each of my nipples in turn. "—they agree to use, so things never go too far."

"So what's ours?" I asked. He told me to choose anything I wanted. "Good-bye," I said. It seemed to fit with the tenor of our relationship.

I groaned when his teeth fastened none too gently onto my right shoulder and made a stinging little pain that bloomed into a tiny point of pleasure so keen it was nearly shameful. He moved to hold my head, long fingers clasped around my nape while he kissed me. I didn't care for the gleam of cunning in his blue eyes. No, I didn't care for it at all. "Ed, I swear to God—"

"The whole point of such games is to suspend sexual release until the last possible moment… to spin out the pleasure till you can't take it anymore." He licked the tip of my cock, then swallowed me whole, and the pulsing in my belly grew and grew until it was as large as the room.

I listened to the gasping sounds of pleasure, and wondered if I was doing that and when I'd become so unashamedly vocal. My fists clenched so hard, the wooden headboard creaked and groaned. The silk ties held fast. I arched my back and pushed my hips toward him, my body aching for completion, but he pulled away.

He sat back on his heels and looked down at me. "Tony?"

"Finish it!" My voice was a strangled croak. "You son of a bitch, finish it."

"That would ruin the demonstration." He moved to untie my left hand, and I briefly considered bashing him in the face with it. "I want to make this last as long as possible." He drew my thumb into his mouth and sucked on it, his tongue tracing the tip in a relentless—*to hell with him anyway*—pattern, over and under. I was pulled back from the edge a little; my arousal was still very much in evidence, but not as violently immediate.

"I want to touch you." My other hand strained the silk tie, reaching for him. I felt as if I were flying apart at the seams. "I want to hold you."

He let my thumb slip out of his mouth. "Is it time for that word?"

"Ohhh… yes, please."

"That's not the word, Tony." He grinned. "Don't you remember?"

"Oh for Christ's sake," I groaned, "good-bye!"

Three strokes, four strokes of his wildly talented mouth, and I went plunging over the edge, coming so hard my vision went, my cock pulsing in time with my beating heart. I felt him tugging at the ties, freeing me. I pulled him into my arms and held him, reaching between our bodies to stroke him until the climax took him. He was silent for a long time, except for the subtle swish and hush of his breath, moving in and out.

"ONE THING I don't quite get," he said, much later, after we'd exhausted our passions yet again. "What about the shoe, the high-heeled shoe? The coroner's report said there were imprints from the heel of a woman's size six dress shoe clearly visible in not only the subdermal layers, but also in the bones of the skull. Somebody hit her pretty hard."

"What about it?" I didn't understand where he was going with it. "A weapon is a weapon. When all's said and done, she's still dead."

"Not like this," he said. He cupped my face in his hand and kissed me. His thumb caressed the scars on my cheekbone and the long one running from my right temple to the point of my chin. "This was personal. Your face is who you are. You don't just beat somebody's face in, unless you're trying to erase them. There had to be a lot of hate, maybe a lot of resentment, or both. Whoever did that to Janet must have hated her guts."

Chapter Seven

LINTON VANDERBILT Stirling not being currently in residence, it was safe for Ed and I to present ourselves at the main house early the next morning. It was a lovely morning, with the sun shining and the night's dew still upon the grass.

We walked past a tall gardener-shaped man who was watering three topiary box trees with a wand attached to a hose. An unlit cigarette hung precariously from his lower lip, and there was another stuck behind his ear. He turned to look as we went by. He had a broad, sunburned face, not quite as large as a car tire. If you turned it on its side, you could roll it like a hoop. "Mister's not home."

"We know," I said.

"Miss Deborah's in there, with her new man." He jerked his head toward the house. "Fancy-pants."

"What new man?" I asked, but Ed grabbed my arm and propelled me up the walk toward the front door. He rang the bell, his finger on his lips. After an appropriate interval, the door swung open, and the unmistakable smell of marijuana washed over us in a soporific wave.

"What do you want?" Pepe wasn't wearing his habitual white jacket. He wasn't wearing much at all, in fact, just a pair of brief swimming trunks held up by rubber and good will, and showing his squat, hairy body to its simian perfection. His eyes were bleary, rimmed with red, and his habitually vague expression had spread, flattening his face.

"We want to speak to Mr. Stirling." Ed leaned over and peered past Pepe, into the house. "Is he in?"

"Mr. Stirling is away." He started to shut the door, but Ed put his elbow in the gap.

"May we see Mrs. Stirling?" Ed asked. "After all, this concerns her too."

"Look. Mrs. Stirling died many years ago. There is no Mrs. Stirling." Pepe's shoulders started a slow creep toward his ears, and his hands bunched into fists. "Nobody is here. It is my day off. You can't come in."

"Oh, let them in, Pepe." The voice was female, of exquisite tone and perfect modulation. "It might be amusing." The door swung open all the way, and there she was, a tall, cool dream of a woman, impeccable in a white linen playsuit, her blonde hair hidden by a turban, and a pair of white, flat-heeled espadrilles on her feet. "So nice to see you again, Tony."

"You sound almost as if you mean it," I said. "Now say the other part, where you tell me what a disappointment I am and how you hate the fact your sister married a drunk."

"Not at all! It takes a brave and brilliant man to get away with murder." She laughed. "Sober, are you? To be quite frank, I'm wildly impressed." She stood back. "Come in." She raked an acquisitive gaze over Ed. "And who is this? Your divorce lawyer? No, come to think of it, he looks much too tough. Wherever did you get him?"

"Ed Malory." Ed showed his credentials, but she wasn't interested. "Mrs....?"

"My sister-in-law," I said. "Deborah."

We sat on the patio near the pool, sipping some kind of chilly, doctored lemonade and watching Pepe perform inelegant arabesques on the end of the diving board. He always seemed surprised when he hit the water. Deborah was in the midst of "a very messy divorce, but you know these foreign types. I'll be lucky to get out of it with my piggy bank intact." Her hands, I noticed, were free of rings, which wasn't like Deborah. Her innate good taste notwithstanding, she liked to be well decorated. She wasn't even wearing earrings. If things were as bad between them as she said, she might refuse to wear the jewelry simply because her husband had given it to her. "I might ask you for a loan, Tony. Would that be all right?"

Ed turned to look at me. He didn't really know what Deborah meant and wasn't sure what to think. "A loan? What does she mean?"

Deborah laughed. "Yes, do tell us what I mean, Tony." And, when I refused to reply, she said, "Tony, as Janet's husband, is the sole beneficiary of not only her life insurance, but her personal wealth as well." She smiled thinly. "Mind you, it's problematic, especially since you're legally dead, Tony, but I'm sure you can find a judge to reverse the whole thing."

"It's a sizeable estate?" Ed asked.

"The whole of it amounts to more than two million," Deborah replied. "Quite the windfall. But then, Janet was always so generous. With everything, really."

"I take it you and your sister weren't close?" Ed asked. The purported size of Janet's legacy seemed to make no impression on him at all. He'd taken out the small, leather-covered notebook he habitually carried and was jotting notes.

"Not particularly, but we got along all right." Deborah had been sitting on the edge of a chaise longue, but now she leaned back, laying out her legs like a flesh-colored bolt of sensuous and very expensive silk. "Are you married, Mr. Malory?"

"No. When did you last see your sister?"

She pretended to think about it. Behind us, Pepe attempted a flying swallow dive, failed, and emerged moments later, furious and coughing water. "Janet came to visit us about a month ago, in Bern. She only stayed three days, but we'd made plans to get together during Christmas, perhaps do a little skiing. You know how it is."

He didn't answer her. "So you had no reason to be angry with your sister? You held no grudge against her?"

"Of course not! Mr. Malory, I must object. Why are you asking me this?" She glanced at me, then back at Ed. "Am I under investigation? And if so, I don't see why the police haven't called. I daresay it's still their jurisdiction."

A door opened and closed and a trim blond man appeared, wearing swim trunks and with a towel slung around his neck. We all turned to look, and believe me, he was worth looking at. He wasn't particularly tall, but he had the broad shoulders and narrow waist and hips of a swimmer. His blond hair was cut short and combed to the side, a small boy's haircut. On him it looked absolutely arresting. He was oddly familiar for some reason I couldn't quite make out.

"Deborah, my dear. Introduce me to your friends." His voice was as beautiful as the rest of him. "Allan Layton." Nice handshake too. Very firm grip.

When we'd all been introduced, he went over to the swimming pool, nodded to Pepe, dropped his towel on the deck, climbed up onto the high board, and proceeded to execute a perfect two and one-half somersault with barely a ripple. Pepe looked like he wanted to kill him, and I suddenly remembered where I'd seen him: he'd starred in *This Gun Speaks Death*, a film many in the "industry" had derided, while the public, bless their hearts, loved it. He wasn't a bad actor and, as far as looks went, he had them. I just couldn't figure out what he was doing with Deborah.

More to the point, where was the doctor from Bern? A pending divorce notwithstanding, I'd have expected him to at least be watching from the wings.

"Very nice," I said. "Any more like him at home?" I'd meant it as a joke, but no one laughed. "So where's your husband, or is it impolite to ask? I find it difficult to keep up nowadays." She could take that last any way she liked.

"We've decided not to draw things out, Johan and I." She stretched the long fingers of her left hand out in front of her and regarded the ring finger. "There are some things my husband never understood about me."

"How long since you and your husband separated?" Ed asked.

Deborah sighed theatrically. "Mr. Malory, you are not a policeman, and I am not required to answer your questions. I do so out of politeness and at my own discretion. Johan and I decided to go our separate ways about a month ago."

"Around the time your sister visited?" He fixed her with a stare.

Deborah stood abruptly. "Good day, Mr. Malory. I believe we've finished here." She nodded to Pepe. "Show these gentlemen out."

We followed Pepe's hairy back (Christ, it was like a natural sweater) through the house and to the front door. He yanked it open and stood glaring at us. "Lady wants you to go. Told you not to come here."

"Just a second." Ed dug the ring out of his pocket and held it under Pepe's nose. "This mean anything to you?"

"*Ladrón*! Thief, you give it to me!" He slapped at Malory's hand, and the ring fell to the floor, tinkling as it rolled away. He dropped to his knees and frantically searched for it, cursing us both. "I hope your fucking balls fall off." He grabbed the ring from where it had fallen, behind a small yucca in a container. "My little sister made this for me. It's mine." He jerked his head toward the pool area. "She saw me wearing it, wanted to see it. This whole family are thieves."

Layton appeared—dripping wet—from outside. He'd obviously heard Pepe yelling. "Is there a problem, gentlemen? Perhaps there's something I can do to help."

Ed looked up. "You know how to use the phone?"

"I think I might." Layton smiled.

"Well, good," Ed replied. "You can call the cops."

Chapter Eight

THE COPS weren't the only reason I suddenly had a burning desire to get out of there, but they were rather high on the list. "I have to leave," I told Ed. "I can't be here when they—"

"Of course." He held out his car keys. "Take mine." He handed them across to me. I couldn't fathom the expression on his face. Obviously the disclosure of Janet's estate wasn't sitting well with him, and I understood, but really, how does one broach a subject like that? Is there ever a right time in any relationship to announce "By the by, I'm richer than Croesus"?

I went out, got into his car, and started it up. It was a late model Oldsmobile, not particularly luxurious but useful and well taken care of. All the way home, I thought about what Deborah had said, about Janet's money, and I felt sick inside because I didn't want a murdered woman's money and because I'd messed things up with Ed. I'd have gotten around to telling him sooner or later—at least I think I would. It's true what I said to him before: I haven't got any guts.

By the time I reached my apartment, I barely had the strength to make it up the stairs. It was still full daylight outside, but it might as well have been midnight. The crushing fatigue that was a hallmark of my disease dragged on me like leaden weights, and once inside the door, I kicked my shoes off and fell onto the couch. A yawning black pit opened its jaws and swallowed me whole.

I WAS freezing cold when I woke up. My cheeks and forehead and under my chin were burning hot, which usually meant a fever. I knew how this would go, how it had always gone. I'd alternately freeze and burn for a day or so, then collapse into profound fatigue and sleep until the inner fire had consumed itself. I ought to undress and go to bed properly, but my mind wouldn't let me rest. I shuffled to the bathroom and washed my face, checked my chin for beard, said to hell with it, and took my medication.

CHLOROQUINE: ANTIMALARIAL it said on the label. I couldn't argue with that, even though my illness isn't malaria or anything like it.

Tony Lionheart, I said, looking closely at myself in the mirror, *a friend to man.* Perhaps that was what I needed—to get out of my own very crowded mind for a while. A visit to the mission down on Fromsett Street might do the trick. I swallowed the two bitter little pills, brushed my teeth, and combed my hair, and went out. I left Ed's Oldsmobile at the curb with the keys tucked under the driver's side visor. I imagined he would be by to pick it up, and he'd prefer not to have to see me, at least not until we'd hashed things out properly. I didn't intend to stray too far from home, just to some little neighborhood bar where the light was dim and the booze was plentiful.

I found a place on Del Amigo where nobody seemed to know me. It was in one of those small, shabby, single-story buildings made of that harsh gray stone that's always in abundance no matter where in the world you go. The sign out front said DAVE'S, and probably should have said DIVE, but there were three things right now in its favor: it was close to where I lived; it was open; it had booze. I went in and sat at the bar, which was a long, dark shelf of old and much-abused wood, its greasy surface worn smooth by the impress of many elbows. "Gimlet," I told the barman.

He sneered at me. "We don't do none of them fancy drinks in here," he said. "You can have beer, or you can have liquor, or you can leave."

"Well...." I felt for my wallet. "When you put it that way...." I dropped a twenty on the bar. "Bourbon. Leave the bottle."

He picked up the bill, crinkled it, smoothed it out, twisted it, and snapped it between his fingers. Satisfied that it was good, he nodded. "Okay."

"Of course it is," I said. "I'm richer than God."

While I waited for him to come back with my whiskey, I took a look around. It was a long, narrow space approximately the size of a tramcar, but significantly dirtier and nowhere near as well decorated. Three hard-faced women in shabby coats smoked next to a brick wall at the rear; now and then a burst of raucous laughter would erupt from one of them, like the cawing of a distressed bird. An old man with the gray jowls and loose, quivering mouth of the career alcoholic was sorting through ashtrays on the empty tables, wearing a stained brown overcoat about three sizes two big and a pair of ill-fitting trousers that might have once been tweed. His shoes were two different colors. I watched him picking up cigarette butts and rolling them into a spotted red handkerchief.

That's you, a nasty voice inside my head whispered. *That's you in twenty years.*

No, I thought. *I won't live that long. My disease will finish me off, unless the booze gets there first.*

Janet used to ask, early in our marriage, why I drank so often and so much. She suspected something horrid in my past, something I'd done, and she assumed drinking was the way to assuage my conscience. She was dead wrong, of course. Nowadays my horrid thing was the same as everybody else's. The war hadn't been so long ended that I could simply forget about it.

IT'S FUNNY how seemingly unrelated things draw you into the past. The sound of dripping water has that effect for me, but not just any water. It can't be water leaking from a tap into a basin, or water down a rainspout in the winter. No, this water has to run in tiny drops from a low stone ceiling where it's been collecting all night long, a courtesy of late-summer dew or April snow melt. There's no container for this water to run into, but you can catch some in your mouth if you're careful and very patient. If you aren't patient, you can lick it off the stones.

"Here." The barman came back with a bottle of Wild Turkey and a glass. He set both down on the bar, along with my change. I counted it carefully, in front of him. If that offended him, I really didn't give a damn. "Anything else?"

"Eternal youth," I said. "Good teeth. Strong bones. A will to live. Life, liberty, and the pursuit of happiness. Did I leave anything out?" He went away muttering, and I sat at the bar for a while, sucking back my drink and half listening to the jukebox.

Time passed, and I'd put away about a third of the bottle when someone sat on the stool next to mine and said, "You don't remember me."

I turned slowly, aware the rotgut whiskey had probably destroyed some of my motor functions. "Allan Layton! Of course I remember you. You're Deborah's... friend." I'd never forget the sight of him in swimming togs. Even in a suit and tie, with a dun-colored fedora tilted over one impeccable eyebrow, he was damned near spectacular.

He grimaced a little but covered it admirably. "Yes, 'friend' is as good a word as any." He unbuttoned the tan overcoat he was wearing and beckoned to the bartender, who ignored him.

"I'd offer you some of mine," I said, "only I haven't got another glass." He held out his hand and I put the bottle in it. "You're a brave man. A very brave man."

He swallowed like a trouper, grinned, and laid the bottle on the bar where we could both reach it. "I've been looking all over the place for you." He glanced around. "Wonder if I can get a martini in here?"

"I wouldn't risk it." I pushed the bottle toward him. "Go on, take another pull. Put hair on your chest."

He laughed. "I wanted to talk to you about Janet," he said. "I have information that the police don't." All of his good humor suddenly fell away. "And I'm afraid it doesn't cast me in a very flattering light." He rubbed his forehead with his left hand. The smallest finger had a patch of lighter skin near the base, as if he'd tanned while wearing a ring. The area was very small and vaguely square, like the impress made by a signet ring. It was the sort of thing you'd easily dismiss as insignificant. Maybe it was insignificant after all.

"Oh?" I poured more bourbon into my glass. There's nothing worse than an empty glass, a glass that has no booze in it. "It sounds serious."

"Yes," he said slowly. "Yes, it sounds serious. It's on the order of...." He stopped, his forehead wrinkling. "On the order of withholding evidence."

Christ.

"If you wanted to consider it that way." His hands clenched into fists, then released. He reached past me for the bottle, took a long pull, and wiped his mouth on the back of his hand. "You're wondering, you and Mr. Malory, who was with Janet that night in the guesthouse."

I didn't wait for him to fill in the rest of it. "It was you." My heart pounded, seemed to grow till it filled my chest and pushed up into my throat. "All along, it's been you."

He saw where I was going with it. "No—Christ, no. Yes, I was there but I didn't kill her. Is that what you think?"

I reached for my glass. My hand almost didn't shake. "I don't know what to think."

"There's more to it, much more." He stared at the bar. "I'd rather not talk about it here, if you don't mind." He nodded toward the barkeep, who was standing nearby rubbing an invisible spot on the bar with a filthy towel. "You never know who's listening."

"So why don't you go to the police?" I asked. "Why come to me?"

"Will you let me tell you what I know?" He stood and buttoned his overcoat, smoothing the cloth down fussily, like a dowager with a piece of Irish lace. "It might help. It probably won't hurt."

"The cops already have their man," I said. "They arrested Pepe, remember? You were there."

Layton shook his head. "Pepe's a patsy. You and I know it. The police know it. That ring was planted. They'll keep Pepe for a day or so, then turn him loose. That son of a bitch sees everything that goes on at that house."

"Including you?" I wondered if he hadn't been doing a little detective work of his own, but I didn't say this out loud. He'd obviously been doing a little thinking of his own, and he seemed to be good at it. I also wondered how he so quickly deduced the ring was planted. "All right. We can talk at my place." I wrote the address on the back of a grubby cocktail napkin that looked like it predated Prohibition. "Park around the back. There's a sort of lane that runs behind the building. There's a man on the desk. He'll want to ring me before he lets you up, but tell him I said it's all right." I handed him the napkin.

He put it in his pocket, nodded a good-bye, and went out.

I waited for a few minutes and had another drink, hoping vaguely that experience would improve its flavor. No hope there—it tasted like rust and engine coolant. If Layton went straight to my apartment, driving, it would take him about five minutes. I'd give him another five to get in. That ought to be plenty of time for anybody who could follow simple directions. Once he was in and had had a chance to open some drawers and turn over some pictures, maybe pour himself a drink, I'd wander over there. It wasn't beyond possibility that Linton Stirling had had me followed by someone ordered to inform him of my every move, but I'd be damned if I'd help.

I tossed four bits on the bar and went out. I could have taken a cab, but the night air was pleasantly cool on my burning face and refreshed me in a way the whiskey couldn't. *You may develop an intolerance to alcohol,* the doctor had said. He'd handed me my diagnosis like a meter maid writing out a traffic ticket. *Many people with this disease are unable to drink.* It was almost funny, if irony happened to be the same thing as humor. The first thing I did after leaving the hospital was find a bar. I spent all that evening and part of the next day drinking; two bouncers brought me home and dumped me on Janet's doorstep. She left me there until I sobered up enough to find my own way to bed.

I passed a corner drugstore (SUNDRIES BEVERAGES PATENT MEDICINES LIQUOR) where two girls languished, waiting. Their eyebrows were pencil-thin, their pale cheeks lurid with rouge. "Hello there, streak," one of them called as I passed by. I expect she meant my hair. Her companion, a tall blonde with bright red bee-stung lips, hooted. "Looking good, Grandpa!"

I'm forty-five years old, I wanted to say. *I'm not old. Really, I'm not.*

I crossed at the corner and headed east, toward home, unconsciously quickening my steps. I thought longingly of the drive Ed and I had taken shortly after we met, following that winding road to solitude and bliss. It was the sort of memory one turns over slowly and with exquisite tenderness. The dive bar's rotgut whiskey was roiling in the pit of my stomach, and I was starting to feel afraid. The buildings took on an unfamiliar aspect, looming above me like static forms from a half-remembered nightmare. I was in a small place, a terribly tiny place, and I had been put there by someone else, a man whose name I knew and whose face was as familiar as my own.

Show me where they cut you, hmm?

You know where, you sadistic son of a bitch.

Fingers, digging into the raw wounds on my face, making a larger pain that would go on hurting forever.

Does it hurt you? Would you like it to stop hurting?

Go to hell.

The alley at the back of my building was commonly used by delivery vans and maintenance crews who couldn't access the front door. At night, when no deliveries were expected, it was empty, providing useful temporary parking if one happened to need it. A car I assumed belonged to Layton was pulled up close to the building but showing no lights.

I approached on the driver's side and tapped the window. Layton was sitting upright, his head bent as if he were reading something on the seat beside him. The darkness inside the car made it difficult to see him, and when he didn't seem to hear me, I tapped again, a little louder. "Mr. Layton?" It was just possible he was ignoring me, but that didn't make any sense. This was his idea after all. "Allan?" I tried the door; it was unlocked. I reached in and laid a hand on his shoulder. "Come on upstairs. We can talk in my apartment."

Slowly, grotesquely, he toppled forward with that horrible grace that is only ever the province of the dead. His beautiful face, so loved by the camera, was fixed in an expression of profound surprise. A wooden handle protruded from the base of his skull like a lurid exclamation point. He was without a doubt absolutely dead. The part of me that should have been surprised wasn't, and the coldly cunning part of me—the seat of the body's primal impulses—told me to run like hell.

"Don't move. Keep your hands where I can see them."

The dark figure of a man stood calmly on the other side of the car. The dark figure had a gun. The gun was pointing straight at me. The man was Ed Malory.

Chapter Nine

"COME UPSTAIRS," I said. "And stop pointing that thing at me." We went up together and I let us both in. The first thing I headed for was the liquor cabinet.

I started to calm down after the second scotch and soda, mixed strong enough so my hands didn't shake. "Stay for a drink," I said. "Just one. Then you can go on your way, and I promise I'll never pester you again."

One drink had turned into two and three, and darkness had begun its diurnal retreat, leaving behind the pale, pellucid skin of very early morning. Ed sat on my davenport, his head in his hands, but whether he was upset or merely thinking, I couldn't readily tell. I felt badly about this—about a lot of things, really—and it led me to address apologetic remarks to the back of his bent head.

"I can't remember the last time I slept," he said. He gazed at me as if seeing me for the first time. "You said Allan Layton was with Janet on the night she died." He shook his head. "Tell me again why he's dead behind your building."

"I don't know." I swirled my drink, the ice cubes tinkling against the glass. "He said he wanted to talk to me—"

"Because he had information about Janet's death." Ed stood up, took the drink out of my hand, and laid it on the coffee table. "Because he was sleeping with her too."

"Why do they call it that?" I asked. "People rarely sleep. They should say 'he was fucking her.' Or she was fucking him." I nodded toward my half-empty glass. "Perhaps I could have my drink back?"

He ignored me. "Layton was with her the night she was killed, and so it's just possible he killed her, although he had absolutely no motive." He tapped his bottom lip with an index finger. "When were you going to tell me about the money, Janet's money?"

I should have known we were coming to that. "We were vacationing in Acapulco and Janet said she intended to leave the residue of her estate to me. I thought she was joking. I laughed it off and didn't give it another thought."

Pour me some more champagne, Tony. Our hotel room faced the beach, and we'd left the windows open so the breeze could cool our sweating bodies. *And come back to bed.* She raised one slim, elegant arm and beckoned me closer. *Fuck me properly, and I'll leave you everything I have.*

Ed sat on the davenport again, rubbing his palms over his face. "You do know it makes you a suspect." He slanted a look at me. "Having that money gives you the perfect motive for murder."

"Except I'm dead. Remember? Who else besides you and old man Stirling even care that I got out of Mexico alive?" I got up and retrieved my drink from the coffee table. "Look here, just because I found her body doesn't make me guilty. You of all people should know that. I expect you've stumbled across your share of corpses."

"Allan Layton is on his way to the morgue," he said. "Which studio was he with? They're going to be spitting nails."

"Layton was Paramount." I sounded weary, even to myself. "They'll be doing a lot of spitting, I expect."

Ed waved it away and glanced at his watch. "I should go. It's getting late. Early. Something." He stood, seeming to be at a loss for words. "Cops'll be here soon."

I stood so quickly I got dizzy. "What? For Christ's sake—"

"—to pick up the body," he said. "There's no way they can connect Layton with you, and I haven't told them anything. The most you'll get is a knock on the door and some poor, dumb flatfoot asking the usual questions."

I could just imagine. "Then they'll see my face and know I'm the man who was in the newspapers. Good Christ, Ed, what am I supposed to say?" We stood gazing at each other like two actors who had suddenly forgotten their lines... except in this case there was no prompter standing ready to hiss them at us from the wings.

Ed shrugged. "You could tell them the truth."

"What? That I fled to Mexico and faked my own death to allay suspicion?" The idea of a jail cell filled me with a bone-deep dread. "I won't go to jail. I won't. I'm never allowing anybody to lock me up, ever again."

"Something happened to you," he said quietly, "didn't it? Something really bad."

"I don't want to talk about it." I didn't need to. That's what my scars were for. As far as information went, they spoke volumes. I was about to turn away when I felt his hand on my shoulder.

"I'm so sorry." He stroked my cheek, then leaned in and kissed me. "I'll see you soon, okay?"

When he left, I sat in my easy chair, the big one next to the window, and lit a cigarette. Time felt strangely distorted and elastic, and I had a queer sense that none of this—the apartment, the chair, the cigarette, myself—was real. A radio was switched on, somewhere else in the building, a thread of music sliding along the walls like captive smoke. I wanted a drink, so I went and got the bottle of bourbon Ed and I had been drinking. I sat in my chair, the bottle cradled against my chest, and sipped its keen, slow burn until the sun was up. I knew I ought to go to bed, but I also knew I wouldn't sleep.

I sat at my typewriter. I'd left my hero and the girl talking in his apartment. In a moment or two, she would burst into tears, he'd comfort her, and they'd end up in his bed. He was that sort of detective. She thought to get her claws into him, but he wouldn't be so easily captured, and anyway, I was pretty sure she, not the escaped convict, was the killer. You can never underestimate the power of a well-dressed femme fatale.

But the words wouldn't come to me. No surprise, that. Finding Allan Layton like I did would put a crimp in anybody's evening, but that wasn't the whole of it. He seemed like a nice guy and I liked him, but something about this—all of this—was seriously off.

I yanked the sheet of paper out of my typewriter and started to crumple it up, but something stopped me. I turned the sheet over and found a pencil. I knew what was bothering me: the plot was all wrong. The facts didn't add up. The sheer number of subplots had multiplied like earthworms after a rainstorm, and there were too many characters. Time to start whittling things down. I sharpened my pencil and, at the top of the page, wrote JANET, in block letters. Then I started reasoning it out, the way I did with my books.

Janet was dead.

Janet was murdered—violently.

Janet's murderer likely hated her. (Who? One of her lovers? One of their wives?)

Most people are murdered by someone they know. Her father? Not likely. He wouldn't get his hands dirty. Pepe? Didn't have the guts. He'd probably screw her, but he wouldn't kill her. Deborah? Absolutely not. They were sisters. True, they didn't always get along, but it was unlikely Deborah's temperament would run to murder, and anyway, what motive could she possibly have? Layton? Moot point, since he was dead and I didn't believe he could do that sort of thing. He'd hardly jeopardize his career for the sake of jealousy or sexual nostalgia or whatever it was.

I drew a line under all this and below it wrote, MOST LIKELY SUSPECT:

Linton Stirling—where had he been, the night of Janet's death?

Pepe—smoking and looking out the window, maybe, while he ruminated on something lodged in his craw, something that made him mad and he couldn't ignore. Maybe he was planning it while he stood there in the kitchen, and maybe he'd told himself he'd go down there as soon as he finished his cigarette. It was his ring I'd found in the scotch bottle. Pepe had confirmed that much himself. But the ring was way too obvious. Even an amateur like me could see that. If the killer had meant it to be planted evidence, it was an incredibly clumsy attempt.

Deborah—Janet had been to visit her a month earlier. There didn't seem to be any enmity between them, or maybe there was and Deborah hadn't mentioned it.

Deborah's husband, Johan—in Switzerland. He was hardly going to make a flying visit to America to murder someone, even someone as irritating as Janet, especially given his personal and professional history. It was in his best interest to keep his head down, maybe move to Argentina if he had any brains at all. Pretty soon the world's justice seekers would be breathing down his neck, wanting to know where he'd been during the carnage of '39 to '45. Some of them already knew.

EVIDENCE?

Linton Stirling might have done it in a fit of rage, if Janet had publicly embarrassed him in some way. He often said he'd kill her if she ever did anything to bring shame on the family. It would explain his sudden departure for the east coast.

Pepe's ring—again, that was too easy, and too much of a coincidence. Most likely it had been planted where someone would eventually find it and draw their own conclusions—planted in a bottle of scotch, which any member of the household could easily access... if they needed to, which they wouldn't, because old man Stirling always kept lots of booze on hand at the main house. Planted as insurance, perhaps, just in case the original plan fell through and they needed a brand new patsy. Whoever had put it there didn't know what they were doing: it was about as obvious as things got. The ring was Pepe's, which fit: if I went to Mexico but somehow didn't end up dead, if that part of the plan fell through, it would be useful to have some other poor bastard to shove under the hot lights. Allan Layton seemed to have access to the house by virtue of his 'relationship' with Deborah. He could have taken the ring. Maybe he'd even worn it for a while, so he wouldn't lose it, just in case the time came when he needed it, to allay suspicion. No, it was too fantastical, too unlikely. I was thinking like a writer, not a detective, servicing the fiction instead of the facts.

Who wasn't particularly welcome at the main house? Who might go crawling around the guesthouse, looking for booze? Who'd make an excellent fall guy, especially when you considered he and the deceased had very recently had their differences?

Me, me, and me. I wasn't stupid. I knew it was a frame from the beginning. My fleeing to Mexico seemed, in the eyes of the police, to confirm my guilt. My being in the guesthouse in the first place could be put down to that old adage about the murderer returning to the scene of his crime. Old man Stirling had no particular love for me, so a frame like this was a useful way of shifting the potential scandal. Janet is killed; I flee to Mexico, making myself look guilty. When I later turn up dead, that's even better. Maybe the two men who'd chased me through the zócalo in Ixtagapa were the same two who'd confronted me in the hotel restaurant. Maybe old man Stirling had sent them after me, just to make sure I was really dead—or really good at pretending.

The whole thing was making my head ache. I checked my watch: what time was it in Bern? I still had his business card, the one he'd given me after my discharge from the hospital. Would he remember me? Would he pretend he'd never heard of me, cut me dead, and hang up on me? I got the overseas operator and listened to the crackle of emptiness coming over the wire. I imagined my call winging its way across a continent and an ocean, navigating the darkness. I imagined Dr. Johan Biertz sitting in his office on some tidy Bernese street, shuffling papers on his untidy desk and wondering when his secretary would bring his afternoon coffee. I heard the call connect and listened to his phone ringing all those miles away.

The call was answered by a man; he spoke in French. His voice wasn't familiar to me. "*Allô?*"

"Docteur Biertz, *s'il vous plaît.*" I hoped my accent wasn't too atrocious.

"Doctor Biertz"—He'd switched to English—"is not in at the moment." It was a delaying tactic, the sort of thing every servant in the world knows how to do, if he is any good.

"Tell him Tony Leonard is calling," I said. "It's urgent."

"Monsieur Leonard, Doctor Biertz is a very busy man. I regret that—"

"Stop yapping, you stupid son of a bitch, and get him on the line." I lit a cigarette with my free hand and sucked smoke. "This is life or death."

A long pause while the line hissed and crackled, a silk-thin filament pulling our voices across an ocean. "Johan Biertz," a voice said crisply.

I told him who I was, but it seemed to have no effect on him. I might have been telling him the price of tea. "I won't keep you," I said. "I wanted to ask a question. I hope you'll pardon the intrusion." Manners were something I'd had drilled into me during my years with the Petit Soeurs, and I've found the English intonation helps. Spin a little of that posh accent, and people automatically extend every consideration.

"How is your face?" he asked. "I have thought about you. I realize now there were certain errors in my surgical execution. You were an experiment, but I expect you know that."

I asked him about Janet's visit to Bern. Of course he'd heard about her death. I didn't try to deceive him on that point, or on any other. His was the keenest sort of intellect; he was a man who noticed any number of tiny details.

You are right-handed, he'd said to me, as soon as I'd woken out of the ether. *You should have known the recoil would throw off the trajectory. I regret I was unable to do anything much about the scar. I am afraid you will have to live with it.* He was so much kinder than the others, so much more civilized. He understood what might drive a man, a former commando, to break out of his prison cell, steal a Luger, and attempt to blow his own brains out. *You are in much pain. Perhaps you are also in despair. You should have said something. You should have asked for help.* He almost sounded reasonable, as if he'd actually arrange for my euthanasia. Of course, they'd herd me into the gas chambers with all the others, as soon as their experiments were done, or stand me up against a wall and shoot me. It was the way of things, and I wasn't merely an enemy combatant—I was a saboteur and spy.

After the war, he'd returned to his thriving practice in Bern and picked up where he'd left off—as if there'd been no interruption and no interregnum at all. Even knowing the Allied governments were scouring the world for men like him didn't seem to bother him. He might have fled to South America, like so many of his compatriots, but he didn't. Perhaps he thought himself invincible.

"She was with us for a few days. The visit was to have lasted for a month, but…."

I heard him rustling papers on his desk. "Did she fight with Deborah? You know how sisters are," I said. "Perhaps they had a falling out."

"I heard a heated exchange one night, in the library. Janet had gone there after dinner, and Deborah followed. I don't know what they argued about. Certain insults were thrown—in gutter language, I might add. One would think two such well-bred women might exercise a little more restraint." He said he was sorry, but he couldn't tell me any more than that. His tone said he wouldn't tell me, even if he did know. I expressed my condolences on the breakup of his marriage.

"I don't follow you," he said. "Divorce? I know of no such thing."

Sometimes in life, certain truths announce themselves with no fanfare whatsoever. For me it usually feels like a subtle tickle at the back of my head. This time it sounded like a tiny but very insistent voice.

Liar, it said. *She's a liar.*

I wondered why I wasn't surprised.

I CLOSED all the drapes, took the phone off the hook, and went to bed. I dreamed I was flat on my back under a low stone ceiling perhaps six inches above my face. The stones were wet with condensation and continually dripped moisture that burned wherever it fell. I tried to push the stones away, but my hands were slick with blood. I heard footsteps, hard heels ringing on stone or concrete, and I called out, but the dark ceiling lowered itself on top of me. I drew a long, deep breath and shouted for help, but the stones were pressing on me and I was coming apart—

I came to myself with a muffled shout. I was lying on my stomach, my face pressed into one of the pillows and both fists clenched at my sides. The room smelled of cordite, as if a gun had been discharged while I was sleeping… but it wasn't real. Just my mind, manufacturing memories.

We can give you water. He'd been so kind, that doctor. *Horst tells me you've been licking moisture from the ceiling.*

What water? When have you ever given me anything? It was a game they liked to play; I knew this. It was one of the things they'd warned us about during our training: *They'll offer you things, food and water and cigarettes. Remember that everything costs. Nothing they offer you is free.* It was easy to discount it, up there in the clear air of Scotland, running about in the gorse and bracken, playing war games. We never for a moment believed, any of us, that what we were doing was horribly, horribly dangerous, and if we were captured by the Germans, it was the end.

Nothing they offer you is free. What was it old man Stirling had said to me? *I'm willing to write you a check right now for any amount you desire... I've got my checkbook here in front of me.* So much more convenient for him if I disappeared again. So much easier to keep the whole mess from bursting if you tie off the loose ends. Ink is easier to get off your hands than blood.

The newspapers were suddenly full of the news of Allan Layton's death, the early editions blaring that he'd been murdered, or he'd been bumped off by the mafia, or it was all a Communist conspiracy. The lane behind my apartment building was regularly full of photographers, reporters, and the curious, all jostling each other to get a better look. Every day it was the same old circus. The police cordoned off the area, and it became so much of a nuisance getting in and out that I eventually gave up my apartment and moved.

I found a small house to rent out near the Hightower Building, set far back on a dead-end street and with an excellent view of foliage and a whole lot of rooftops. I didn't care. The property was at the top of a rise and practically buried in trees, so I could see out but other people couldn't see in.

Whenever it rained—the winter rains had by now begun—I liked to sit at my desk in front of the big windows and write, lulled into a state of near somnambulance by the thunder of falling water. My femme fatale had killed her husband and was busy laying traps for the detective, but I didn't think he'd fall for it. I hoped he'd have more brains than that. I didn't see or hear from Ed for several days. I told myself he was busy and didn't have time to come looking for me. I told myself it had nothing to do with me, but I knew—just like you always know—he was thinking about Janet's money, my inheritance, and he was maybe a little disappointed that I hadn't seen fit to tell him about it.

I was sitting in front of my window one Wednesday morning, hammering away industriously at my typewriter, when the doorbell rang. Since I wasn't expecting anyone, I ignored it and hoped they'd give up and go away. I hadn't counted on the stubbornness of your average religious nut, because they kept right on ringing. Obviously their need to tell me all about God overrode my need to work. I got up and yanked the door open.

If I hadn't seen it with my own eyes, I would have never believed it. Pepe was on my doorstep, carrying a paper bag that could have only concealed a bottle of hooch. He jerked his chin toward the house. "I come in?"

"Sure." I stood back and let him come inside. He was dripping wet, the ends of his hair streaming water; he shrugged out of his coat, and I hung it near the heater to dry. "How on earth did you know I lived here?" I ushered him to a chair and offered him a cigarette, which he declined. "I'm not in the book."

"That dick told me." He produced a thin cigar from an inside pocket and lit it with a fancy gold lighter, turning the tip in the flame until it had caught. "What's his name? Malory."

"Ed told you where I live. How did Ed know?"

He gave me a look that could have melted glass. "*Zurramato*! He is a private cop. Maybe he follows you." He puffed on his cigar, looking at me but not saying anything more.

"Yes, well, I may be ugly, stupid, and all the rest of it—*zurramato*—but that hadn't occurred to me." Ed had told me I made a good suspect, especially since Janet had left me all her money. I indicated the bag Pepe held under his arm. "What's that? My Christmas present?"

He pulled out a bottle of mescal and held it up so it gleamed greenish gold in the pale winter light. "You wanna snort?"

It was barely ten in the morning, but I hadn't yet taken a drink. I prided myself on being able to hold off till noon some days, if the sun shone and I behaved myself. Then there were the other days when I woke out of a feverish, nightmare-haunted sleep to suck whiskey at four thirty in the morning. "Sure. I'll get some glasses." I went into the kitchen and pulled two tumblers out of the dish drain. "So to what do I owe the pleasure of this visit?"

He reached a slender brown hand across and plucked a glass from my grip. He was standing right behind me, smiling in that sneaky way people do when they want something from you. I hadn't even heard him. "I was in the neighborhood, señor." He tipped the bottle, and golden liquid gurgled its way into my glass. "Besides, I have information."

I took my drink and went back into the living room. He followed me. "What's it going to cost me?"

His grin widened. "Not so much. You can afford it." He nodded at the typewriter. "Working on a new book?"

"Yes," I said. "It's about a nasty woman who gets herself killed under mysterious circumstances."

Pepe laid his glass on the small table beside his chair and leaned forward. "Your sister-in-law," he said, "is a very strange woman. All day yesterday, people were coming and going, cleaning the guesthouse. Just this morning, she moved in." He sat back and drew meditatively on his little cigar. "She asked me to help carry her things down there. You wouldn't recognize the place."

Deborah had moved into the guesthouse? "What do you mean?"

"New rugs, new curtains—the whole shot, man. She even brought in a decorator, some pansy from Laurel Canyon. He's gonna do it over like the *Arabian Nights*." He lifted his glass and downed the contents in one go. "She says she's not going back to her husband."

I couldn't say I blamed her. Although he had good manners, as far as war criminals went.

Pepe poured himself another shot. Already the level of liquid in the bottle was dangerously low. "You were in the war, huh?" He touched the side of his face and nodded at me. "That where you got the scars?"

"In a manner of speaking." *Horst tells me you were licking moisture from the ceiling.* "It's rather complicated."

He nodded. "I was in the war." He tapped ash off his cigar. "I joined up right after Pearl Harbor, you know? They put me on a destroyer, down in the galley peeling potatoes. I told them to go fuck themselves, and I went to England. I wanted to kill some Germans." He leaned back in his chair, taking his time with the story. "We were in the Faroe Islands. Goddamn, it was cold. The local resistance needed training. They needed someone to help them get it together." He poked a thumb into his chest. "The channel was mined, but somehow the Germans got their submarines through, now and then. Lot of fishing boats sunk that way. Lot of men got killed, innocent people."

The back of my neck had begun to prickle in the way it often does when something of importance is happening. It's a trait I've written into several of my literary characters, simply because I rely on it so much myself. "If you came here to read me a history lesson, you can leave."

He laughed and poured another shot of mescal. "After a while, we started to hear reports of German submarines getting blown out of the water, their ships being wrecked and no survivors. The Germans kept trying to get ashore, but whoever they sent got chopped to pieces. Then we heard it was three guys, hiding somewhere near Tórshavn, two Americans and one other. These three guys, they were making absolute fucking havoc, man. Keeping the Germans on the run. Except nobody knew who they were."

"I don't see what this has to do with me." I got up and went over to the bottle, poured myself a shot and downed it, then poured another. "You can check for yourself, if you like. I haven't any war record." I went to stand by the window. It was still raining, but not as heavily as it had been. The water had collected in the gutters and was being sucked down into the drains.

"This one time, near the end of the war, me and some buddies were sent up the coast to escort some big military jefe back to Tórshavn. We were met by three men who got out of a Jeep, all very quiet, all of them in black. One of them was you."

"Who was the big military boss?" I asked. "Since we're telling stories." My hands were shaking. I stuck them in my pockets. Outside, the wind had picked up, tossing the branches of the eucalyptus trees wildly to and fro. They flailed damply, like the limp arms of dead men.

"I never knew his name. They didn't tell us things like that." He'd somehow crept up behind me again, in that soundless way he had. Yes, I could easily believe he'd been a commando. "After the war, I got a bit messed up in the head." He didn't bother with a glass this time, but drank straight from the bottle. "I didn't want to go back home, so I came here and wandered around for a while. I got pretty down and out, ended up at the mission down on Fromsett Street." He stood back and looked me straight in the eye. "I saw you there. At first I couldn't believe my eyes, and the scars threw me off. But I'd know you anywhere. I got that kind of memory, you know? I never forget a face."

I drew a slow breath, calming myself. When my palms weren't quite as sweaty, I said, "Did you see the man who was with Janet in the guesthouse, the night she was killed?"

He laid the empty mescal bottle on the windowsill. "No."

"Pepe, who tied her up with ropes?"

He went to where I'd hung his coat. He took it down and shrugged into it. It was still wet. "I did," he said. "But I didn't kill her." He gave me a funny little smile, and stepped out again into the rain.

Chapter Ten

DEBORAH WAS at home when I called on her before eleven the next morning. She emerged from the pool, flicking her wet hair from her face. It was an unusually warm day, and her white one-piece bathing suit left about as much to the imagination as a sheet of wet tissue paper. She saw me and waved me over, then pretended to embrace me while she kissed the air on either side of my face. "Tony, darling! Come in, come in."

I followed her through the louvered doors into the house. She'd had the original wood flooring torn up and replaced. The rugs were all new as well. She'd taken the closet doors off, the contents disgorged—albeit neatly—onto the floor, clothing stacked in precise piles and shoes laid in pairs against the wall. I counted twelve pairs of very expensive footwear and one single shoe, a black high-heeled pump with an ankle strap.

"Will you have a drink?" She'd had a small bar installed opposite the bed. "It's five o'clock somewhere, right?" She pressed a hand to her forehead. "God, I need a break. Maybe a spa vacation." She examined her fingernails. "Steam all the badness out of me."

"Gin gimlet, if you've got it. Scotch if you haven't." The interior of the small building had been completely changed. Where Janet had favored a colonial look, Deborah preferred modern. Everything was geometric patterns and shiny melamine edged in chrome, and colors so bright you could hear them shouting from thirty feet away. "Pepe said you'd moved down here. I quite like what you've done with the place."

Deborah was busily agitating a cocktail shaker. "I wanted somewhere of my own." I could hardly hear her over the insistent rattling of ice. "The main house is all well and good, but I always felt like a child, living there, subject to my father's whims." She decanted the drink into a martini glass and handed it to me. "Try that."

I took a tentative sip. "Very nice. You know, most people offer you coffee this hour of the morning."

"You'd rather have coffee?" She raised an eyebrow in my direction, a gesture I'd seen Janet use. "By the way, does my father know you're back from Mexico?"

"Since I've spoken with him on the telephone, I assume he does, yes." I wandered into the kitchenette and watched her peel an orange. "Although I daresay he'd prefer it if I'd stayed dead. He's terrified I'm going to give the game away." I fortified myself with another sip of my drink. "You'll have heard about Allan Layton?"

"Of course. One of the women I play tennis with said the mafia was involved, that he'd annoyed some bigwig at an industry party." She dug her thumbnail into the soft, rounded belly of the fruit, tearing it open. The juice ran down her wrist and dripped onto the floor. She didn't seem to notice. "Do you think that's true?"

Her sangfroid just about took my breath away. "I thought you two were close. You don't seem very upset."

"Oh, for Christ's sake! He was good in bed. That's the extent of it." Deborah dropped the peels into the sink and turned to face me. "We hadn't made any long-term plans, if that's what you think. He had a nice body. I liked it."

"I wonder if you mourned this hard when I disappeared in Mexico," I mused, only half aloud.

"About that, Tony…." She split off a section of the fruit, bit into it, and chewed thoughtfully. "I can't get the real story from anyone, especially Linton." It amused her to call her father by his first name. "That was quite a stunt you pulled. What the hell happened down there?"

"I rather think it was a stunt you pulled," I countered, "putting up twenty thousand to make sure I stayed tucked away in Mexico, out of the old man's reach. I'm touched. I didn't think you cared."

She flushed red to the roots of her hair. I was impressed. "When I heard what had happened, I…." She glanced away, then back at me. "We're practically family." She uttered a brittle little laugh. "It's the least I could do."

"It's a lot of money." I watched her face for some flicker of emotion, but there was nothing. "Don't you think people would be wondering about it?"

There it was, that flicker I'd been looking for. Only for an instant, and then she pulled the shutters down behind her eyes. "What people?" She lifted one shoulder and let it drop. "It's neither here nor there."

"What people? How about anybody? Since I was supposed to be dead and all… and you paid out a lot of money to make sure I stayed that way." I smirked. "Still taking it in the neck for dear old dad, I see."

She ignored the jab and sank her teeth into another section of fruit. "So tell me, what really did happen in Mexico?"

I told her, leaving out the bit about the two men who'd chased me in the zócalo—who I suspected were Linton Stirling's hired goons—and also the part about the zombie powder. "I assumed I was the main suspect." I sipped my drink, wishing I had another. The balance of lime to gin was very near perfect, and ice cold. Gimlets are only good if they're really cold. "What can I say? I panicked."

"Good God, Tony. If it had come to trial, you'd have been acquitted. There was absolutely no evidence, for or against anybody." She finished eating the orange and rinsed her hands under the tap. "I want to change out of this wet bathing suit. Won't be a minute." She went into an adjoining room, untied the straps from around her neck, and pulled the suit down, letting it drop to the floor. Then she stepped away from it and stood, naked as a babe, in the middle of the room. She was inviting me to stare.

I stared. "Is all that for me?" I asked.

She turned so I could admire the view from the other side. "If you like."

I laid my glass down on the counter and went to where she was. "So is it every man for himself, or do you take them in order of appointment?"

"That is a disgusting thing to say." Twin spots of red appeared on her cheekbones. "If I were a man, I'd punch you." She came and put her arms around my neck. Her skin was cold, and the nipples of her small breasts were hard and pointed. She pulled my face down to hers and kissed me. It was like being kissed by a corpse. "Don't be angry with me, Tony. I've been so terribly lonely. Johan was never any kind of husband to me." She slid a hand between us, groping at my crotch, but I pushed her away. I'd been to bed with women before—Janet notwithstanding—and I'd enjoyed it very much. But there was something hard and cheap about Deborah, something all her money and her tasteful clothes—or lack thereof—couldn't compensate for. "So the rumors are true." She stepped back, her face twisted in anger. "You can't respond to a woman, can you? Or is that something else that happened in the war?"

"For Christ's sake, Deborah." I tried to keep a note of disgust out of my voice, and failed. "Put some clothes on."

She snatched up a robe, shrugged into it, and tied the belt savagely around her middle. "I practically offer myself to you on a platter—"

"It isn't that." I went into the kitchen and started mixing drinks. "God knows, there was a time when I'd have had you without so much as a by-your-leave." I dropped ice into the cocktail shaker and dumped the gin in after it, not bothering to measure. "I didn't come here for that."

"Then why did you come?" She stood by me, waiting for her drink. "It's not like you, Tony. I'd hardly expect you to darken my door any time of the day or night."

I handed her a glass, and she snatched it eagerly, like a child with a new Christmas toy. "I wanted to ask you something."

She gazed at me over the rim of her glass. "Like what?"

"Where were you the night Janet was killed?"

"I was up at the main house with Dad. Why?" She went and sat on a white leather couch against the opposite wall. Her robe fell open, exposing her naked legs, but she didn't seem to care. It went well with her new façade of shameless hussy.

"Did Janet give any indication she was entertaining?" I couldn't think of a more euphemistic way to put it. "She was with someone, a man. I want to know who."

Deborah leaned back and peered at me as if she were seeing me for the first time. "Good lord, Tony! You are taking this detective stuff rather too seriously, aren't you? I suppose you think this is like one of your books."

"I want to find out what happened. The police aren't getting anywhere, and nobody else seems to give a damn."

"Why do you care?" she asked. "You were hardly soul mates, even at the best of times."

"She was still my wife when she died." I drew a slow breath. "The way she died was horrible. No one should die that way."

"I suppose you think I did it," she said coyly. "Put the handcuffs on me, Tony. You never know, I might like those sorts of games." And, when I ignored her invitation, she said, "From what Pepe has told me, there were loads of men constantly in and out of Janet's house… probably in and out of Janet as well. How she managed to avoid the clap, I've no idea. Anybody could have done it, Tony. The police haven't stopped looking, but in a city this size, it's easy for anyone to disappear, no matter how guilty their conscience." She lifted her drink to her lips and smirked at me over the rim. "Even you."

I MET Ed Malory that night at the Melody Room over on Sunset and told him what Pepe and Deborah had told me. It was a Friday night, and we were drinking whiskey sours, and he was still mad I hadn't told him about the money. The weather was unsettled, and thunder cracked and boomed overhead, competing with the three-piece band and the tall redhead wailing about how her man had done gone. Ed was in a reflective mood, sipping his drink slowly and leaving wide pauses in our conversation. This latter concerned me, so I asked him about it.

"They've closed the books on this one," he said. "The cops, I mean. For a while there, it looked like it might break, but they've been at it for weeks and none of their leads have panned out. It's not priority anyway. Sex crimes like these never are."

"You sound disgusted."

"I am. Nobody should die that way." He'd left the maraschino cherry in the bottom of his empty glass and was rolling the glass between his hands, tipped up on its edge. I kept watching the cherry, waiting for the moment it would slide out and spread its sticky wetness on the bar. "Problem is, it's easy to disappear in a city this size. Too easy."

"That's what she said." I tossed back the rest of my drink and signaled the barman for another. "Deborah. She lied about splitting from her husband too. Makes me wonder what else she lied about." There was that insistent tickle in my mind again. It felt like a rubber band snapping at the back of my skull. "And there was something else...."

Ed leaned toward me. "Something else?"

"When I was there... it was a little thing, nothing really significant, but it stuck in my mind." I shook my head. "Anyway, it's gone now." I looked up as the bartender laid a fresh drink in front of me. I put some bills down on the bar and told him to keep the change.

"Spending Janet's money?" Ed's face was expressionless, but there was something in his tone I didn't like. It got my back up, so I took my time answering him.

"You seem to have trouble getting past that," I said. "And no, it isn't Janet's money. It's my own." My fists clenched on the edge of the bar. "From my writing. Believe it or not, my books are bestsellers."

The anger on his face melted away and was replaced by a temporary shame. "Tony, I'm sorry." He closed his eyes and pinched the bridge of his nose. "It's been a hell of a week. Things have been real slow. I was on a job in Santa Monica, for this guy who owns a racetrack—millionaire, but he's an ape. Doesn't like anything I do. Thinks he could do it better."

"So he's all talk," I said. "I hear they still make them like that."

Ed nodded. "I'm tempted to give him back his money and tell him to go hell… except I've already been to hell and I still need his money."

A woman in very high heels came clacking across the wooden floor toward the bar. She was quite tall and quite dark, and very beautiful. She was wearing a gold dress that shifted and sighed around her like a pauper's dream of everlasting wealth. "Vodka martini," she told the barman, who hurried to get it for her. I didn't blame him. She was the sort of woman worth hurrying for. She turned and caught me staring and lifted an eyebrow.

"That is one hot piece," Ed remarked. "If you like that sort of thing." He leaned over to look at her legs, and she turned her back on both of us. "She looks like a million bucks and worth every penny."

The woman ignored us, accepted her drink from the bartender, and clacked off back to her table. Her shoes were black and looked like suede, with the kind of ankle straps that are all the rage nowadays, and stiletto heels that could take your eye out. The redhead on the stage had gone and the jukebox, previously as mute as a mannequin's rage, gargled into life with a muffled thump.

I swallowed the rest of my drink, aware I was taking them too fast and too close together, but I couldn't work up the energy to care. "I think I've had it." I pushed back from the bar and stood. "Walk with me?"

Ed glanced at his watch. "Yeah, why not." He tossed some money on the bar, and we went out. It had been raining but it was stopped now, and the streets had that glistening surface that reflects neon like a film set. We walked about a block in companionable silence, and then he said, "Do you want to stay over at my place?"

A city bus roared by, and a siren wailed somewhere in another part of town. In the wan streetlight, he looked younger and absolutely innocent. "Do you want me to?"

"Keep walking," he said, and "Yes." Three men on the opposite side of the street had noticed us and were matching their pace to ours. To a casual observer, they might appear perfectly harmless, but I'd been mugged before, and once, when I was drunk, I was violently rolled by two men and spent a week in the hospital. I wasn't eager to repeat the experience.

We turned a corner and waited for the signal change. It seemed to be taking an awfully long time. The whiskey I'd drunk felt like it was curdling in my stomach. They would confront us, and we would have to fight them, and I didn't want to. I didn't want to because I knew what would happen if we did, and it wouldn't be heroic like you see it in the movies. It would be bloody, and nasty, and grim.

They started to cross to where we were, and halfway there they ran, washing up over the curb and pushing us against the wall of a nearby building. They were young, all of them tall men, wearing dungarees and leather jackets with white tee shirts underneath.

The whiskey I'd drunk was beating in my brain along with something else, something much more primitive and violent. Cornered, I was trapped. Trapped, I reacted out of sheer animal instinct.

The tallest of the three came at me, and I lunged for him, hooked fingers clawing at his eyes and drawing blood. He staggered backward, howling, and I went after another, grabbing his shoulders and shoving him headfirst into the wall. Someone was shouting something, but it was far away and had nothing to do with me. The one I'd thrown was on his knees now on the sidewalk, holding his head and wailing like a banshee while I kicked him. Behind me, Ed grappled with the third one, and I saw the flash of a knife and heard a shout.

Somebody fired a gun.

That was my cue to get away. I turned and ran in the opposite direction, but a small cinema down the block disgorged a multitude of people, all of them heading my way. The crowd streamed past me, all laughing and talking. Watching them pass was like waiting for a herd of elephants, all of them stepping to the thundering beat of my heart.

Someone's hand touched my shoulder; Ed Malory. "Okay?" he asked.

My palms were bleeding. "Yes, I think so. What happened to my hands?"

"You tried to push him into the wall. You missed."

"Where are they?"

"Gone," he said grimly. One of the men was more gone than the others: he'd been shot through the head. Whoever had done the shooting had disappeared. Just another night in the City of Angels.

We took a cab back to his place, where he picked the dirt out of my shredded hands and cleaned the wounds. It was a warm night, and the rain had started again, making a reassuring little patter we could hear through the open windows of Ed's house.

He poured cool water over my palms and dabbed them dry with a soft cloth. A radio played in another room, the volume turned down low. "I've heard it called 'shell shock,'" Ed said quietly. He glanced up to see if I was listening. I was. "I saw how you reacted to those guys back there."

"I was in the Faroe Islands." My voice seemed to echo strangely in my head. The room seemed to be full of hard edges, and the chairs and other furniture were sharply outlined, as if they'd been just then drawn with a marking pen. "During the war. I was part of an English commando unit."

He looked up at me and grinned. "Is that where you got your accent?"

"No." Despite myself, I laughed. "I cultivated that all on my own, thank you."

"Hold still." He applied Mecca Ointment, using just the tips of his fingers, but it still hurt. "I think we should bandage these, even if it's just for tonight." He rolled clean gauze around and around, trapping my thumbs and my wrists. I looked like a hand model for King Tutankhamun. The wounds on my palms pulsed with a ragged red pain that felt like being cut with broken glass.

"We thought we were so clever... we kept them on the run, the Germans." It had been so cold that winter, a bitter chill that felt like it would break your bones. We never stayed in any one place for very long, but kept moving, concentrating our efforts on the coastal areas where the Germans had been trying to set mines. They regularly made incursions all along the coastline, so it was relatively easy for us to harry and harass them, and drive them off. "We were doing something," I said. "We were helping to win the war."

Ed had gone into the kitchen to make coffee, and he brought it out now and laid it on the cocktail table. "What happened?"

"The Gestapo got me." Even now, with the distance of many years, it bore a patina of incongruity. Sitting with my comrades in the early morning light, drinking hot coffee out of metal cups and telling jokes, I had made the fatal mistake of assuming my own safety, and the safety of my fellows, was guaranteed. "Ambush. It was a long time before they let me go." I took the cup Ed passed me. "Thank you. They didn't just get me, understand. They got all of us... most of us. A couple of chaps tried to make a run for it." I shook my head. "I wonder which was worse. Sometimes I think the ones who got it in the back…." I let it lie.

"You survived."

"Not really." I glanced over at him. "I don't mean that in a self-pitying way. It's more a statement of fact. I was with them for a year. They tried to break me." I sipped my coffee. "This is really good. You make good coffee."

He shrugged. "I use a vacuum pot. I think you get more flavor that way."

"Were you in… I mean, did you… during the war?" *Christ, Tony, do try to master the language, there's a good chap.*

"Yes. I was in the Army." He'd been stationed to Newfoundland, he told me. "Helluva place. I spent the war spinning records for Armed Forces Radio." He laughed. "One of the locals called up the station to tick me off about mispronouncing Bix Beiderbecke."

The conversation faltered, and the night was quiet between us. We put our coffee cups in the kitchen sink and went to bed. We left the windows open and lay in the dark, not moving or speaking, holding tight to each other.

Chapter Eleven

I WAS sitting at my desk one morning, about a week before Christmas, putting a final polish on my novel's chapter four, when the telephone rang. Thinking it was Ed, I picked it up. "Tony Leonard."

"I would very much like to come and visit you," a man said. He had a South American accent, and for a moment, I wondered if Pepe had decided on a return engagement. "Are you free now?"

"Who is this?"

"You mean you don't know?" He laughed. "I'll be there in about ten minutes. Make some decent coffee, okay?"

I turned back to my typewriter, but the morning's mail slid through the door slot with a hiss, and I got up to go look. Two utility bills, a postcard, and the newspaper: SECOND MAN SLAIN ON FROMSETT. The front page carried a picture of an elderly man with a shock of white hair and the empty eyes of a wet-brain alcoholic. His face was as wrinkled and seamed as an old boot. His expression indicated the photograph was a mug shot. The accompanying text identified him as George Pocius, a frequent visitor to the seaman's mission on Fromsett Street and an occasional musician. I remembered seeing him play the accordion on the corner of Fromsett and Arbogast for pennies. If business was good, he'd walk down to Larry's Liquor to buy a fifth of vodka. If business wasn't so good, he'd end up behind the mission with a can of Sterno. I expected any day to hear his body had been washed up somewhere, or stuffed into one of the old cage elevators in the Bosco Building. That was the sort of thing that happened around Fromsett. The brief accompanying story had few details and merely said he'd been shot in the back.

But *two* men murdered? I didn't remember hearing anything of the kind. True, I hadn't been down to the mission recently. Maybe someone had a vendetta against down-and-outers, or maybe one of the old wet-brain alcoholics took exception to the coffee and decided to go on a rampage. If old Pocius was one of them, who was the other?

The postcard had a picture of Honolulu on the front and the slogan: ALOHA FROM HAWAII. On the back, written in ballpoint by a not-very-steady hand it said, MERRY CHRISTMAS—REMEMBER ME? It was signed, *Love, Janet.* Obviously someone with a sick sense of humor thought to instill a little holiday cheer. I knew Janet wasn't in Honolulu. She was in the ground. Whoever thought it appropriate to send me such a thing was a very sick chicken.

I was on my way to the kitchen to throw it in the trash when I stopped and decided to keep it. Ed might be interested in it, or able to make something out of it where I couldn't. I stuck it behind the toaster for safekeeping. I pondered whether it was too early for whiskey, decided it was, and made coffee—not nearly as good as Ed's, but not bad—and drank it black, with sugar. I stood at the kitchen window with my cup and watched the traffic slipping by down on Alta Loma Terrace, and I thought about nothing.

That was when the doorbell rang. A young man, maybe thirty years old, stood on the porch holding out a leather wallet with a badge in it. I must have looked idiotic, standing there with my mouth open, but this was the biggest shock I'd had in ages.

"Special Agent Rafael Sequerra, FBI," he said. "It's good to see you again, señor."

"Seeker." I stepped back and held the door open for him. "For Christ's sake, come in."

"SEEKER IS a nickname, as I am sure you know." He grinned. "It sounds like my last name, Sequerra, which is my father's name. My name is actually Rafael Abano de Loma Sequerra, but the Bureau couldn't fit it on my identification card." We were drinking coffee and sitting together on the davenport in front of the window. "So I am Agent Sequerra."

"I'd have never thought…." I shook my head. "I'd no idea. You told me in Mexico that you were a Federale."

"You could say I am both. Many of our agents trained with your FBI and received American qualifications. We found it useful to have certification on both sides of the border."

"I often wondered if that badge you had was real," I said. "Part of me thought you were some local ne'er-do-well with dubious connections and far too much time on his hands."

He'd been working out of the Los Angeles office, he said, when the news of Janet's murder reached them. It wasn't so much her murder that interested them, but the way she'd been killed. The Bureau had been watching Linton Stirling for years because of certain business deals he'd made, and it was strongly suspected he had ties to organized crime, drug smuggling, and cross-border prostitution, although they'd never been able to uncover any hard evidence. When I fled to Mexico, the Bureau sent Seeker after me, thinking I might have useful information. Seeker was charged with my care.

"And the zombie powder," I said, "was that your doing?"

He grinned. "Yes. We used a pharmacological preparation of curare. You were never in any real danger, but the drug effectively mimicked death. We wondered what Linton Stirling might do if he thought you were dead. We wondered, also, if the police might turn to other suspects once you were out of the picture. We thought having you killed could draw them out."

"Remind me to never get on your bad side," I said. It was good to see him again. "But I don't think you've come here to reminisce."

"No." He reached to take an envelope from his pocket. "Do you recognize the man in this photograph?" He passed me the picture and waited while I studied it.

"Not right offhand." I passed it back to him. "Should I?"

"I would be surprised if you remembered him. His name is Hector Vargas. He came here to Los Angeles five years ago, from Corraio, a small town near Juárez. Although he was married, he came alone, looking for work." Seeker paused to sip his drink. "He wrote faithfully to his wife every week, on Sunday morning after Mass. About a year after his arrival, the letters stopped coming."

"And that's an FBI matter?" I asked.

Seeker shook his head—a little impatiently, I thought. "He ended up at the seaman's mission on Fromsett Street. Local police found him dead last week, in an alley behind a liquor store. His killer sliced up the right-hand side of his face."

My hands were suddenly shaking. I wrapped them around my cup and tossed the rest of the coffee down my throat. "Sliced it up how?"

"Three deep cuts. One starting at the temple and running in a shallow curve to the chin, one running parallel to that but about half its length, and the third starting under the right eye and curving towards the ear, ending in a puncture wound."

I touched my face. I couldn't help it.

"Yes," Seeker said. "Just like your scars. That's not what killed him, though. He was shot in the back." He regarded me intently. "Are you sure you don't remember him? Witnesses at the mission said you had helped him—that you regularly gave food and shelter to men considered incorrigible alcoholics."

"Well, I do... I m-mean, I d-did." I was stammering like a frightened schoolboy. "I haven't lately."

"The first victim, George Pocius, had similar cuts. Is he another you helped?"

"Yes." I got up and went to pour more coffee. "I've been down and out myself. I wanted to help if I could." I wondered if this was why he'd come, to try and force a confession out of me. He'd obviously made up his mind about certain aspects of the situation. "Why would I kill someone I'd helped? I felt for these men. I'd been there myself. I'm... still there."

Seeker got up. "I make no accusation, Señor Leonard. I'm simply trying to find my way to the bottom." He shrugged. "The waters are murkier than I expected."

I offered him a second cup of coffee, but he refused. "Too much work to do. May I come and see you again?"

"Thank you for helping me... in Ixtagapa," I said. "It was a unique solution to my problem."

He came into the kitchen, buttoning his jacket. "It was my pleasure and my privilege to help." He gazed at my scars. "Forgive me. It is a rather unusual set of marks." He leaned in and rested his hands on my shoulders. "If ever you need anything, please...."

I thought about showing him the postcard, but decided against it. I wasn't sure why. "I'll remember."

He dropped his hands and stepped back. "Then I hope to see you soon."

The screen door banged shut. Ed Malory stood there, in his habitual tan raincoat, his hat pushed back on his head. He glanced at Seeker, then back at me before his gaze slid away into the middle distance.

"Excuse me." Seeker slipped past him and out the door—rather quickly, I thought.

Ed watched him go. "I brought—" He took a small yellow envelope out of his inside pocket and dropped it on the table in the living room. "Never mind." He turned away.

I heard his footsteps going down the stairs, fading in the distance, diminishing to nothing. I picked up the little envelope and opened it: two tickets to the Tommy Dorsey Christmas show at the Casino Gardens. These would have cost him a fortune—a fortune I knew he didn't have.

I felt like the world's biggest heel.

I WENT back to my typewriter and tried to pick up where I'd left off. Chapter four involved the femme fatale and her weak and ineffectual brother, a dissolute mess who passed his time getting to the bottom of a gin bottle. It looked like he might have killed the leading man, but I was pretty sure he'd try to get away with an insanity plea. I tried a few lines of dialogue, hoping to steer him in the right direction, but it wasn't working out.

I pushed the typewriter away and pressed the heels of my palms against my eyes. I wanted a drink. There was whiskey in the cupboard, I knew, and a bottle of Tanqueray in the icebox (gimlets are always better when they're ice-cold). I could even make my way back to that dive bar and spend some time among the lowlifes and the desperate, except they watered the booze and I wasn't so lonely that I needed that sort of company.

I called Ed's house and let the phone ring a dozen times, but nobody answered. It was a quarter past eleven in the morning, so he could have been anywhere. I decided to chance it and caught a cab over to the Luden Building, where Ed's office was.

I took the old cage elevator up to the ninth floor and stepped out into a narrow, tiled hallway lined with doors. Each door boasted a frosted glass panel with a business name etched on it in stark black lettering. I passed IAN BLESSING, DENTAL SURGEON AND ORTHODONTIST and MAUDE FRIST, EMPLOYMENT AGENCY FOR LADIES and a lawyer's office right next door to a dealer of rare coins.

At the end of the corridor, a door marked ALL-AMERICAN RUST INHIBITER stood slightly ajar while a bald man with a wrinkled neck was arguing with someone inside. I tapped on the door. Three people—the bald man, a tall man with an unpleasant expression, and the young blonde at the reception desk—turned to stare at me.

"Help you with something?" The tall man was about forty, with sandy hair cropped very short on the sides and a cowlick in the back. His eyes were a blue so pale as to be almost colorless; he seemed to be peering at me from the bottom of a goldfish bowl. "This is a place of business."

"I'm looking for Ed Malory, the detective," I said. "I believe he's in this building?"

"Go back towards the elevators, then turn left. He's the last door on the right." He turned his back, and just like that, I was dismissed.

I did as he said and retraced my steps to the elevators, then turned left. This took me into a shadowy secondary corridor that ended in a T-shaped recess with five doors, all closed, all exuding the same air of cynicism and thwarted hopes. The door to my right was embossed with ED J. MALORY, PRIVATE INVESTIGATOR. A piece of card was taped to the glass and it read PLEASE WALK IN. I did as it said, stepping into a bare, rather shabby little anteroom with a wooden bench, a water cooler, a coat tree, and a small table with a pitifully meager selection of magazines, most of them several months—if not years—old. A second door, this one marked PRIVATE, obviously led to his office. The setup reminded me of a field commander's temporary headquarters in wartime, spare but efficient, and I knew if Ed Malory had been the kind of detective who took graft and accepted bribes, he'd put up a more luxurious front than this. Ed Malory's office was like Ed Malory himself: poor, but very, very honest.

I waited for perhaps ten minutes, and then the door to the inner office opened and Ed was there, one hand on the doorknob and the other resting comfortably in the curve of a woman's back. She was a redhead, tall and slender, with what photographers like to call "good bones." She apparently considered herself entirely responsible for this lucky hereditary accident, and her resulting air of hauteur stuck out so far you could have broken off a mile of it. "Thank you for coming," Ed was saying. "If you remember anything else, please don't hesitate to call me." He saw me but didn't acknowledge my presence, walking the girl past me and out the door.

She was the girl singer from the nightclub, the one who'd been wailing about her man being gone. As far as torch singers went, she didn't have great pipes, but I figured the patrons of her kind of bar probably didn't notice, or care. The Melody Room wasn't exactly a dive, but the booze still got you good and drunk.

"Well?" Ed stared at me the way you stare at a spider you're thinking of killing. "Since you're here, you might as well come in." He stood aside and I went in.

This room was just as bare and spartan as the other, except this one had Ed's desk and three filing cabinets. The window behind the desk read

SNOITAGITSEVNI YROLAM .J NIWDE, presumably so it could be read from outside. The desk had a blotter, a telephone, a Los Angeles area directory, and an empty coffee cup full of pencils.

He gestured to a chair in front of the desk. "Have a seat."

I sat. *I want to explain*—that was what I meant to say. Instead I said, "I don't think this is going to work."

He lowered himself into the swivel chair behind the desk and stared at me. He looked tired, even haggard. "Is that right." It wasn't a question.

"I keep disappointing you." My heart thumped unpleasantly. "You… I let you think… when I was in Mexico, I could have contacted you—"

He stood and went to the door. I heard the subtle snick of the key as he locked it. He came to where I was, grabbed me by the arm, and yanked me up out of the chair. We were standing toe-to-toe, our faces barely a hand span apart. "So all of a sudden you're the one who gets to decide?" He shook me, none too gently. "You're the one who gets to call it quits, and it doesn't matter what I think?"

"I thought you wanted it that way." I felt distinctly like an idiot, having said that. Standing so close to him, I could feel the heat of his body, smell the slight odor of his cologne. He was warm and alive and achingly beautiful to me.

"Did you?" He took hold of my other arm, squeezing gently. "Just because we've stumbled a couple times here and there, made fools of ourselves and each other?"

I said the only thing I could think of: "You have the bluest eyes I've ever seen." *And I'm in love with you.*

He cupped my face in his hands and kissed me—the hard, almost brutal kiss of a man trying desperately to hold on to something dear to him. When the kiss ended, he held me that way, our foreheads touching, our faces close together.

"I'm sorry," I said. "I'm an idiot." I drew a shaky breath, suddenly— and humiliatingly—close to tears. "He's an FBI agent, the man you saw standing in my living room. He helped me in Mexico."

"I know who he is," Ed replied, "at least to some degree. Rafael Sequerra. Would you listen if I told you to stay away from him?" He squeezed my arm. "Let's have a drink." He unlocked the bottom drawer of his desk and took out a bottle of Macallan.

"I'm impressed," I teased, "considering how down-at-heel the rest of this place is."

"Gift from a grateful client," Ed said. "If you're honest in this business, you don't make very much money." Ed poured a generous portion into each of our glasses.

I smiled. "Are you honest?"

"Painfully." He had a copy of the *Post-Dispatch* in front of him. He turned it so I could see the headline. MURDER AT THE MISSION. "Did you know about this?"

"Yes." I tossed back the whiskey. It burned its subtle fire all the way down. "There's a disturbingly personal aspect to it." I touched my face. "That's why Seeker—Agent Sequerra—came to see me."

"I talked to McAvity down at Central Homicide. He told me about the marks on their faces." His gaze lingered on my damaged cheek. "Obviously you knew these guys—through the mission, I mean."

"Not personally," I said. "I sometimes volunteered down there. I remember the first guy, Pocius. He used to raid the trash cans all up and down Fromsett. The other fellow, this Hector Vargas?" I shook my head. "Maybe I gave him some money once. I don't remember." It bothered me that the two men had been cut to resemble me. It bothered me a great deal. "Why do you think they cut them that way? It couldn't have been mere coincidence. That only happens in bad novels." I laid my glass down on the desk, and Ed obligingly refilled it.

"That's not the worst of it," he said. He reached into his desk drawer and brought out a large manila envelope. It had a Santa Monica postmark and was addressed to a Lydia Race. The handwriting was small, crabbed, and very untidy. Ed peeled back the flap and pulled out a handful of photographs in various sizes. He spread these on the desk like playing cards. "Recognize anybody?"

I leaned in and took a long look. Several of them featured a fetching redhead—the same redhead who'd just been here, unless I was very much mistaken—wearing nothing but her earrings and a smile. In some pictures she was alone, but in others she posed with a beautiful young man who bore a startling resemblance to—"Allan Layton."

Ed nodded. "Uh huh."

"I don't see the connection," I said. "What's this redhead have to do with Allan Layton?"

"That's Lydia Race. She's the singer at the Melody Room. She got her start in Reno, at the Blue Danube—Vic Ramirez used to own it, back in the day." Ed gathered the photos and stuffed them back into the envelope. "Somebody sent her these, last week in the mail."

"I gathered that. I think the postmark gave it away."

"Don't be a wisenheimer, Tony." But he was smiling. "Lydia Race and Allan Layton used to do some work for this guy, before the war."

"Pornography?" It didn't surprise me. Along with the casting couch, posing for nude photos was practically de rigueur in Hollywood these days. "Layton's publicist couldn't have been too happy when these surfaced." I wondered aloud why somebody would bother sending the photos of Layton. Surely they couldn't do him any harm now? "Never mind that the poor bastard's dead."

"Miss Race is being blackmailed." He replaced the envelope in the drawer. "That much is readily apparent. She just doesn't know who's doing it. She has no idea who'd want to blackmail her."

All this was making my head hurt. "So if she's the one being blackmailed, why bother sending the photos of Layton? Unless someone is trying to damage his reputation, postmortem."

"That's what I intend to find out."

I took the postcard out of my coat pocket and dropped it on his desk. "Here's another mystery for you. That came in this morning's mail." I waited while he read the brief inscription. "Bit sick, isn't it?"

"Disgusting." He turned it over. "Hawaii. Where's Linton Vanderbilt Stirling these days?"

"You don't think he sent this?" I laughed. "He's got enough money that he could have me killed. I hardly think he's got to stoop to sending silly postcards."

He looked thoughtful. "And you're certain it's not Janet."

"Ed, I found her." An image of her battered face, its features utterly destroyed, flitted across my consciousness. "Believe me—she was dead."

"So were you." He wasn't smiling when he said it. I felt lower than the arches on a fat man. We were quiet for a little while, sitting there together.

"Ed, I'm so sorry." I thought about sitting alone in that stuffy little hotel room in Ixtagapa, wondering if the next knock on the door was going to be the police, or the Federales, or someone with explicit orders to shoot me. "I didn't know what else to do. I figured they'd come after me. I didn't know Linton Stirling would pay good money to make it seem like I was dead. Number one suspect tops himself, case closed."

"How much did the estimable Mr. Stirling pay?" Ed scraped a match across the surface of his desk and lit a cigarette.

"Twenty thousand dollars," I replied. "Deborah paid it to Sequerra. She didn't know he was a Fed, obviously. She must have followed me to Mexico—or had me followed."

"Are you sure Sequerra wouldn't take a bribe?" He drew on his cigarette, exhaling smoke slowly.

"I'm positive. He could have killed me, but he didn't."

Ed tapped two fingers on the postcard. "Mind if I keep this?"

"Not at all," I said. "If you can pick apart this particular Gordian knot, I'd be grateful."

Ed took another drag off the cigarette. "Cut, you mean. The Gordian knot was cut."

"Cut." I gave him back the yellow envelope with the tickets. "And by the way, I'd love to go with you… if you still want me to."

I DID all the right things, made all the correct romantic gestures. I even brought him flowers when I showed up for our date, a huge bouquet of heliotrope. I didn't even know if he liked them, but they were my favorite flower. He answered the door on the first ring. "Tony. Flowers."

"Very good," I said. "You're beginning to master the language." I closed the door behind me and pushed him up against it. He tasted like heat and good scotch. "Sure we haven't got time…?"

"We haven't got time." He caressed my face. "Come on. It'll be hard enough to find a decent parking space."

We traveled in companionable silence, broken only by occasional exclamations, comments, anecdotes. It was a clear night, cold for Southern California, and the stars were out, clustered around the peaks of the distant San Gabriel range. We pulled up in front of the club, and Ed handed the keys to a uniformed valet, who whisked the car away without so much as a word.

"Very efficient here, aren't they?" I observed. "You'd think he intended to strip it for parts."

We offered our tickets to an absolutely massive doorman, who lowered his enormous craggy face long enough to examine them before ushering us inside. The club was decorated for Christmas, all tinsel and colored lights. "I think I see an empty table up here," I said, starting toward the stage.

"Let's sit in the back," Ed said. "I'd rather see the entire room."

We found a table near the back, against a wall, Ed with an almost panoramic view of the entire room. Each table sported a tiny Christmas tree, complete with miniscule lights that flickered on and off, just like the real thing. The tablecloths were red and green, as were the candles.

"Festive," I said. The room was full of the murmured buzz of a hundred different conversations, overlaid by a tinkling chorus of piano music from somewhere far away.

"They hire Fleisher every Christmas, or so I've heard." Ed shook out his cigarettes and lit one. "To play the piano. He used to play at Terry Rider's place in Vegas, right there on the strip. Remember it? El Rancho Vegas."

"I don't remember," I said, "but then again, I never was much for Las Vegas. Janet always said it was tacky. She went to Monte Carlo when she wanted to waste money." I signaled a passing waiter, who appeared at my elbow, his tray carefully balanced on the fingertips of one hand.

"Something to drink, sirs?" He was a tall, stringy sort of character, with narrow shoulders and a large nose and a thin, rather drawn face. He looked like someone who'd been firmly grasped at either end and stretched.

"Bring us a bottle of your best champagne," I said. "Chilled, if you please."

"Right away, sir."

"Why did you do that?" Ed asked. His relaxed, open expression had hardened into something much less pleasant. "I'm capable of paying for drinks."

Christ, I thought, *here we go again.* "You like champagne. I don't see what the problem is."

"I can pay my own way," he said. Obviously this was a problem with him.

"I know you can," I told him gently. "I've never doubted it for a moment." I reached under the table, beneath the hanging cloth where my hand couldn't be seen, and squeezed his knee. "Please let me do this."

He sighed. "I'm sorry, Tony. I guess I don't like rich people very much." He fiddled with his napkin, twisting it into various shapes.

"What happened?"

"Nothing." He wouldn't look at me. "It's nothing."

I lit a cigarette of my own and smoked in silence for a moment or two. "One of those nothings that haunts you for the rest of your life?" I never heard his answer. The waiter arrived with an icy cold bottle of Bollinger and the moment was lost—but I kept turning his answer over in my mind all night long. Ed wasn't the sentimental type. If he had something to say, he'd generally say it.

His earlier good mood had evaporated, and he was much too quiet all through the evening. He drank champagne and smiled at me, even asked a couple of women at a nearby table to dance. He was a wonderful dancer, graceful and light on his feet, adept at charming them with conversation and the benefit of his attention.

It was 1:00 a.m. when we finally rose to go. I sent the valet to retrieve Ed's car while we waited at the entrance.

"Do you want to drive?" Ed asked. His expression told me nothing, but he was more able than most at disguising his feelings. "I'm kind of tired." It was the first time I'd ever heard him admit fatigue, and I wondered what else was going on. Ever since our disagreement about the champagne, he'd been uncharacteristically reticent—not remote, exactly, but removed.

"Sure." I got in and started it up. Ed slid in on the passenger side. "Where are we going?"

"Home." He kept his face turned away.

"Mine or yours?" I pulled into the steady stream of traffic, merging with the cars heading north, into the Hollywood Hills. I expected him to bark something about having to go home because he had work in the morning, but he didn't.

"Can we go to your place?" That surprised me. He usually preferred to go straight home, I suspected because his own four walls represented something like safety to him.

"When we get there, will you tell me what's bothering you?" I lit a cigarette from the dashboard lighter and reached to turn on the radio. A flood of contemporary swing filled the car's interior with false levity, like too much icing on a birthday cake.

"Tony, would you ever knowingly lie to me?" He turned, his face still somewhat hidden by the darkness. "If you knew something was going on, something you didn't like... would you lie about it?"

I merged onto the Santa Ana highway and accelerated, aware I was doing rather more than the posted speed limit and hoping there weren't any motorcycle cops around. I wanted to get home as quickly as possible, and I wasn't sure why. Something was wrong with Ed, and I didn't know what it was. I only knew that it was making me very uneasy.

"Would I ever lie to you?" What the hell had brought this on? "I suppose that depends."

"On what?" He flicked cigarette ash out the passenger side window. I hadn't even seen him light up.

"Ed, what's this about?" The tiny knot in my stomach began to bloom into a larger knot. "Have I done something wrong?"

"You said Rafael Sequerra was an FBI agent."

"He is." I stopped for a red signal and looked across at him. He looked like he probably did when he interrogated bad people: hard-faced, cold and resolute, remote. It made me quite uneasy. I wondered whether I was about to lose the only real friend I'd ever had.

"I ran his particulars past McAvity, down at Central Homicide," he said. "They liaise a lot with the feds, especially on cross-border stuff. He never heard of Rafael Sequerra. The LA bureau never heard of him either. McAvity sent a wire to the Mexican Federales. He went to college with one of their senior officers. They haven't heard of him."

"I saw his identification card." My heart began beating in a dark and nasty rhythm.

"Maybe," Ed said, "you wouldn't know what to look for."

"I'm not a bloody idiot!" For some reason, that flicked me on the raw. "I've been to university, you know. Under appropriate conditions, I can even read and write."

"Identification can be faked. There's an underground economy right here in the city that specializes in it. Unless you know what to look for—"

"I know what to look for," I said. "I know all about it." The signal changed to green, and I accelerated rather more sharply than was necessary. A taxicab came charging out of an alley, hell-bent on beating the next set of lights, just up ahead. I swerved, leaning on the horn, and stomped on the brake. We came to a juddering halt; Ed threw out a hand to stop himself slamming into the dashboard. "If he's not FBI, who is he?" I asked. "Some random stranger who showed up in Mexico, in exchange for twenty thousand dollars?" I put the car into gear. "He said it was all taken care of, that a blonde, Spanish-speaking woman had given him twenty thousand dollars. She told him she was my sister." I pulled up to the next set of lights and stopped. "Ed, I haven't got a sister. As far as I know, I've got no other family at all, so it was most likely Deborah."

He considered this for a moment, while the light switched from red to green. "A complete stranger handing over twenty large for your safekeeping didn't bother you?"

"Are you accusing me of something?" I asked. "Because if you are, I'd rather you didn't dance around the subject."

"Did you kill her?" His voice was very quiet.

"Oh, for Christ's sake, Ed." I pulled over to the curb and set the parking brake. "I'll walk from here." I was reaching for the door handle when he caught hold of my wrist.

"I'm sorry," he said quietly. "I've been following Janet's case from every angle I can think of. That includes questioning you as a suspect. Tony, there's so much about this that doesn't add up."

"I know." It still annoyed me that he'd even ask me if I'd killed Janet. "Do you want to hear my alibi?" He nodded. "I couldn't possibly have killed Janet," I said, "because I was nowhere near her at the time she was killed."

"Where were you?" he asked.

"I was with you."

He squeezed my arm. "Come on. Let's go to your place and have a couple drinks."

As apologies went, it wasn't the best I'd ever had, but I was willing to overlook it. Part of me wondered if he was still working for Linton Stirling. If he was, then this entire friendship of ours was nothing but a smokescreen, a way to get close to me in order to glean necessary information.

It wasn't a pleasant thought.

We drove to my rented house and I put the car away. My house didn't have quite the number of steps that Ed's did, but it was still a bit of a climb, and I was already tired to begin with.

As soon as I put the key in the door, I knew something was wrong. It was just a feeling I had. The door swung open without my having to unlock it. All the living room windows were wide open, the net curtains twisting in the breeze. The house had been ransacked. The cocktail table and the davenport had been turned over, and the throw cushions torn apart. The desk, usually situated under the living room window, had been dragged into the center of the room and had all its drawers ripped out. The carefully stacked pages of my new novel were scattered everywhere, helped along by the draft from the open windows. My typewriter had been upended onto the floor.

I looked at Ed and tried to smile. "Damn literary critics," I said shakily. "Haven't got enough to do." I reached for my typewriter but he stopped me.

"Fingerprints," he murmured. "Don't touch anything." He clasped my shoulder briefly before reaching inside his coat and removing a gun from his shoulder holster.

"You wore that under a tuxedo?" I asked. "Who the hell wears a gun to a Dorsey Brothers concert?"

He slanted a look at me. "It's part of my clothes." He waved me back, closer to the door. "Stay put until I make sure nobody's here."

"If you think I'm staying here and waiting for you," I said, "you're completely mad." I took up a position just behind his right elbow and followed him down the hall. The house was arranged so the bedrooms and bathroom branched off a narrow central hallway. At the end of the hallway, there was a small storage room that held nothing very much, but I habitually kept the door closed. It was closed now. I tapped Ed's shoulder and nodded toward the room. He pushed me back against the wall with his gun hand and put a finger to his lips with the other. I waited in an agony of suspense as he slid forward, crouching low and keeping close to the wall.

The storage room door burst outward so violently that it nearly came off the hinges. A small dark-skinned man with very shiny black hair leaped out at us, firing his gun in rapid bursts and shouting something I couldn't quite make out. He ran down the hall and into the living room, heading for the open door. Ed followed him, squeezing off several rounds and shouting at him to stop. He did stop, at the door, grinning widely, as if the entire thing was a joke only he understood. He grabbed his crotch in that universally vulgar gesture and pointed at me. "*Los muertos vivientes.* Ha! *Los muertos.* Tell the old man I said soon." He vanished into the darkness.

The wind whistled through the open windows.

"What did he mean?" Ed asked. "*Los muertos vivientes.* Do you know him?"

"I saw him, once." The figure of Death, balanced precariously on stilts, staggered across my inner vision. "I–In Mexico." I was trembling uncontrollably, an unwieldy marionette. "He was… it was the Day of the Dead… the festival."

"Yes, I'm familiar with it." Ed closed the front door and locked it. He slid the gun back into his shoulder holster. "What I don't understand is why he said it to you. And what did he mean by telling the 'old man'?"

I gazed at him as if I'd never seen him before. "I don't know. He must have followed me here from Ixtagapa. I-I d-don't know." I was suffused with a sudden and violent weakness. I reached for a chair, turned it over, and sat on it. "We… it was a festival."

Ed shook his head. "It makes no sense. Why did he call you 'the living dead'?"

"I honestly don't know," I said. "He wasn't there. It was just Seeker, and me, and Papa Loi. He wasn't in the room when any of it happened."

Ed crouched down so he was on eye level with me. "Tony, I need you to think very carefully." His voice was gentle but insistent. "He wasn't where when what happened?"

"He wasn't in the room," I said. "In Ixtagapa, the night I died."

Chapter Twelve

"THE POSTCARD didn't come from Honolulu." Lieutenant Hank McAvity tossed it down on the desk in front of me. "The postmark's smudged, but I had one of our guys take a look at it. He does that sort of thing." He was well past forty, but he'd kept himself in fighting trim. He didn't have the flabby gut most cops his age usually sported. His hair was dark auburn, turning gray at the temples, and his face had the lean, almost hungry look of a career cop. He wore glasses, which he seemed to need only for reading. He kept putting them on and taking them off.

"What sort of thing?" I asked. It was ten in the morning, and I desperately wanted a drink. I wanted one so badly that my teeth ached.

"Forensics. Questioned documents is the fancy name for it." He went back behind the desk and sat. "Near as he can tell, it was posted from up near Santa Rosa, little town called Thermalito. Used to be some kind of health spa there, back in the day. There's still a couple of places the rich wives like to go when the strain of it all gets too be too much."

"So who mailed it?" I asked. "It's a bit of a sick joke, don't you think?"

"We checked the fingerprints," McAvity said. "Nothing showed up. Whoever sent it, they don't have a criminal record."

"Not helpful," Ed said. "It could be anybody." There was an edge to his voice, a thin sliver of something palpable and sharp. I guessed he and this McAvity had some kind of history.

"Yes," McAvity said evenly, "it could be." He lit a cigarette, sat back, and looked at us both. "Every time there's a high-profile murder, some sicko decides to try his hand at a little creative writing. He finds out where the family lives, where the husband lives, and starts sending out these little invitations." His lip curled. "If we could catch the bastard, we'd nail him. But good luck trying to catch him. He probably stayed in Thermalito long enough to mail the postcard, then lit out for somewhere else. I'm sorry, gentlemen, but there's not much I can do."

"Thanks for trying." Ed stood up and reached to shake McAvity's hand. "I appreciate it."

I added my thanks to his, and we went out. It was a clear, sunny day, but it might as well have been pouring down buckets. In three days' time, it would be Christmas. I couldn't remember ever really looking forward to the holiday—Janet and I usually lit out for some warmer climate, not necessarily together—but now the impending festivities made me want to crawl inside a bottle and stay there.

We went down and got into Ed's car. He seemed to be in an equally somber mood, because he didn't speak until we were a block from my house. "Christmas in three days."

"Yeah." It was a warm day. I dangled my hand out the window, enjoying the sensation of air slipping over and under my fingertips. If I cupped my hand, it felt like I was holding on to something, a tangible object about the size of a tennis ball.

"Don't sound so excited." Ed looked across at me, not quite smiling. "Not a fan of the jolly old fat man?"

I lit a cigarette from the dashboard lighter. "Are you?"

He shook his head. "There wasn't much to it when I was a kid. Some of the charities used to donate presents, and I remember one year the local Pentecostal church filled stockings with candy and religious tracts."

"Religious tracts?" That made me laugh out loud. "What did they say?"

"Oh...." He stopped at a red light, and for a moment, the only sound was the clicking of his turn signal. "Things like Jesus was coming back and was your heart right with God, that sort of thing." The light changed and he turned left, onto Camrose Drive. "I remember one in particular that stuck out in my mind. It was that Bible story about the rich man who couldn't get into heaven... remember that one?"

"I think so." On Sunday evenings we were assembled in the dining hall, and the Petits Soeurs read Scripture to us, usually chapters about sin and damnation and hell. It was intended to strengthen our moral fiber. "Didn't it say something about a camel and a needle?"

"That's the one. It really stuck with me." He went quiet, and I didn't pursue it further. I had the strongest sensation he wasn't with me just then—that his body was in the car, but his thoughts were somewhere else. "Rich people." He pulled up in front of my house and set the parking brake. "Okay?"

"Thank you." I reached across and briefly clasped his hand. "Come in for a bit?"

"Maybe later?" He grinned. "I'm working on a case downtown. I need to go and harass some people."

"Ed…." I hesitated. "Who could have sent the postcard?"

"Does anybody have a grudge against you? That's where you need to look. People—reasonable people—don't do such a thing. But somebody eaten up alive with resentment, maybe hatred? I'd start there."

I shut the passenger side door and waved at him as he pulled away from the curb. It wasn't even close to noon, but I felt the urge for a drink like a keen-edged, palpable ache. I unlocked my door and stepped around the morning's mail that had fallen through the slot: a utility bill, a reminder about municipal water taxes, and another postcard.

This one was from Acapulco. It had a picture of the Hotel Majestic on the front, showing the poolside. Whoever had sent it had drawn two stick figures in the pool, with only their heads above the water. One of the figures had long hair; that one held stick arms in front of its face, a defensive posture. The other figure was holding a crudely drawn hammer over its head. On the back the sender had written *Fuck me properly and I'll leave you everything I have.* It was postmarked Ixtagapa, but Janet and I had spent our honeymoon in Acapulco, at the Hotel Majestic.

I got a bottle of whiskey from the cabinet and cracked the seal.

I WAS lying on something that had bony fingers. They were sticking into my spine. There was something vaguely rectangular under my left buttock, and it seemed as though I might not be fully dressed. My mouth was dry, and every one of my teeth had its own coat of moss. I lay there for several long moments, wondering where I was and trying to recall how I'd come to be lying on someone's bony fingers.

A telephone was ringing, somewhere in an empty room. I lay very still and listened to it. The noise went on and on, and then it stopped. Between one breath and the next, it started again, and I heaved myself up and went to find it. The bony fingers turned out to be a hair brush. The thing under my ass was a book. The telephone was in my bedroom.

"Yes?"

A voice, crackling with disuse and vaguely female, blasted my ear. "Who's this?"

"Tony Leonard." I cleared my throat. "It's Tony Leonard." My shorts were itchy, sticking to me, and I smelled like I wanted to be alone.

"Good. I got the right number." She coughed noisily. "You know anybody named Ed?" I told her I did. "He lives in Betty's old house," she said, "just across the street from me. I see him coming and going all the time. He's a nice-looking man. Handsome." Another rattling cough that sounded like she was hacking up a lung. "Something going on over there."

"Something like what?" My watch was still strapped onto my wrist. I held it up in front of my eyes and squinted at it. Four thirty in the afternoon. Jesus. I'd drunk the entire day away.

"Four men went in there around noon, maybe a bit later. I always listen to the Robert Jamison show at twelve thirty every day. He's got a little bit of everything—music, jokes, contests. You name it." She paused for another racking cough. "I was sitting in my front room waiting for Robert Jamison to come on. They had some program with Edward G. Robinson, but I don't really like him. All that gangster stuff."

The pain in my head intensified. My skull felt like a balloon that was being blown up with a fire hose. "These four men…?"

"Well, like I said, I was waiting for Robert Jamison. I see everything that happens around here."

I'll just bet you do, I thought. There's one on every street. "They went into Mr. Malory's house?"

"Yeah. All four of 'em. I heard a lot of ruckus, so I went out to see what the problem was."

A cold fist of fear was moving inside me, dragging its icy grip along my vitals. "What was the problem?"

"That's just it, sweetie. I got no idea. I went over there after they left and let myself in," she said. "The door wasn't locked, nohow. I didn't go through the house. I just stood in the doorway and called out for Mr. Malory, but nobody answered."

"How did you find my telephone number?" I asked. "Did Mr. Malory tell you?"

"Like I said, I called out but nobody answered. I didn't touch nothing, mister. You can just write that down in your little book."

"Of course not," I reassured her. "But you found my telephone number."

"Mr. Malory had it written on a pad by the telephone. I took the number, I come over here, and I called you. Did I do wrong?"

105

"Not at all," I said. "And thank you for letting me know."

"Well, aintcha gonna do anything about it?"

"I'll go see Mr. Malory myself," I told her. "No need for you to worry further."

"The name's Louise Morrison," she said, "just in case anybody's asking."

I hung up the phone and got the quickest shave and shower I'd ever had in my life. It amazed me I managed not to cut off an ear. I made some coffee and drank three cups black, then tossed down two aspirin. My head was still pounding, but I was fairly certain I'd survive. I took the shortest route I knew to Ed's house, not knowing what I'd see when I arrived and expecting just about anything—but his street looked the same as always, and there were no police cars parked at the foot of his stairs. I went up at an almost-normal pace and rang the doorbell. I heard it echo inside the house, but there were no corresponding footsteps. I rang it again, holding it down this time. Still nothing. I knocked, but that didn't get me anything either.

Old Nosy said she'd gone right in, that the door wasn't locked and she'd just let herself into the house. I turned the doorknob. It clicked open. I pushed, and the door swung back on its hinges.

"Ed?" I walked into the living room. A lamp had been left on over one of the easy chairs, and an open book lay facedown on the floor nearby. I read the spine: *Captains Courageous*. The book was scuffed, its pages hopelessly dog-eared, and certain passages had been underlined in pencil. He'd obviously read it more than once—read it and loved it, if its physical state was anything to go by. Over in the corner, near the bookcase, a potted yucca sparkled with Christmas lights, a star nestled precariously among its spiky leaves. A radio was on in the kitchen, playing "Smoke Gets in Your Eyes." It sounded surreal and disembodied, like the music from a dream.

I went down the narrow hallway, peering into each room I passed. The bathroom was at the very end of the hall. The door was half open, the exposed mirror reflecting a slice of the opposite wall. I grasped the knob and pushed, but something was blocking the door from the other side. "Ed, are you in here?" Perhaps he'd felt ill and had lost consciousness, or maybe he'd fallen in the shower and hit his head. I stepped around the door, and he was there, lying naked in the bathtub, his head and shoulders a mask of congealed blood. I knelt by his side, touching him with hands that, for once in my life, didn't shake. "Ed, if you can hear me, don't move, all right? I'm going to call an ambulance."

He caught my wrist. "Call... McAvity. Central Homicide." He coughed—a ghastly, rattling noise. "Tell him... four of them. Vic Ramirez's boys...."

"Please don't try to talk." I wanted to hold him, to comfort him, but he was covered in blood and I didn't dare. Both eyes were swollen shut, and there was a bump on his forehead the size of an ostrich egg. His lips were grotesquely engorged; the bottom one had been split wide open, revealing the bloody interior flesh. "I'm going to call an ambulance."

LOUISE MORRISON—Old Nosy from across the street—stood with me on Ed's front steps while two ambulance attendants conveyed him down to their waiting vehicle. The senior attendant had given him a shot of morphine, so Ed wasn't physically able to tell the police anything. I could only tell them what I knew, which was how I'd found him and what Mrs. Morrison told me.

"It's a damn shame," Louise said. She looked exactly as I'd expected: a short, skinny old lady in a lime-green pantsuit thirty years too young for her, her face heavily made up and her overrouged cheeks almost the exact same shade as her obviously dyed hair. She smoked incessantly while she waited with me, lighting one off the tip of the other. She could have been anywhere between seventy and pre-Cambrian.

"And you noticed these men going into Mr. Malory's house shortly after noon?" Hank McAvity looked as if he'd been dumped out of a brown paper bag. An unlit cigarette was stuck to his lower lip, bouncing as he talked. He looked haggard, exhausted, and deep lines of fatigue cut into the flesh of his lean face. "Four of them." He jotted this down in a small notebook, the same type that seemed to be issued to every cop in any jurisdiction in the world.

"Four of them, that's right." She nodded at McAvity, at me, at traffic passing in the street below. "Big men. One of them was wearing a lot of jewelry, I remember that. Necklaces and such, big rings."

Big rings. Probably knuckle-dusters, which explained the state Ed's face was in.

McAvity thanked Mrs. Morrison and signaled a nearby officer to help her down the stairs. "Every time somebody is injured or killed lately," McAvity said to me, "you turn up. Is there something going on, Mr. Leonard, or are you just lucky that way?" He ushered us both into

Ed's house but left the door open. Already a veritable squadron of police officers was busy dusting the place for fingerprints, but McAvity didn't spare them a glance. "I normally wouldn't be telling you this, but you already heard Malory say it. These hoods were Vic Ramirez's guys—punks, button men, you know the kind." He flipped the notebook closed and stuffed it into a pocket. "Vic Ramirez only ever passes through LA, kind of a flying visit to check up on his various business interests. He never stays any longer than he has to. He'd rather send his goons to do his dirty work." He nodded toward the hallway of Ed's small, tidy house. "That's what happened here." He sighed. "Damn shame." He caught my expression and said, "Oh, he'll be fine. He took a hell of a beating from these guys, but Malory's as tough as they come. He'll be okay."

"Why would a guy like Vic Ramirez bother with Malory?" I asked. "Do they even know each other?"

"Malory would have gotten too close to something Vic was interested in," McAvity said. "Ramirez plays his stuff close to his vest. He doesn't want trouble. If he had something brewing on the side, and Malory started nosing around...." He raised his hands to shoulder height and dropped them.

Hank McAvity would have made a decent enough actor, I thought. "What are his business interests?"

McAvity shrugged and lit his cigarette. "You name it: gambling, girls, smut. Whatever the market will bear." He drew meditatively on his cigarette. The smoke disappeared inside him and didn't come out for a long time. "Ramirez isn't dumb. He never gets his hands dirty if he can avoid it." He shook his head, smoke trickling out of his nostrils. "He's got lots of wise guys to yank the strings for him—ex-cons, hustlers, low-level operators out of places like Reno or Pescadero, maybe the East Coast even. I heard he's in tight with a couple of the local wise guys in Jersey City. He supplies them with smut in exchange for services." The word "services" might as well have had quotation marks around it.

"Could one of Ramirez's Jersey boys have done this?" I asked.

"Maybe," McAvity allowed, "if Vic wanted to be careful and if he didn't want to get his name in the paper." His gaze was keen and insistent. I had the feeling Lieutenant McAvity didn't miss much. "You thinking of looking for retribution?"

"I want to find these guys. I think—"

He shook his head. "Don't." The hand holding the cigarette stabbed the air in front of him. "You keep out of it. This is a police matter. Obviously Malory was being warned off. You can see what it got him." He turned his wrist to look at his watch. "I gotta get going. When the guys finish dusting, we're closing the place up. This is a crime scene now." He pushed past me and charged down the steps.

I thought to wait around for a while, but the fingerprint boys decided I was getting in their way and put me out. When I got home, my house smelled like cigarettes and stale gin, so I opened all the windows.

I SPENT half of Christmas Eve trying to see Ed at the hospital, but they wouldn't let me in. Then I went by his house, but the cops McAvity had stationed were still on the door, promising dire punishment if anybody set foot on the premises. I sat in my car for a while, pondering the imponderables of life until I was very thirsty. The only thing for my thirst, I decided, was an ice cold gimlet at the Melody Room.

It was about five in the afternoon and there were perhaps nine people in attendance, most of them deeply in their cups and brooding over their cocktail glasses. Lydia Race was fronting a three-piece combo—piano, bass, and drums—while a skinny man with all the vigor of a neurasthenic push broom watched her with his one good eye. A string of colored lights adorned the front of the bar, blinking on and off in jagged bursts while a tube of neon blushed red and green above the jukebox.

I waited while Miss Race sighed and groaned her way through "Jingle Bells" and "My Heart Belongs to Daddy." When she finished her set, I had a Gibson waiting for her at the bar.

"Thanks, pal." She raised the glass—"Here's to ya"—and downed the whole thing in one go. "Gotta keep the pipes wet, know what I mean?" She drew a crumpled pack of Luckies out of her cleavage and fitted one in her mouth. I struck a match off my thumb and leaned toward her, but she waved me away. "I never let guys light my cigarette," she said. "Makes 'em think I'm easy."

"Really?" I forced a note of sincere disbelief. "I can't imagine why." I signaled the bartender for another Gibson and told him to make it a double.

Lydia lit her own cigarette and sucked on it enthusiastically while waiting for her drink. "You look familiar to me," she said. She scooped up a handful of peanuts from a dish laid out on the bar and rattled them in her hand like dice. "I see you somewhere before?" The peanuts went into her mouth one, two, three, like mice disappearing down a drainpipe.

"I'm flattered that you remember me."

"Riiiight!" She nodded. "You were with that detective, Ed Malory, the day I was there." She tilted her head to one side. "You friends or something?"

Or something, I thought. "Mr. Malory has been helping me with a delicate personal problem," I said. "I'd rather not discuss it, if you don't mind."

"Sorry, fella." She glanced at her empty glass pointedly. "No offense." She sat back and looked me over. "Juicer, aren't ya? I can always tell. You had a drink yet today?"

"No."

She told me she was sorry—again—and reached into the bodice of her dress to adjust herself. "So how come you're hanging out here on Christmas Eve? Ain't you got nowhere else to go?"

"I wanted to ask you a question, actually." I took out a picture of Victor Ramirez. I'd found it among the files in Ed's office—I suspected it wasn't a recent likeness—and showed it to her. "Do you know this man?"

"That's Vic Ramirez." She handed the photo back to me. "What do you want with Vic?"

The bartender laid down a gimlet and a double Gibson and stood there waiting. I took out my wallet and put some money on the bar. It disappeared into his meaty fist and from there into the cash drawer.

"A couple of days ago, Mr. Malory was attacked in his home by four men. He's in hospital."

"Jesus!" She put her hand over her mouth. Her nails were long and painted a dark red, the polish chipped and peeling at the tips. "You think Vic's boys did this?"

"The newspapers say the men identified themselves as working for Mr. Ramirez." This was rubbish, but I needed something to goad her with. "I'd like to hear your thoughts on the subject."

She grabbed her glass hard, thin flesh stretched white at the knuckles. "I ain't got no thoughts on the subject." Her lips made a wet, sucking noise as she siphoned up the gin. "Tell your friend to stay out of Vic's way."

"Wait a minute." I caught her by the arm. "Don't rush off." I waited till she reseated herself. "What's Vic Ramirez got on you?"

She drew back, her mouth a hard line. "Nothing."

"So why would Vic's boys pay Malory a visit? Was he being warned off?"

She shook her head like there was a spider in her hair. "I don't remember."

If I was at all inclined to violence, I'd have shaken her silly. "Did Vic Ramirez tell Ed to lay off the Janet Leonard case?" Maybe Stirling had underworld connections and he'd decided to call in a favor.

"I don't know!" She sipped her drink. The glass rattled against her teeth. Maybe she was the type that needed a shot or two first thing in the morning, I didn't know. Some drunks are like that. "What you're asking me, I don't know anything about it. I swear to God."

I extracted a fifty dollar bill from my wallet and laid it on the bar. She reached to take it, but I slapped my hand down, trapping the money. "I'm willing to help out," I said. "There is more where that bill came from."

Her gaze flicked to the money, then away. She spread one hand in front of her and picked at her nail polish. "Where'd you get money like that?"

"I earned it."

She raised her head. Her lids were heavily painted, and she'd drawn a thick black line across them, near the lashes. Heavy pancake makeup fought a losing battle with the network of fine lines fanning out from the corners of her eyes. The flesh of her cheeks had begun to sink. Miss Race was hardly in the first flush of youth, and in a business where her looks meant as much or more than her voice, she was running out of time. "I can't help you," she said. "If it got around that I talked to you about Vic, my life wouldn't be worth a wooden nickel."

"So you know Mr. Ramirez."

"Everybody knows Vic." She dipped her cigarette into the cold ashtray in front of her. "Yeah, Vic's a real popular guy. Got a lot of pull in this town. Got lots of pull anywhere, really."

"You sound bitter." I watched her face carefully for any sign she was considering my offer. "What did he do to you?"

The corners of her mouth turned down hard, like she'd just tasted something sour. The tip of her cigarette went around and around in the spent ashes, the detritus of a hundred ancient smokes. She didn't say anything.

"I'm not asking you to name names." I slid my hand back, so she was free to pick up the money if she wanted to. "I'm looking for information."

"Everybody's looking for something." She laughed, but there was no joy in it. "Everybody wants what they can get."

It would help, I thought, *if I could tell her what I already knew*—but that would compromise the progress of Ed's investigation and expose his client. It could end up with him losing his license. "What time do you finish work?"

She shrugged. "Whenever." She glanced around the place. "Looks like it'll be early tonight, but you never know what's gonna come screaming through the door."

"How about I wait for you? I've got a car. I could drive you home."

She slid off the barstool. "Don't do me any favors."

"I can protect you." It was all I had, and as far as closing gambits went, it was pretty damn weak. Protect her from what? It was all I could do most days to push through my hangover. "Is Vic Ramirez involved in the Janet Leonard case?" It was a weak and tenuous connection, but I had to at least try.

"I gotta get back to work."

"Why would Vic want Ed Malory off the case?"

"I told you already." She raised her hand and brought it down hard on the bar. "I don't know anything."

"What time do you get off work?" Maybe this time she'd give me a straight answer. "I could wait for you."

She didn't. "Go on, get out of here." She walked away and disappeared in the darkness near the stage. By the time she'd started the first bars of "Good Morning, Heartache," I was already out the door.

The Melody Room had no posted hours, but I figured it wouldn't do any harm to come back after twelve, when the other bars were closing. Midnight on December 24th marked the beginning of the holiday, and nobody was open on Christmas. In a lot of ways, LA was hopelessly parochial.

I drove around for a while, headed nowhere in particular but wanting a change of scenery to clear my head. The words of Lydia Race's last song were floating through my brain, making a nice puddle of sentiment and gin.

For some reason it reminded me of the war: the sound of a scratchy, tinny radio inside a wooden communications hut at the edge of the civilized world… drinking bad ersatz coffee we'd stolen from the Jerries… smoking endless cigarettes and waiting. Always waiting. When we got word that a German transport had been sighted, we'd pile out, nerves strung taut with anticipation and fear. It was just like Scotland, we told ourselves. Just like our training days in Scotland, running wild in the mountains, playing at soldiers.

Playing at soldiers… that was the trouble. Pretending what we were doing wasn't dangerous, wasn't liable to end about as badly as anything could.

What happened to your face? Janet wasn't afraid to ask. She'd asked it the first time we went out together. *You're all cut up.*

The Gestapo got me.

I turned off Sunset and headed up into the hills, thinking to take Mulholland at some point. The road rises slowly in that part of the city, and as you climb, you leave the congested streets and car-choked boulevards behind. It all falls away, and you can kid yourself that you're climbing up into some rarer air, where everything will suddenly make sense and every problem you ever had will crumble away in pieces.

Utter rubbish, of course.

I pulled off the road above a scenic overlook and got out of the car. The city lay spread out below, a living, pulsing organism adrift in a sea of lights. Down there, people were crying, being beaten to within an inch of their lives, being disappointed and abandoned, having their bluff called, letting their hair down. Somebody was sitting in an empty room watching the pulse and flicker of disenchanted neon and waiting for a moving bar of light to fall at a predetermined point along the dank, rumpled sheets of someone's lonely bed. People were being crushed, being knifed, stabbed and shot; people were bawling their eyes out, and people were sitting in a bar drinking themselves into oblivion. People were laughing, celebrating, eating, toasting, gasping, breathing, and dying, and all the while, the luminous flesh of the palpitating city didn't give a sweet goddamn.

I stood there and smoked a cigarette, thinking of nothing in particular, watching the glowing ember of hot tobacco burn itself to ash, and then I got in my car and drove back down the hill.

AT A quarter to twelve, I parked across the street from the Melody Room and watched its disenchanted habitués straggling out. Lydia had changed out of her evening gown into a more practical dark suit. She wore a pillbox hat with a veil, a string of fake pearls, and low-heeled pumps. She was carrying a purse and a brown paper sack that might have booze in it. She stood on the sidewalk and looked up and down the street, like women do when they're interested in hailing a cab. There weren't any cabs, not just then, so I got out of my car and walked across to meet her.

She didn't seem surprised to see me. "I didn't think you'd come back."

"I was on my way home and thought I'd swing by and see if you needed a lift." I held the door open for her and waited while she slid in. "It looks ready to rain any minute and I notice you haven't got an umbrella."

She sat primly, with her purse held on her lap like old ladies do. The brown bag she put on the floor. "I don't live so far away. I figured I could do without one." She produced a cigarette and lit it. "You know, most nights I get a cab home."

I pulled away from the curb.

"I live on Glencoe," she said. "Out near the Hightower, you know? Me and another girl are renting a place."

"That's rather a nice neighborhood." I slid a glance at her. "Nightclub singing must be more lucrative than I thought."

"Go spit in your hat!" she said. "And here I thought you were a gentleman."

"So Mr. Ramirez is helping with the rent?" I figured that was going to get me something—either a proper answer or a smack in the face.

"Mr. Ramirez owns the building." She drew on her cigarette like she hated it and wanted it to suffer. "But maybe you already know that." She blew smoke and peered at me the way you'd peer at something you cleaned out of your fingernails.

"You seem pretty loyal to the big guy, all things considered. What has Vic Ramirez got on you?"

She stabbed her cigarette out in the ashtray. "You got all the answers. Why don't you tell it?"

"I think Vic got you out of a jam once. I think he helped you out, and you've been paying him back ever since." There was scant traffic that hour of the night, and we were nearly at the turn for Glencoe. I took my foot off the accelerator. "Maybe there's terms attached. Maybe what Vic wanted in the beginning was more than you could pay." I glanced over at her. "Am I even close?" I turned the wheel and let the car drift to the curb. I set the parking brake and let the engine idle.

She gazed out the window for a moment. Her hands worked the cheap plastic purse, squeezing and releasing the clasp. Her breath rasped a little in her lungs. "My sister found herself in some trouble a few years ago."

"What kind of trouble?"

She gave me a look that could have curdled milk. "What kind do you think?"

"I see."

Her sister had been a showgirl at Ramirez's joint in Vegas. She made good scratch flashing her gams for conventioneers from places like Peoria and Dubuque, and she was invited to all the swanky after-hours parties back at Vic's place. She liked the life but made the fatal mistake of getting involved with one of Vic's businessman friends from back East. A bad decision all the way around, and especially when she found out Junior was on the way. "You can't stuff a belly into those costumes, you know?" Lydia lit another cigarette. "She wasn't showing, but that was only a matter of time."

"I'm assuming Mr. Ramirez stepped in and made things happen." I lit a cigarette of my own and rolled down the window.

"He knew a guy... a doctor." Lydia shrugged. "So Vic fixed it up. Next week, just the same as always, she was in the chorus line." She flicked cigarette ash out the open window. "I made a deal with Vic, but I couldn't pay up. I don't make that much money, if you can believe it."

I made sympathetic noises and advised her that, yes, I could absolutely believe it. "I suppose there were alternate arrangements?"

She opened the door, got out, dropped the cigarette, and stepped on it. "I'll walk from here if you don't mind."

"Did Vic Ramirez farm you out?" I half expected to get my face slapped, but instead she laughed.

"Yeah. Pictures, some home movies, that sort of thing. Nothing weird."

"And now you're being blackmailed." I wondered if she regretted her decision, but I didn't say this out loud. I wasn't interested in being her father confessor. "Do you have any idea who's doing it? And why?" I figured she knew something about Ramirez, something really damning, and the big boss was keeping her mouth shut with the blackmail angle.

"At first I thought it was Layton—Vic had him in pictures too, long before he made it big. But now he's dead."

"Did he get in trouble too?" I asked. Christ, this was starting to play out like a soap opera.

Lydia leaned against the car door and gazed into the middle distance, as if measuring the dark horizon with her eyes. She didn't look at me when she spoke. "Layton was a pansy. Nobody knew it, except Vic. Layton was keeping this guy in a nice apartment out in Westwood, and he'd go visit when he got the itch. Layton's the big six, and everybody knew it, and Vic figured he'd be an easy touch. Some of Vic's friends wanted something a little different, if you get my meaning, and Layton was glad enough to help out." She shifted her weight and looked in at me. "Vic promised to keep Layton's boyfriend out of it, if Layton would make some films for him."

"I can just imagine what sort of films those were," I said. Perversely, I wondered if any were still around. Seeing Allan Layton in flagrante with some young stud would make my year.

She shrugged. "I don't know. All I know is what I was told." She reached in and took the brown bag from the floor, tucked it under her arm, and walked away.

I had a horrible feeling it was the last time I'd ever see her.

I RANG in Christmas with a bottle of Teacher's I'd stowed away for a special occasion. It was a warm night, so I opened my door and sat on my front steps, listening to the rumble of traffic from down below. I felt like I was listening for something in the darkness, but I couldn't imagine what that might be. I was lonely, sad, and growing old. I'd asked questions of everybody I could think of, but I was no closer to finding out who'd killed Janet. Perhaps I'd never know. Perhaps that was something best left to the professionals—except the police seemed just as stymied as I did. If they knew anything, they were keeping it to themselves.

There was a rustle of noise to my right, and then the sound of footsteps on the wooden stairs. Old Nosy—Mrs. Morrison—materialized out of the night. She might have walked all the way from her house, or she might have flown, or maybe distances seem longer when you're drunk, like I was. She was carrying a newspaper and a bottle of bourbon.

"Forgot to pick up yesterday's paper," she said. She came near and dropped it into my lap. "Paperboy doesn't even bring it to the mailbox nowadays. Goddamn lazy little fucker." She peered at me, her head on one side. "You don't look so good. Have a drink?"

I went and fetched two glasses out of the kitchen. When I came back, Mrs. Morrison was sitting on the steps, smoking a long cigarette in an ivory holder. I offered my bottle of Teacher's, but she made a rude noise.

She took the glasses from me and poured a healthy slug of bourbon into each. "Damn shame what happened to your friend," she said. "How's he doing?"

"They won't let me in to see him," I replied. "I'm not family."

"Huh." She grunted her disdain. "You're as good as family. What the hell's wrong with people nowadays?"

"Damned if I know." I took a drink of bourbon and unfolded the newspaper. The headline was bold and black, solid enough for a blind man to see it in the dark, but I still didn't believe it.

HEIRESS CONFESSES TO SISTER'S MURDER.

"Christ." It was all I could do to draw a steady breath. Deborah had just confessed to Janet's murder.

Chapter Thirteen

"LEONARD, GET out of my hair. I couldn't tell you anything if I wanted to, and trust me, I don't want to." Hank McAvity pushed past me and toward the water cooler. The corridor outside his office was jammed with people, all clamoring for a glimpse of Deborah arriving from the cell for her arraignment. She'd been brought in on Christmas Eve, but the district attorney had been vacationing in Santa Monica, leaving Deborah to cool her heels until after the holiday. That gave the popular press enough time to whip themselves into a froth of righteous indignation, and now they were practically slavering with it.

"Yes, but she is my sister-in-law." I knew this argument wasn't going to cut it, not with McAvity, who was about as flexible as concrete.

"Immediate family only." McAvity dumped cold water down his throat. "I got my orders."

"You and everybody else," I grumbled. "I only want five minutes with her."

"I'll be generous," McAvity said. "I'll give you no minutes with her." He went back to his desk and sat. "Get lost," he said. "And shut that damn door on your way out."

I stood outside on the steps, basking in the winter sunshine and wondering what to do next. I thought I might try to get a word in with Linton Stirling, but I doubted the old bastard would even return a phone call. Ever since he'd lit out for the family's Long Island retreat, he'd been unreachable, preferring to bury himself inside the walls of his Georgian revival mansion. Even the New York press, notoriously persistent, couldn't find a way to breach the old man's defenses. Whatever Linton Stirling thought about his daughter's confession, he was keeping it to himself. Maybe he wasn't even in New York; maybe he'd returned to LA by now. It didn't matter. He'd enjoy a visit from me about as much as a hot gasoline enema.

I drove downtown to the mission on Fromsett Street and parked my car near a drycleaners. The air was heavy with a chemical scent, the odor a cross between printer's ink and automobile paint. They'd left the front door open, maybe to vent the steam.

An old man sat behind the counter, mending something by hand when I went in. "You want your shirts done?" he asked, not looking up. "Take two days. We're backed up now. Holidays, you know."

"I was going to ask how much you'd charge to clean my dress and polish my pearls," I said.

That got his attention. "Funny guy." He looked me over. "You got no dry cleaning? Nothing to pick up?"

"No dry cleaning," I said. "I'm like a snake: I simply molt my old outfit."

"Don't waste my time." He turned toward the back room.

I took out my wallet, extracted a ten-dollar bill, and laid it on the counter. "Mind answering a few questions?"

He looked at the bill and licked his lips. "What kind of questions?"

"The mission next door." I tilted my head in its direction. "Ever notice anything odd happening there?"

"Like what? Bunch of drunk guys singing hymns?" This was funny. He was a comic genius. He drew back the corners of his mouth, revealing shrunken, toothless gums. "Get it?"

"Unfortunately." I reached to take back the ten.

"No!" He slapped his palm down on it. "I just remembered something." He tightened his fingers on the bill, drawing it slowly toward him. "These two old guys, they used to sit outside with tin cans, ask people for money."

"Lots of guys panhandle. Is that the best you can do?"

"Yeah, but these were the only two from that place." He nodded at the open door. "They always had lots of good food in there, hot soup on cold days, the works."

"So why do you think they were panhandling?"

He looked at me, his lower jaw hanging slack. "For booze?"

"Uh-huh. So these two were different from the others?"

"Well, they were all drunks in there... most of 'em, anyway." He shrugged. "These two didn't mix with the other ones. They just kept to themselves."

It was too much to hope for, but I decided I'd ask anyway. "Do you remember their names?" He didn't. "Are they at the mission today, do you think?"

119

He laughed. "They ain't anywhere!" His fingers crumpled the ten-dollar bill into the palm of his hand. "They got bumped off by some crazy. Both of 'em. Dead."

"When did this happen?" I asked. I knew—I'd read it in the paper—but I wanted to see if he'd bother lying to me. "Did you see it?"

"I don't see nothin'." His tone made it clear that was the end of the conversation.

I let him keep the money and went next door to the mission. One of the volunteers, Marion, was there—she usually took the breakfast shift—clearing away the dishes and folding up the tablecloths. The mission insisted on tablecloths for meals, and napkins, and proper silverware. Marion believed that just because a man was down-and-out didn't mean he wouldn't enjoy a bit of civility. I liked Marion. Before the mission, she'd been a nun, lived in a cloister and everything. She once told me she'd taken a vow of silence, but even in a convent, it was harder than she'd thought to keep quiet. "So I left," she said. "Figured I could do more good out here in the big, bad world."

"Tony!" She hugged me so hard I could feel every bone in her skinny chest. "Tony Lionheart! Where have you been keeping yourself?" I explained about Janet, leaving out the gorier details. "Oh, I am sorry," she said. "How terrible."

"I hear you've had some problems." I lit a cigarette. "It's all over the news."

"You mean Hector and George?" she asked. "Could I have one of your cigarettes, do you think?"

I lit it for her. "So why them? Why those two and not anybody else?"

"I don't know." She coughed, then carried on smoking. "They certainly weren't the only panhandlers on the street. There are guys selling pencils up there on the corner. Gerry Arbogast is still sitting on the sidewalk in front of the Chinese grocery, pretending to be blind. He's been doing that for the past five years." She stared at a spot on the floor, rubbing the toe of her shoe over it. "Did you hear how he cut them?"

"Yes."

"Do you think he had something against you? You personally, I mean."

"How could he? He doesn't know me—at least I don't think he does." This last was mere conjecture. I knew no such thing, not for certain. The idea that he might know me, might have some grudge against me, was too twisted to consider.

"Well, there's one small comfort in all of this," she said. "Hector and George were almost always drunk. I mean, absolutely blotto." She took one last drag and stubbed out her half-smoked cigarette in a nearby ashtray. "They probably didn't feel a thing."

THE CHARGE nurse objected strongly when I pushed past her onto the ward, insisting I see him. "Immediate family only!" She pointed to a sign over the door. "You aren't related to Mr. Malory."

I turned on her, suddenly tired of all the various rigmarole. "Mr. Malory's parents are both dead. He has no family. I am his only friend. Now, if you'd prefer he have no visitors—"

"He's had a visitor," she snapped. "A policeman was here to see him last night."

"In or out of uniform?" I asked.

"Well, we don't allow people to roam the hallways in the all-together," she huffed. "Mr. Malory's room is right past the elevator. Room 604."

"Thank you." I tried to keep the sarcasm out of my voice, but it was a struggle. "I appreciate it."

Room 604 was, just as she'd said, past the elevator. It was one of those kinda-sorta wards—a long, narrow space the size of a small bowling alley, with six or eight beds crammed in it. Ed was the first one closest the door; he was awake and sitting up.

I had to restrain myself from leaping forward and crushing him in my arms. "There you are, you silly bugger."

"Tony." He smiled. I was glad to see that smile. "Hey, it's nice to see you."

"It's amazing, the lengths some people will go to, to get a day off," I said. I had to say something. It felt like my chest was about to cave in. "I want to hug you," I murmured, "but this is an open ward." Most of the other patients were sitting up reading or listening to the radio. Two men near the end of the long room were playing checkers, and a man across from Ed was slowly and deliberately walking a quarter up and down his knuckles.

"You can hug me when I get out." His expression said he was looking forward to it. He touched his cheek. "How's the old man look, anyhow? They won't let me have a mirror in here."

He looked—to put it plainly—terrible, like he'd stuck his face in an electric fan just to see the pretty blades go round, but I wasn't about to tell him that. "Not too bad, considering."

"Considering what?"

"Considering you were an ugly bastard to begin with," I said, laughing. I pulled a chair close to his bed and sat. "Guess you've heard about Deborah's confession?"

"Yeah." He pulled a copy of the *Times* out from under his pillow. "Do you think she did it?"

"Deborah? Not bloody likely." I took the paper from him and reread the handful of details the police had released to the press. "She's a cold-hearted bitch and a bit too free with her favors, but I can't see her beating Janet's head in."

"So she's protecting somebody," Ed said.

"Could be. They're arraigning her today. I tried to see her, but McAvity kicked me out."

"He was here, to see me. Brought me a box of candy and everything." He grinned.

"Did you hear the latest about the two hoboes from the mission?" I turned up an inside page of the *Times* and showed him the single paragraph detailing several previously undisclosed details about the murders. "What gets me is how they were cut." I fingered my scars. "It's no coincidence, Ed. It's not even close to coincidence."

"Were they cut before or after they were killed?" He sat up straight, and I reached to put another pillow behind his back. "If he cut them before, it's one thing. Afterwards...." He shrugged. "Interference with a corpse, the law boys call it, but it points to some personal motive, usually revenge. If he cut them beforehand, he'd have probably just killed them that way."

"This is why you're the detective," I said, grinning, "and I'm the crap novelist."

He reached out, his hand carefully hidden, and tugged at my shirt. "You are not a crap novelist." His blue eyes were wide and slightly moist in his ravaged face. My heart turned over in my chest. Goddammit, I loved this man. "The papers all say they were shot in the back."

"Yes. They were two of the more recalcitrant cases I'd ever seen. Both of them seemed to be perpetually intoxicated."

"Both of them were men you'd personally helped," he said. I could tell by his expression that he was putting certain pieces together. "And both were incorrigible drunks." He tapped the paper with his index finger. "Had any more postcards?"

"Acapulco," I said.

"Where you and Janet spent your honeymoon, I believe."

"How the bloody hell did you know that?"

"When old man Stirling hired me to investigate… things, he let me have a peek into the family Bible, you might say." He folded the newspaper and returned it to its place behind his pillow. "What did this one say?"

I told him.

"It's a bit crude," he said, "but I approve of the sentiment." He made to say something else, but the charge nurse was moving down the ward with the inevitability of a demented juggernaut. "Look, I haven't got much time, but I can tell you one thing: whoever killed those two men from the mission doesn't approve of your charity work—or anybody's charity work, for that matter… at least not when drunks are involved."

"He hates drunks?" It seemed like rather an extreme reaction.

"Or he hates you." Ed glanced up at the woman glowering down at us both. "Mrs. Keegan, this is my long-lost brother." He wasn't quite smirking.

"Your long-lost brother has to go," she said. "Visiting hours are over."

And just like that, she put me out.

I WAS sitting at home that night, mulling over the developments in my latest chapter, when the telephone rang. My telephone didn't ring very often; when it did, it was usually a wrong number.

"Tony? They told me I could call you. I hope that's all right. They always allow the condemned one telephone call, isn't that right?"

"Deborah?" This was novel.

"Yes, it's me." She laughed, but it had the sound of a sob in it. "Isn't that funny? Who would have ever thought I'd be calling you from jail?"

I flashed on an image of the corridor outside McAvity's office, the milling press and spectators, all eager for a glimpse of the fallen woman. "Was it bad?" I asked. "The arraignment."

"Oh no, it was quite a picnic." Her voice was harsh, brittle, just hovering on the edge of the entitled hauteur I knew so well. "That's why I'm calling. To see if you remembered the lemonade."

I didn't answer. There was no point.

"Tony? You are still there, aren't you?"

"Yes." I drew a couple of slow breaths. Losing my temper with her wouldn't serve either one of us. I think she realized that as well. When she next spoke, her voice was polite and her tone restrained and well-modulated.

"I wonder if you could come and help an old friend out." A self-deprecating laugh. "I'm afraid I've got myself in a bit of a jam."

"I'm listening."

"I need someone to bail me out," she said. "I'm think you're it, darling." She sighed—a little theatrically, I thought. "Could you, do you suppose…?"

"How much is it?" I was trying my best not to sound angry. I was failing.

"Well, good God, how would I know?" Her voice went away. I could hear her talking to someone in the background. "Five thousand dollars, Matron says. Only five thousand. Apparently I'm nobody. Can you help?" And, when I didn't immediately respond, she said, "I thought, considering that you *are* Janet's only heir—"

My gut clenched. "All right." It was only a matter of time before she brought that up. "I'll be there as quickly as I can."

THE HALL of Justice was still reasonably crowded when I got there, although the hordes of reporters and various sensation-seekers had moved off. Deborah was being held in the women's block of the Los Angeles City Jail. They'd taken her personal belongings, as well as her belt and the string of pearls she'd worn. I don't know what kind of person wears pearls to get arrested. She was smartly dressed in a pale blue linen suit, with navy and white open-toed pumps. She'd spread her overcoat on the filthy bench of the holding cell, although they'd taken the sash off it, supposedly for her own protection. People have killed themselves with much less, but I didn't think Deborah was the suicidal type. She waited till we were in my car before saying anything.

"Tony, darling, light me a cigarette." I did; she took it and drew on it gratefully. "I swear to God—" She exhaled a long stream of smoke into the space between us on the front seat of my car. "If I had to spend one more hour in that place, I'd have gone off my rocker." She stretched her arms above her head, the lit cigarette dangerously close to the ceiling. "Take me home and fuck me properly." She laughed at my expression. "Fuck me properly, and I'll leave you everything I have."

I nearly ran the car up on the sidewalk. I only just missed a mailbox and an old man sitting in a folding chair next to a barbershop, enjoying the cool night air. I yanked the brake so hard the handle nearly came off. "What did you say?" It was the exact same thing Janet had said to me on our honeymoon... and the exact same thing that was written on the postcard. I felt faintly queasy.

"I'm joking, you ninny." She slanted a look at me. "Although, if you really wanted to...."

"For Christ's sake!" I released the brake and pulled back onto the street. It was a while until I felt calm enough to talk to her. "How did you know?"

She regarded me queerly, her head on one side. "How did I know what?" I explained it. "Oh, that," she said. "Janet told me."

I didn't believe her. Deborah had a very finely honed sense of irony, and of cruelty as well. Perhaps she'd sent the postcards. It was the sort of thing she might do, thinking it great fun. She was the sort of person who enjoyed pulling the wings off flies.

When I pulled up to the main gate of the Stirling residence, half the lights in the big house were on and the other half were out. We'd passed linesmen a ways back, suspended on the tops of the electric poles and fiddling about with rubber gloves and wire. "Looks like they're having problems with the power." The guesthouse, too, was dark, even the perpetually lit safety lights lining the walkway.

Deborah huffed out an irritated breath. "Oh, for Christ's sake. Take me up to the main house." Her tone was commanding, petulant—the spoiled rotten little girl too used to getting her own way.

I pulled the car up in front of the huge double doors, hoping against hope that old man Stirling was not in residence just then.

"What you doing here, man?" Pepe appeared at the side of my car. "You know old man Stirling don't want you here."

"Go chase yourself," I said. "I simply gave the lady a ride home." *And five thousand dollars*, I thought, but I didn't tell Pepe this. He was just the sort to touch me up for a loan. "Will you be all right?" I asked

Deborah, but it was mere politeness. I don't personally believe in the fragility of females, and Deborah was about as helpless as a buzz saw.

"Don't run away mad," she said, getting out of the car. "Come in and have a drink." She smiled brightly, as if we'd just returned from a shopping trip instead of the city jail. "Do you want a drink?"

The house echoed with the sound of our footsteps. The lights in the foyer were out, casting the space into a sinister half-darkness. "I'm going to run up and have a quick shower," Deborah said. "You don't mind, do you? You can roam around if you'd like. I think my father has some decent cigars in a box on the mantelpiece—just there in the sitting room." With that, she scampered up the stairs and vanished into the upper reaches of the house.

"You want anything?" Pepe hovered nearby, grim-faced and surly. "I get it for you."

"Thank you, no." I waited till he'd also disappeared, then went into the sitting room and had a little poke around.

I could lie and say I'm not at all the inquisitive type, but I think every writer is. We aren't easily satisfied; we must peel back every single layer of a thing and find out what's underneath. I could also lie and say I'm not the type of man who snoops in somebody else's things, but snooping happens to be one of my favorite pastimes, one I've gotten particularly good at. You can tell what sort of person somebody is by examining the minutiae of their lives—the tie clips and loose change, the broken fountain pen leaking ink like blood into the pocket of a fine silk shirt. People leave little bits of themselves in the most unexpected places. It pays to examine every nook and crevice, every hiding place, so I did.

I found a bobby pin, half a Tootsie Roll, two pennies, and a lot of dust. I also found a pamphlet, cheaply printed on a single sheet of paper and folded. On the front was a grainy photograph of a vaguely Spanish house, set in a grove of scrub pines against a backdrop of some mountains. LUDLOW VALLEY RETREAT, it read, WHEN REST IS ALL YOU NEED. I wasn't so soon out of the egg that I couldn't see it for what it was: a rest cure for drunks.

"When I said wander around, I didn't mean you should entirely upend the place." Deborah was suddenly at my elbow, wrapped in a terrycloth bathrobe, her hair wet. "Oh, you've found the family secret. May I?" She took the pamphlet out of my hand. "Ludlow Valley… I believe that's up near Carmel." She reached for the decanter on a side table, poured two fingers of amber liquid into a glass, and handed it to me.

126

"Family secret?" She'd lost me.

"Oh, Dad used to be quite the soak. Whiskey, I believe, was his poison. It got so that he couldn't function." She splashed some whiskey into a glass for herself and added ice and soda. "When he was really out of control, he'd take a run up the coast and stay for a few days... or a few weeks, depending." She turned the pamphlet over and peered at it. "Quite a pretty spot, isn't it? If one wanted to escape the city."

"Dirty weekend?"

She burst out laughing. "Are you asking, or telling?" She handed the Ludlow Valley leaflet to me. "You might like to check it out sometime, Tony."

If this was a joke about my own drinking, I wasn't laughing. Like others of her social station, Deborah was adept at uttering small epithets that turned out to be damning indictments. To hell with her; I had epithets of my own. "Go there often, does he? Your old man." I opened the leaflet and read aloud from it. "'For those who are accustomed to the best.' Did you write this?"

"Don't be absurd." She picked a cigarette from a small glass box and lit it. "Perhaps you really ought to run up there for a look." She glanced at me, and there was something afraid and tenuous in her expression. "Never hurts to have a fallback plan."

Something that might have been an idea fluttered briefly in the back of my brain. "Deborah, why did you do it?"

"You're babbling." She blew smoke in a long plume toward the ceiling.

"Why did you confess to Janet's murder? You and I both know it's rubbish." I took a cigarette from the box. "Even if you hated her, she was still your sister. There's no way in hell you'd beat her face in."

She smirked. "You seem awfully certain."

I lit the cigarette and drew smoke. As expected, it was Turkish tobacco, very fine and gorgeously blended. Linton Vanderbilt Stirling would, of course, insist on the best. "You might be a lot of things—" *A rich man's wife, a spoiled brat, the heiress to her old man's fortune.* "—but you're not a murderer."

"Well, no. I'd be a murder*ess*, and I'm sure you've heard that the female is deadlier than the male." She crossed to a wingback chair set near a large french window and sat, arranging the bathrobe to cover her knees—an interesting show of modesty quite unlike the Deborah I knew.

"So you've read your Conan Doyle." The rich taste of the cigarette was making me slightly ill. I stubbed it out in an ashtray. "Who are you protecting, Deborah? Because it occurs to me that you're hiding somebody." This last was a bluff, but I was certain she didn't realize it. "Is it your husband? Seems rather a long way to travel, just to kill a sister-in-law he hardly even knew."

She laughed. "Don't play detective, Tony. You're not good at it."

"The servants are blameless, of course, and I know Pepe didn't do it."

She stiffened, the skin of her face drawing taut over the bone. "How do you know he didn't do it?"

"He told me."

She tilted her head and drew her fingers through her wet hair, separating the strands. "Of course." She peered up at me through her hair. "One's servants are always so dependable and trustworthy nowadays." The corners of her mouth turned up, a little at a time.

"Pepe didn't do it, Deborah. He had no reason to. Neither did you. So who did?"

"You know, Tony, I'm dreadfully tired. Being locked up does wear one down. I trust you can find your own way out?"

"What did dear old Dad say he'd give you, if you kept your mouth shut? A quickie divorce from that husband of yours?"

"Really, I've heard quite—"

"He was a Nazi until 1945. Did you know that? Rather a distinguished career as I recall."

Horst tells me you've been licking moisture from the ceiling. We can give you water.

"I didn't know that." An obvious lie; her voice sounded like it was coming from a long ways off. "I think you must be mistaken, Tony."

I crossed to where she was, grabbed her arms, and yanked her up out of the chair. "I am not." I turned my face so she could see the scars. "See this? I know you've seen this. You've been looking at me for years."

She struggled to free herself, but I refused to let go. "Johan would never do something like that!"

"Ask him." I shoved her away from me. "I was taken by the Gestapo and held prisoner for over a year. While I was there, they thought it would be amusing to experiment a little."

"That's nonsense," she said. But her voice trembled. "Johan wouldn't hurt—"

"Johan did." My heartbeat was thundering in my ears, and my chest felt tight. I had to get out of that house.

I left and drove around for a while, thinking to clear my head—then I realized I was headed north, away from Los Angeles and into the hills. I was going to the one place right now that had answers: Ludlow Valley.

Chapter Fourteen

THERE WAS no street lighting where I was going, but I didn't really care. I drove with one hand on the wheel, chain-smoking with the other. Once I nearly hit a deer, after which I slowed down. The monotony of the endless road started to get to me after a while, and I found myself nodding off a couple times. I opened all the windows and let the breeze blow in on me.

Near Paso Robles I stopped to buy gas from a rickety service station, open late. The owner was a well-fed Mexican in his late fifties, who pumped the gas for me himself and gave me the strongest cup of coffee I've ever tasted. But it did the trick, that coffee, and kept me awake for the remainder of the drive. I made a mental note to go back some time and thank him for the unexpected boost.

It was starting to get light out when I got to Salinas, the false dawn spreading slowly over the wide, arable land of northern California. I found a narrow dirt road leading off the highway and pulled over, reclining as far as I could in the seat and using my coat for a pillow. The rising sun slid its level rays into my eyes, so I pulled my hat brim down and slept.

I dreamed Janet and I were on our honeymoon, but instead of staying in a hotel, we'd erected a tent on the edge of a precipice overlooking the sea. All night long we listened to the crashing of the waves, and whenever I tried to speak, Janet shushed me: *Shhh... I need to understand. Don't speak. I'll explain later.* I leaned far out over the precipice. Something was down there, something I needed to see.

I woke midmorning with the feeling of having slept too long. It was 10:00 a.m. by my watch, and the sun occupied a fair space of sky. I felt like something spat out by a sick dog, so as soon as possible, I found a gas station where I could get a quick wash and a drink of cold water. After I'd finished, I went inside and ordered breakfast at the lunch counter.

The waitress was middle-aged and tired-looking, as if she'd spent all night there. "Whatallyahave?" And, when I ordered ham and eggs, "'Kay." She disappeared through a set of swinging doors, and in a minute, I heard her arguing with someone back there. The doors swung wildly on their hinges, and she was back with a pot of coffee, which she poured into my cup in a long, undulating stream. "Minute."

Someone had left a copy of the local newspaper on the counter, so I paged through it while I waited for breakfast. The news was all of the "man bites dog" variety, with the biggest story being Mrs. Fiander's azaleas.

The waitress came back and slapped a plate down in front of me. "Anything else?"

"No, thank you." I tagged her sleeve as she turned to go and asked her about the Ludlow Valley clinic. Was it still in operation? Did she know who ran it? She frowned, and the longer I talked, the deeper her frown got.

"You mean Biff Straker's place?" She jerked her head in a vaguely eastern direction. "Up there on the hill? Big sign in front. Used to take in drunks."

"Do you know if Mr.... uh, Biff takes in anybody nowadays?"

"You a cop?"

"No."

"I don't know much about it. You'd best go on up there and look for yourself." The kitchen doors swallowed her, and that was that. Apparently conversation was a poorly appreciated skill in these parts. The food, however, was excellent, and after I'd cleaned my plate and had another cup of coffee, I left a generous tip.

I drove into Carmel a little while later, feeling well pleased with myself. The town was one of those fairytale-looking places with little cottages set on well-kept little streets, cozy neighborhoods made to look like they'd come from Victorian England. North Americans are fascinated with England to an unnatural degree, something I've never understood. Many of them have never even visited there, let alone entertained a lingering knowledge of the culture. They seem to assume the Englishman is a slightly higher breed, more refined in his tastes and attitudes. Pity they've never seen him in his natural habitat.

I took the road north, out of Carmel, following the vague descriptions listed in the brochure, which I'd foolishly assumed were correct. At a four-way intersection, I annoyed innumerable other drivers, trying to decide which way to go. The chorus of car horns had risen to a cacophony by the time I picked a direction and turned left; several people treated me to various descriptive gestures as they pulled around me. I drove for some distance, seeing nothing that looked anything like the pamphlet. The countryside was very pretty, and by now I'd got up into the hills, where there was a surfeit of open space and considerable distance between houses. There were plenty of roadside signs offering land for sale, but nothing to indicate a place where drunks might go to dry out. I was ready to turn around and try another direction when I saw a narrow dirt road leading into some trees. A crude, hand-lettered sign read: STRAKER.

The road grew narrower the deeper I got into the trees, until it was little more than a path with grass growing thick in the wheel ruts and the foliage leaning in precipitously on either side. At the end there was a low-roofed, ranch-style house painted red, with a wide porch at the front. There didn't seem to be anyone around.

I parked near the steps and got out. The air was absolutely still, with scarcely a sound except for the occasional halfhearted chattering of some small bird. There was a scent of pine in the air, of greenness and growing things, and the raw, damp smell of the earth.

"Hello?" I called. "Is anyone here?" A scrub pine creaked in response, and two birds began a furious disquisition in a nearby bush. I walked around the back of the house, my shoes crunching loudly on the gravel. "Anybody?" I'd just turned when a screen door slammed and a young woman came down the steps. "Marvelous," I said. "You certainly seem to be somebody."

She was tall and red-haired in a way that appeared entirely natural, except nowadays you can't always be sure. Her beautifully shaped face was clean of makeup, and her lips, slightly parted just then, looked soft. "Can I help you?" She offered me her hand. "Dr. Sylvia Kane." She examined the clipboard she carried. "Have you a reservation, Mr....?"

"Gandy," I said hastily, "George Gandy. No, I'm here looking for my brother-in-law, actually." I laughed, as if this were all a fine adventure, or a fine misunderstanding.

"His name?" One of her eyebrows arched, but whether it was a natural gesture or suspicion, I didn't know. "We have very few patients in residence right now. Much of the facility is being renovated."

I didn't even blink. "Linton Stirling. Of course, we call him Harry." If Linton Stirling was here, I'd eat the front bumper off my car. I didn't even know why the hell I'd asked. Did some part of me—the drunk part, probably—still believe in magic?

"Sorry." Her smile was perfunctory and meaningless. No doubt she put it on each morning like her perfume. "We haven't anyone here by that name."

"Would Mr. Straker be in residence?" It was the longest of long shots and bound to fail.

"I am Mrs. Straker, née Kane." There was that smile again. "Is there anything else, Mr. Gandy? Only we are rather busy…."

"But you said there was hardly anyone in residence." I peered around her. "Or am I mistaken?"

"Good-bye, Mr. Gandy. Please don't oblige me to have you escorted off the property. We wouldn't want that."

"No," I agreed, "we wouldn't. Good-bye, Mrs. Straker."

I hadn't honestly expected to receive a straight answer, but at least I knew where the place was and could come back—say, after dark. I left Mrs. Straker standing in the yard, and I hightailed it back to Carmel. I'd been on the road nearly twenty-four hours. I was tired, dirty, and smelled like a whore's week-old underpants. It was no wonder the woman put me off the property.

I stopped at a modest department store and bought a change of clothes: underwear, socks, trousers, shirt—the whole business. I found a small hotel on a tree-lined side street close to the town center. As far as hotels went, it was nothing special, but it was clean and well-kept, and the shower was hot and needle sharp. Afterward, I lay down on the bed for a while and dozed, hoping a rest might sharpen my mental faculties. I wanted some strategy to take with me when I went back to Ludlow Valley—preferably something that would get me information, and lots of it.

Maybe Linton Stirling's drinking had nothing to do with a mountain rest cure, and maybe it did. It wasn't his drinking that bothered me; it was what he did as a result. Was he a reformed drunk, one of those inveterate do-gooders who are persuaded by steps nine through twelve to "take the message" to all the other poor slobs who've never heard of Bill W.? Or was he filled with self-loathing as a result of his addiction and compelled to punish every other drunk he met? I'd met a few of those, the ones who hate everything—most of all themselves. I didn't for a minute believe Linton Stirling was blameless; I knew for a fact he wasn't. I'd gone to Mexico under my own and Ed Malory's steam, but it was old man Stirling's money that kept me there—or tried to. Was he afraid of what I might tell someone, if I chanced to make it back?

I set my alarm for midnight and went to sleep. I must have been especially tired, because the alarm clock had run itself down when I finally woke up. It was ten past twelve and a lovely night for a drive. I pulled my clothes on and went down to my car, and within minutes, I was heading north to Ludlow Valley.

I've often wondered how they choose names for these places. Just after the war, I stayed at a clinic in Switzerland, a manor house belonging to some minor noble who'd committed suicide back in the thirties. It was an absolutely massive structure, set on the edge of a lake and glaring down at the faintly greenish water with an ill-concealed hatred. It was a very posh sort of place, with private rooms for all the patients, and an especially quiet floor if you were particularly ill or recovering from surgery, like I was. The nurses wore white uniforms without any starch, to prevent them from rustling, and special shoes with heavy rubber soles to mute the sound of footsteps. It was so quiet that the silence became a kind of oppression, and I waited eagerly to hear rain against the windowpanes, or the radiator in the corner ticking out heat.

The clinic was called Les Jardins de Dieu—God's Gardens—and it was a very pretty spot to recover from extensive facial surgery. They'd had to suture together the torn and damaged tissues before they could even touch the skin, and some muscle had gotten sacrificed along the way, flesh so necrotic it could not be saved. When the internal damage was sewn back together and the external tissues repaired as well as could be expected, I was left with a trio of raised, livid scars, corded and sinuous but ultimately better-looking than the raw hamburger I'd previously had for a face. An honorable war wound, they said. The medal was in the mail.

By then I'd met and married Janet, and I didn't care about wounds or medals. I just wanted to forget the war. The best way to do that was with alcohol, and so for the first six months of our marriage, I was utterly and absolutely soused. I'd start the day with whiskey and end it the same way, but in between there might be wine or beer or gin, all quaffed with great enjoyment and abandon. By noon I was pleasantly buzzed; by six I was drunk; by midnight I was deep in my cups, half-asleep and often surly. The very next morning, I'd start the entire process over again. It went on like that for years.

Once I got out of Carmel, I had no trouble finding my way to the ranch, and before too long, the dirt road appeared and I obligingly turned onto it. It was deathly quiet, and I cringed as my tires crunched over the loose gravel drive. I'd doused my lights just before the turn off, but there was a full moon, which provided ample illumination for someone trying to sneak onto the grounds of a clinic for alcoholics. I parked under a clump of trees, hoping they would provide some little camouflage. All the lights were out except for one at the rear of the building, and I went to it, keeping to the shadows, my back against the wall. It wasn't a particularly hot night, but I was sweating bullets. I found an overturned metal bucket that made a decent stepstool and pulled myself up to peer cautiously in the window.

The room was occupied: a tall, stoop-shouldered man bent over a small wooden desk, writing something with a pencil. He had the emaciated look of a dying man, or someone who'd gone a long time without a decent meal. He wrote with his right hand, the left held close to his side; now and then he would reach up to a shelf in front of him and take down a book. I watched him for close to ten minutes, and all the while, he did nothing but write.

I was beginning to wonder if I'd wasted my time when he turned very suddenly and brought his face up close to the wire netting that covered the open window. "What do you want? What do you want here?"

I froze as if someone had nailed my feet to the ground. At first I wasn't sure if what I was seeing was even real. Perhaps the ravages of war had left him unnaturally changed, or he'd been altered by disease. It could be the window netting distorted him, so the face he presented to me wasn't his face at all, but a grotesque simulacrum. "It's you." My pulse sped up, my heart shuddering in my chest. "I haven't seen you since—"

"The war." He called me by the name I used back then, not my real name. Could I even remember what that was?

"I go by Leonard, now," I told him. "Tony Leonard."

"Tony Leonard." He grinned, a wide and savage rictus of his ravaged face. "Tony Leonard, the war hero. Yes, I read the papers. Tony Leonard, the coward who deserted and left his men to die." He thrust his face forward till the wire netting pressed into his skin. "Remember me, Tony Leonard? I hear you're doing charity work among the down-and-outers."

I backed away from the window, my mind clanging a warning.

Somewhere inside the building, a door slammed, and then another, and someone clattered down the stairs. He rounded the corner, his heels skidding on the gravel drive. "Tórshavn! You remember that word, don't you?"

I ran for the car, leaped inside, and started the motor.

"Tórshavn," he said again, "do you remember?" As he drew near, I saw he was brandishing a tire iron, holding it above him and to the side, like a club. "You're a drunk," he spat. "You were a drunk then, and you're a drunk now."

I put the car in reverse and stamped on the gas, but nothing moved. By now he'd attached himself to the passenger side door and was struggling to get in. Luckily I'd locked it, and the window was rolled up. "Let go of the car." I found the hand brake and released it, backing down the hill and onto the main road. He followed me, brandishing the iron and shouting obscenities, but by then I was too far away for him to do any genuine harm. I turned the car south, toward Los Angeles, and went back the way I'd come.

IT WAS morning, or close enough, when I pulled up in front of the police station and put the car in park. I'd driven almost straight through and felt like someone had smashed me in the face with a mallet. Worse, I wanted a drink like nobody's business.

I went in and found Lieutenant McAvity at his desk. He looked like he hadn't even bothered to go home. "Leonard." He poured me a cup of foul precinct coffee and offered me a cigarette. "Suppose you heard about Malory."

"No, I haven't." I drew hard on the cigarette and let the smoke meander around inside me for a while. "Is he all right?" Maybe he'd taken a turn for the worse while I'd been gallivanting around up north. Just thinking about it made me feel sick.

"Oh, sure," McAvity said, "but there's something different cropped up with his case, so they decided to hang on to him for a while longer." They'd be releasing him in a few days, McAvity said, but until then he was on strict bed rest and quiet. During a routine check, the charge nurse had noticed him behaving oddly—agitated, nervous—and had called a neurologist in to consult. He diagnosed a rather significant concussion and had Ed moved to a quiet ward. McAvity warned me to stay away. "Last thing he needs is an impromptu visit from you. He's had one helluva knock on the sconce. I mean it, Leonard. Don't make me run you in."

I brought McAvity an account of my encounter with Donald Whitlaw—that was his name, although I'd heard that after the war he'd taken to calling himself something else—up north, at Ludlow Valley.

"Why are you telling me this?" McAvity asked. His expression said it had better be good, or else.

"The men who were murdered, the ones from the mission? Whoever killed them cut them first." I turned so he could see my scars. "Like this."

"And you think he did it, this Whitlaw guy?" McAvity sipped his coffee and made a face. "And I'm supposed to send my guys out to arrest him on your say-so." He rose from his chair and dumped his coffee into the trash. "Leonard, you've been trying my patience ever since that beating put Malory out of commission. Now you tell me that some Army buddy of yours has been killing bums down on Skid Row to get back at you."

"It's true. I just have this feeling in my gut." Christ, I wanted a drink. I drew a couple deep breaths and told myself it would pass, the craving would pass in a few minutes. "He cut them exactly the same as—" *Forget it*, I told myself. *He doesn't believe you, and he thinks you're wasting his time. Go home and have that drink you want.* I got up and headed for the exit.

"Wait a minute." McAvity's voice crackled like cornered electricity. "Come back here, Leonard." He waited till I'd sat before pulling some pictures out of a file and sliding them across the desk to me. "Crime scene photos," he said. "The very latest. Do you know how he killed them?"

The men in the photos weren't what I'd call close friends of mine. Still, I'd known them, however fleetingly. "How?"

"Manual strangulation. Not shot like last time. He was pretty strong too. Their larynxes were crushed." He gave me a moment or two with the photos, then took them back. "I don't particularly care for your version of events, Leonard, and I don't particularly care for you." He sat back and lit a cigarette. "As far as I'm concerned, you're a pain in my ass." He breathed smoke. "But the way he cut them, and the fact that you and he are old Army buddies…." He shrugged. "I'll look into it."

I got up to leave. "Do look into it soon, Lieutenant. And thank you."

"Yeah," he grumbled. "Get out of my office."

The sun was coming up when I pulled into my driveway and turned off the engine. It was a beautiful morning, clear and bright, with birdsong and just a hint of the late night's leftover dew clinging to windowsills and fences. I felt about a thousand years old, and all I wanted to do was take my medication and tumble into bed for a couple of hours. I unlocked my door and dropped my clothes as I went, not caring where anything fell. I pulled back the covers on my neatly made bed (I didn't remember doing that, but never mind), and by the time I remembered my medication, I was trembling on the edge of sleep.

I dreamed it was the war again, and I was back in the Faroe Islands. It was hellishly cold, with intermittent snow showers. We were crouched in our camouflaged hut, drinking the weak coffee we'd brewed over our tiny camp stove, listening to the wind and waiting. We were always waiting.

We thought maybe if we were clever enough or attentive enough, we'd evade any attempt at capture, and anyway, the Jerries weren't too keen about landing anywhere ashore. They'd heard about us. Word had come from Berlin that the Allies had dispatched small groups of highly trained commandoes, stationing them at various strategic points close to—or inside of—enemy lines. It had the effect of redoubling German reinforcements at these locations, so basically anyone who volunteered for the assignment was signing his death warrant. Stories of other units falling to sabotage and ambush had begun to trickle down to us. Since we were located literally under the Germans' noses, it was only a matter of time before it happened to us.

I was in the hut with Whitlaw, crouched around the feeble warmth of our camp stove. We burned Sterno because it was portable and readily available; it had the added benefit of being virtually smokeless. We figured we had taken all necessary precautions and were reasonably safe from ambush—well, as safe as you can be under such circumstances—so perhaps we weren't as attentive as we ought to have been. Perhaps that finely honed soldier's instinct had become dulled by the seemingly endless weeks and months crouched in a frozen hellhole, drinking ersatz coffee and waiting for orders.

Corcoran—the third member of our little soiree—had gone outside to take a look around. We'd gotten in the habit of scanning our surroundings at predetermined intervals—intervals that changed every day. It doesn't do in wartime to make oneself predictable, and whatever else the Germans were, they weren't stupid. Lately we'd begun to notice their patrols sweeping closer and closer to our location, and twice now they had nearly surprised us on our doorstep. It would soon be time to leave and take up residence elsewhere. The last thing any of us wanted was to get caught and spend the rest of the war rotting away in an internment camp, or being tortured by the Gestapo.

I'd been pondering a second cup of coffee when I heard a shout from outside: *Hey! Toss us a bog roll, would you? This fecking grass is killing me.* We weren't supposed to reply to any hail not within a direct line of sight, but I knew it was Corcoran. I'd recognize that County Wexford accent anywhere. I clambered up out of the shelter, which we'd erected under an overhanging lip of sod, and cautiously raised my head above ground level. A wave of relief washed through me: it was merely Corcoran—

He wasn't alone. Another man stood behind him, a knife at his throat. The man with the knife was grinning, a wide, toothy, madman's grin, and the knife he held never wavered. "Where are the others?" he asked. His English was perfect, with a neutral accent that might have been London or Surrey or Kent. He'd probably been educated at Cambridge or Oxford in the years before the war and retained a deep respect for England as an abstract entity.

"Don't know what you mean," I'd said. I had no illusions that would make him go away. I'd have to kill him, because if I let him live, he'd go back to his own encampment and someone would get on the radio-telephone to Berlin, and we'd have all the Nazis in Norway down on our backs. No, I'd have to kill him before he killed Corcoran, even though I knew he would kill Corcoran anyway, because there wasn't time enough for me to get up onto level ground and draw the knife that was clipped to my belt. There wasn't enough time, and Corcoran would die because of that....

I dreamed I was there again, that I was struggling to hoist myself out of the hut while unseen hands grabbed at my legs and feet, pulling me down again. Corcoran was trying to free himself while the Nazi officer sliced his throat across, again and again. I saw it in slow motion: the hand drawing the knife from left to right, as easily and gently as someone slicing a bow across the taut strings of a violin or cello. The blood flowed from Corcoran like a dark, sticky river and rose around me, trapping me and pulling me under—

I woke, the scream still echoing in my ears, my heart pounding fit to burst. The clock by my bed said it was half past three in the afternoon. I'd slept most of the day away. The sky outside my window was a deep, louring black, with an ominous rumbling to the southwest that meant heavy rain.

I shuffled to the bathroom to take my medication. The man in the bathroom mirror peered back at me with a certain hostility I found unnerving. "You know what you can do, and all," I murmured. His expression didn't change. Some people are arrogant that way. I swallowed the quinine tablets with half a glass of tepid tap water and went through to the living room. My typewriter was where I'd left it, the manuscript of *A Sad Farewell* neatly stacked beside it. I'd have to get back to it sometime, perhaps if I had a free afternoon.

I didn't know what Whitlaw would do, not really—if he intended to do anything. After all, he'd chosen to scar and kill complete strangers in some twisted scheme of vengeance, when he and I were in the same city and he could have come after me at any time. Where I lived was a matter of record, and my telephone number was certainly in the book. If he wanted to repay me for a wartime ambush that was nobody's fault, he knew where to find me. Why not just take the bull by the proverbial horns and have done with it—instead of picking off people who knew me and had some stake in my existence?

I desperately wanted a drink, but all I had was a half bottle of Wild Turkey, and I wasn't desperate enough for that. I got in the car and found a halfway decent place that served drinks I could recognize. I ordered a gimlet, very cold, and took my seat at the bar. The door was open to the street, to the thunder and the rain, to an unexpected cooling breeze that helped clear my head. I remembered being in a bar the night Allan Layton had approached me, and how that had turned out. Was I the proverbial Jonah, the jinx? Did people get hurt because they were close to me?

I was working on my third gimlet when a body interposed itself between me and the bar: Donald Whitlaw. He was significantly more composed than he'd been during our exchange at Carmel, almost civilized. "Why Tony Leonard?" He signaled the bartender and ordered a double whiskey with a beer chaser. "Surely you can come up with better than that. Perhaps a character from one of your books?"

That got my attention. Nobody knew crime novelist A. J. Dunbar was really Tony Leonard. Ed had found out by dint of his investigative skills, but he and Deborah were the only ones who knew besides my publisher. It was kept under very tight wraps. "How did you know about that?"

"But that's not your name either, is it?" He turned on the barstool and gave me a weak smile. "What were you calling yourself during the war...?" He tapped his lower lip with his finger, like a man reaching to retrieve some information he can only barely remember. "Edgar something, wasn't it?"

The bartender laid a glass and a bottle on the bar in front of Whitlaw.

"I don't remember." I downed the rest of my drink and stood up. "Excuse me."

"How is your sister-in-law?" he asked, apropos of nothing. He'd turned around to watch me leave. "Shame about that family. With their money, you'd think—"

"Deborah is none of your business."

"She confessed to murdering her sister, though, didn't she?" He grinned. "Did they tell you how Janet died? Oh, my mistake. You already know."

"I didn't kill my wife."

"Of course not. You simply found her body." He turned back to his drink. "Unless you did it when you were drunk and now you can't remember."

"I'd remember." A cold thrill ran through me. "I'd remember a thing like that."

"Don't go." His tone was cordial, almost friendly, if you didn't look at his face. His face was a mask of hatred, features twisted almost beyond recognition. In this light, he looked nearly as scarred as me. "Stay a little while and I'll tell you how Janet died." He winked, a grotesque parody of good cheer.

My pulse beat in my temples, the hollow of my throat. I wanted another drink. I wanted all the drinks they had. "You're lying. You don't know anything about that." The room's dark interior seemed to press on me, the walls closing in. "You don't know anything about anything."

"Don't you care?" He signaled the bartender for two more drinks, and I moved to sit on the stool beside him again. "I'd think there was at least some small measure of sympathy between you. I mean, surely she was more than just a good lay." He laughed at what must have been my stricken expression. "She was a good lay, wasn't she? She opened her legs and you were halfway to paradise." The bartender put two drinks down on the bar, both whiskey sours. Whitlaw slid one toward me. "Of course, all this was after the fact. You never knew. Now, I was in favor of telling you, but Janet wouldn't hear of it."

"She had other lovers," I said. "I knew that. She made no secret of it." From the very beginning, I was given to understand this was an open marriage, that Janet would have gentlemen friends—just as I would. *An open-door policy, Tony. That's what we'll have.* "Janet was hardly a blushing virgin."

"She waited for me, you know, after the war." Whitlaw lifted his drink and put it down, making wet circles on the dark wood of the bar. "She promised she would, and she did."

"Why are you telling me this?" I asked. "It's neither here nor there now. The woman's dead."

"Yes." He gazed at himself in the mirror behind the bar. "I could have done what you did—changed my face, changed my name, vanished for a while."

After the war, I'd spent some time in London, a city in which I always felt comfortable. I wasn't born there, but in the years since childhood's end, I'd made it my residence as often as I could. What I liked best about London was its size. One could easily disappear for days, weeks, or months on end, with no one the wiser. One could drown in the Thames or drink oneself into oblivion, if that's what one wished to do. "The face I could do nothing about. It wasn't my choice." My hand strayed to the scars, feeling them with my fingertips, remembering the shape and their contradictory smoothness. "So why Janet? Or was that to get back at me?"

"Sleeping with her?" he asked. "Or killing her?"

A silence seemed to fall over everything around us, a silence with form and texture, an encompassing shape. The bartender was washing glasses at the small bar sink, and three men at a corner table were smoking cigarettes and drinking beer from the bottle. At first I thought I'd misheard him, and then I didn't know where to look, so I gazed into the mirror behind the bar, seeing myself. I looked like someone who'd just then seen the imminent end of the world.

"You killed Janet?" My lips were numb; I could barely form coherent words.

"I don't actually remember." He nodded and lit a cigarette. "I'd have done a better job of it, though." He shrugged. "She probably didn't feel a thing."

My skin prickled like ants were crawling over it. "You—"

"I had nothing against her." He carried on talking. "But I'd heard you were in Los Angeles, and I'd been waiting a long time...." He turned to look at me. There was nothing in his eyes but emptiness. "...waiting a long time to make you understand."

"Understand what?"

"I always said I'd pay you back." He spread his hands, the kind of gesture that said he didn't really care. "And he paid me very well. It's hard finding work nowadays. People are starting to look at us funny. Guy comes back from serving overseas, and they ask a lot of questions, like

Where were you? and *Why aren't you working?* No good trying to explain that you had things to take care of back in England, people to see."

"Did they pay you?" I asked. "Who was it?"

"Don't you know?" He blinked in what seemed like genuine astonishment, an astonishment that gave way to laughter. "If old man Stirling wanted someone taken care of, don't you think he could find a way to make that happen?"

Chapter Fifteen

I WAS sitting in front of the manuscript of *A Sad Farewell* a couple of days later when the doorbell rang. This was so unusual an event—especially for that time of evening—that for a moment I wondered if I'd hallucinated it. When it rang again—much more forcefully this time—I got up and went to the door.

Hank McAvity was standing on my doorstep, both fists crammed in the pockets of his overcoat, his expression at once tragic and irritated. He didn't wait to be invited in, but pushed into the house like I wasn't even there. He stalked back and forth for a while, glancing in my direction but not saying anything. "Leonard, I am only going to ask you this once." He stopped in front of me, fists clenched. "Once." He picked up the first couple pages of *A Sad Farewell*, glanced at them, and dropped them back on the pile.

I slid toward the sofa and sat. "Right."

"Day before yesterday, around four in the afternoon, you had drinks with a Donald Whitlaw at the Black Door tavern over on Grenville Street?"

"Yes."

"Where Whitlaw insinuated that he killed Janet, your ex-wife, at the behest of her father, Linton Stirling?"

"He said something like that, yes." I was sweating. "He didn't come right out and confess to anything—"

McAvity pulled a crumpled newspaper out of his overcoat and held it up so it unfolded in front of me. "Read it."

MILLIONAIRE LINTON STIRLING DEAD.

"Fell off his yacht," McAvity said, "in Long Island Sound." He refolded the newspaper and stuck it under his arm. "Queer time of year to be out on a yacht, especially in New York. I hear that water's freezing in the winter."

"I wouldn't know." I finally found my voice. "It's been a while since I've been on a yacht, actually. Perhaps they've changed the way they do things."

"Goddammit, Leonard, this isn't funny!" He fumbled for a cigarette, found one in the crumpled packet in his shirt pocket, drew it out, and lit it. "They're already saying it's suicide—that old Stirling went to New York because he killed his own daughter."

"Maybe Stirling didn't kill her," I said. I sounded tired, even to myself. "Not in the way you think."

"We had Whitlaw in half an hour ago for a nice, cozy chat." He laughed humorlessly. "You can't even talk to the guy. He doesn't make any sense. Meanwhile, somebody drove an ice pick into your wife's skull—"

"But I thought…." The image of her slowly toppling body, the blood on the bed, on the floor, the wooden handle sticking out the back of her neck….

"I'm a cop," McAvity said dryly, "I find out things." He took a long drag off his cigarette. "Most likely her old man hired somebody to do the job. Whoever did it, he was a professional."

"But her face," I said. "Her face was beaten to a pulp. I thought that's what killed her."

McAvity shook his head. "Nope. Ice pick."

I told him to sit, and I went and made a pot of coffee, extra strong, the way Ed taught me. I brought it through to the living room on a tray—very civilized—with cream and sugar. I poured for both of us, and when he was seated across from me, I told him about Donald Whitlaw, our wartime service together, how I'd found him—quite by accident—at the Ludlow Valley ranch, and all the rest of it. To his credit, he didn't interrupt; he listened as if I were giving him a confession. That disturbed me more than the rest of it, to be honest. I figured he'd take me in, since I'd known about Whitlaw—at least initially—and hadn't told him.

"I'm hurt," McAvity said, but not very convincingly. "I thought you and I had some kind of rapport. I thought you knew you could come to me with anything. You should have come to headquarters as soon as you left that bar—with Whitlaw in tow, if possible." He swallowed his coffee in three large gulps.

I reached across to refill his cup. "How did you know I was drinking with Whitlaw?"

"You've had a tail on you since the start of this thing. Malory asked for it. He figured you were good at getting yourself into trouble, not so good at getting out of it, and he couldn't watch you every goddamn day." He lit another cigarette. "Thing is, Leonard, we knew you were involved in this. We just didn't know how. We had to wait till our guy turned up pay dirt." McAvity drained his cup and laid it, rattling, back in the saucer. He seemed to have finished his little speech.

"So what now?" I asked. "Do you take me in, or can I have some leeway to finish my book?"

"The only thing you're guilty of is withholding information." He sounded crestfallen. "I could book you on that, but why bother? This way I'm saving the taxpayers' money." He dropped his cigarette butt into the coffee cup and stood up. "Whitlaw is a pain in the ass. The state he's in, he probably can't remember what he had for breakfast." He coughed ostentatiously.

"I had nothing to do with that," I said. "I only had coffee with him." I was lying.

"Right," McAvity said. "And you only had coffee with me." He stood up. "Did you hear about that Lydia Race dame? Bar singer. Nice legs, I've heard."

I couldn't think what this had to do with anything. "Hear what?"

"She's dead. They found her in La Tuna canyon. Whoever did it cut her throat so deep they nearly severed her head."

My reaction didn't seem to matter. He was gone before I could say anything at all.

I cleared away the coffee things and sat in front of the typewriter again, but I couldn't concentrate. I kept thinking about Whitlaw and Corcoran and me in that foxhole, shivering and freezing, smoking cigarettes to stay awake, and drinking horrible ersatz coffee while we waited for the Germans to blow us to kingdom come. Whitlaw killed Janet because old man Stirling wanted it that way. Maybe her latest round of sexual excess was making him look bad, or maybe he was tired of pretending his eldest daughter wasn't a tramp. It hardly mattered now. He'd killed his daughter by hiring someone to shove an ice pick in her skull....

...which didn't explain the state of her face when I'd found her.

Deborah wasn't in the pool house when I got there, but I hardly cared whether I had her permission or not. I started in the bedroom, where I'd found Janet's body. They'd done a good job of cleaning the place up since then, but there was one thing they couldn't possibly have noticed. I opened the clothes closet: there were Deborah's shoes, all lined up neatly side-by-side, like evil sisters waiting to go to the ball. There were high-heeled pumps and low-heeled pumps, shoes with open toes and shoes with various glittery decorations. There were cowboy boots and a pair of rubber Wellingtons and Roman sandals with strings that laced up the calf.

There was one high-heeled shoe—black, with an ankle strap. It was intended for the right foot. I sat down on the bed with it in my hand. I felt weak and almost sick. I felt like I needed a drink.

Whoever did this to Janet must have hated her guts. Ed Malory had said that.

"So you found it." She was standing in the doorway, wearing one of those after-dark caftan things. It was dark blue and had tiny silver-colored bells sewed onto the hem. The bells tinkled gently when she moved. "I noticed you worrying over it the last time you were here." Deborah came and sat beside me. She took the shoe out of my hand. "Designed by Adam Culpepper," she said. "Five hundred dollars a pair."

"Expensive," I observed. "Nice."

"They were Janet's," she said quietly. "Nothing but the best for Janet. Everybody loved Janet."

"Except your father and you."

"Bravo, Tony." She smiled. "You figured it out." She leaned in and coyly put her head on my shoulder, as if we were teenagers lost in the throes of first love. "I always said you were too good for Janet. Did you know I was in love with you?"

I didn't know what to say to this, so I simply grunted.

"You were so handsome, even with these scars." She caressed my face. "A war hero. I thought if I could catch the attention of a man like you, I'd really be worth something."

"Deborah, I'm not sure this is appropriate."

"You know, I never planned it, not really. I know Daddy had hired that man. I thought that would be the end of it. So I came down here to see. I very much wanted to see. You can understand that, can't you?"

"There was a shoe on the floor when I found her." I pushed her off my shoulder and stood. Being close to her was making me sick. "I thought that was mud on the heel."

"Oh no, not mud." She tilted her head to the side. "You can't imagine how hard a human skull is. The skin, the muscles underneath, the bones, and all of it. It's only really satisfying when you get right down to the bone. Once I started, I couldn't stop." She blinked like a woman coming out of a trance. "Have I shocked you?"

"Where did you learn your cruelty?" I asked. "Is it inborn, or did dear Doctor Biertz offer to teach you?"

"When Janet and I were still quite little, Daddy thought we should have swimming lessons. He didn't want just anyone, though, so he decided to teach us himself." She nodded at the open door and the swimming pool just beyond. "In the pool up at the main house. We got brand-new swimsuits and everything. Daddy thought the best way to overcome our fear of water was to simply toss us in—at the deep end, of course. Janet caught on right away, but I wasn't quite as coordinated."

Chilled through and through, I simply nodded.

"I got into a bit of trouble and started coughing. Janet came to try and help me, but Daddy warned her back. 'She's got to do it on her own,' he said. He kept saying it. 'She's got to do it on her own.' He couldn't seem to grasp that I was just a little girl, and I couldn't—"

"That was a vile thing to do to a child."

She looked up at me. She seemed surprised I was still there. "It is, isn't it? I always thought so. I always thought it was an awful thing to do. There were lots and lots of lessons like that, lessons I always failed and Janet always—" She was quiet for a long time, her eyes fixed on something only she could see. "He was like that. Janet was the golden girl. She always got first place in everything she did, and Daddy admired that, you see. It meant she was like him." She drew a breath. "Then she discovered boys, and... well, you know the rest."

"Is that why you beat her head in with a shoe?" I dropped it on the bed beside her. "Because you were jealous of her?"

"Jealous of her?" She stood. We were just about toe-to-toe. "It wasn't mere *jealousy*, Tony! She took everything that was mine—everything I worked for and wanted, she came and took it from me. Johan was... the final straw. She was working on him when she came to visit us. They'd taken to having drinks every evening in the library, just the two of them, alone together." She turned away and went to stand in the door, gazing out, her expression set and inscrutable. "She was pregnant when she died, you know. She told me." Deborah moved so her back was against one of the lintels and she was looking into the room where I was. "Allan Layton's baby. He knew. He even offered her money to take care of it, but she wouldn't. Janet wouldn't hear of it." She drew a shallow breath that sounded like a gasp. "I didn't kill her. Daddy always hires someone to do the really dirty work. But I wish I had."

"And your confession?"

She was smiling vacantly now, like someone in the throes of an opium hallucination. "I wanted them to believe I'd done it, that I was that sort of person... tough and hard, not afraid."

"Like your father."

She nodded. "It would make him pay attention to me. He could hardly fail to notice something like that."

I wondered, then, if I should tell her or if she'd already heard. "Your father's dead."

"I know. One of the family lawyers wired me." She came and put her hands on my shoulders, as if we were friends and intimates. "What do you think they'll do with me, Tony? Will you come and see me in prison?"

"You aren't going to prison!" I thrust her hands from me and moved away. "You'll probably get a warning and a fine, if that. At most it's interference with a corpse. It isn't murder, Deborah."

"No," she said quietly. "It isn't murder. She really was dead when I...." She looked up, holding my gaze like we were challengers in some obscure form of duel. "What will happen now? To the estate? I mean, the house and grounds...."

"I don't know."

"But you'll be all right," she said. "You've got Janet's money."

"I don't want Janet's money." Just thinking about it made me weary. "And as far as I know—unless your old man made other provisions, which wouldn't surprise me in the least—the entirety of his fortune should go to you." I laughed aloud at the irony of it. "You're a very wealthy woman, Deborah." I turned away to pick up the shoe. "You can go anywhere you like, live the sort of life most people envy." I laid the shoe next to the cowboy boots. "I'd drop a word in McAvity's ear, though, about Janet's face. I think—" But I was talking to myself. Deborah had already gone.

I found a bottle of Macallan in the little fridge and sat by the pool to drink it. It was a clear winter night, with a few stars hanging near the horizon, unobscured by smog or the city lights. I thought about Ed, wondering how he was doing in the hospital. Maybe I'd go see him later, with some chocolates or a big bunch of flowers....

And I'd finish my novel, too, supposing it killed me. Maybe I still had enough juice left in me to write a real crackerjack ending, with betrayals and gunfights and tearful good-byes. I'd make the main character much more sympathetic, write him as a war hero with an indelible wound, a misanthrope with a heart of gold. I'd give him an honest best friend, an upright man who always did the right thing and whose advice was dispensed in glasses of fine alcohol. I'd layer on the clichés and leave 'em weeping in the aisles. It would be the apogee of my career.

Or something.

A movement in the bushes to my right caught my attention. I smelled cigarette smoke and saw the tiny pinpoint of red light as it moved toward me. Pepe came to sit beside me, dangling his bare feet in the swimming pool. "You tell her about her old man, huh?"

"Yep." I passed him the bottle of scotch. "She already knew."

"She's cold, that one." He took a long swallow from the bottle and passed it back to me. "Like ice. I bet her *concha* freeze your dick off."

"I wouldn't know."

"That's right." He grinned. "You don't like the concha. You like it the other way."

"If you say so." I had left my watch at home, so I asked, "What time is it?"

"Quarter past seven. You got somewhere to be?"

Visiting hours at the hospital ended at eight o'clock. "Yes, as it happens, I do." I stood and handed him the bottle of Macallan. "Here—a token of my esteem."

"What's going to happen to all this?" He gestured at the house and grounds. "Miss Deborah?"

"I don't know, Pepe." I turned to go. "You'll have to ask her."

THE HEAD nurse treated me to a warning look when I arrived on the ward, but made no move to kick me out. Ed was sitting up reading the newspaper, a cup of coffee on the table beside him. He glanced up, saw it was me, and smiled. "Tony." He reached out a hand to me, and I took it and squeezed his fingers.

"You look fantastic," I said. He looked better than that. The period of rest had done wonders for him. "Good enough to eat." This last was murmured quietly, for his ears alone.

"Is that a promise?" The look he gave me was hot enough to set my shorts on fire.

"You're an evil bastard." I squeezed his hand and let it go before another of the ward occupants saw me. "I may have plans for you when you finally check out of here."

He sighed. "I hope that's sooner rather than later. I've had my fill of this place."

I pulled a chair up next to his bed and sat. I wanted some way to tell him about Janet's murder, but once again words failed me. I decided to dive right in. "Linton Stirling's dead," I said. "He hired some vigilante to kill Janet—turns out he's the same one who killed those two bums down on Fromsett Street."

"So he's a bum who knew you." Ed shifted in the bed, and I saw a flicker of pain cross his face. "Which makes it revenge... am I right?" He reached to position a pillow, but it slipped onto the floor. I picked it up and wedged it behind his back. "I've been trying to train them," he said, indicating the pillow, "but they aren't the brightest creatures."

I told him what I knew about the Fromsett Street murders and the clinic at Ludlow Valley. "He was in my old squad during the war. We were caught in an ambush. He... blames me. He's been waiting all this time for his revenge."

Ed's hand drifted toward my face, not quite touching me. "And that's where these"—he indicated my scars—"came from."

Something inside me cringed a little, the way it always did whenever anybody said anything about my face. "Yes." I pretended to gaze out the window. "I was.... The ambush, remember, we were captured. I spent a year as a guest of the Gestapo. I told you." I didn't tell him the scars on my face were nothing compared to the ones he couldn't see. "Ancient history."

"Oh, Tony... I'm sorry."

"Not so bad. I've heard of chaps who went through worse." I didn't care for this line of conversation. Talking about the war always made me maudlin. "Look, I just had an idea. When you get released, why don't you come and stay with me for a while? I daresay there's things you can't quite do for yourself, and that way I'd be able to help you." I grinned. "Besides, I'd enjoy the company." I expected him to reject the idea outright, but he seemed to be considering it.

"I might do that," he said. "If those dames at the nursing station ever let me out of here. It's like a bad movie."

A movie.... Something occurred to me. "He never did tell me," I said. At Ed's inquisitive look, I continued. "Allan Layton. He met me in that dive bar and said he had something to tell me, something important... but he never did." Instead, he'd ended up in an alley with an ice pick in his skull.

"Tony, stay out of it." He raised a bandaged hand to his face. "I thought Vic's guys were going to kill me. I'm reasonably sure they'd do the same to you. Let the cops handle it."

"Do you care?" I asked, but my tone was teasing and he understood.

"No." He laughed. "Stay in close contact with McAvity. He knows things. If something turns up on your doorstep and you aren't sure what to do, call Hank." He yawned, a hand over his mouth. "Hank will be able to shed some light on it. Trust me."

I GOT back home and put my car away, made a pot of coffee and sat at the typewriter again, but I couldn't stop thinking about Allan Layton. I couldn't figure out why someone had targeted him for an ice pick job. I'd seen that sort of thing before, but it was almost always gang related, and as far as I knew, Layton had no such affiliation. I'd done some research on his background, scouring the movie magazines and the local library. It was all of a piece: born into extreme poverty in Arkansas, left home for the bright lights of Hollywood. He'd hoped to make it big, but instead found himself wandering around the back lots, vying for attention with all the other young and handsome hopefuls. Despite what was printed in the magazines, he wasn't an overnight success, starring in a number of B-pictures and low-budget flops. It wasn't until *This Gun Speaks Death* that his career finally gathered enough steam to get him off the back lots and into movie theaters. His character—a sympathetic, baby-faced assassin—got him noticed by the studios. Allan Layton was on his way.

Before all the hubbub and hullaballoo, however, there was another Allan Layton story, a lesser-known and heavily suppressed rumor about secret assignations on deserted sound stages and clandestine meetings with other handsome young men that extended well into the night. There were films the magazines never wrote about, featuring a younger Allan Layton—smut films, poorly funded and badly lit, with minimal scripting and a notable absence of costume. These weren't, of course, commercially available, and the few that survived remained in the hands of wealthy collectors—or so I'd heard. I'd made discreet inquiries, but not even the police—according to McAvity—had copies or knew where they could be had.

Maybe the films were the key to Layton's murder. Lydia Race was being blackmailed over them, and both she and Layton were veterans of Vic Ramirez's smut mill. It could be that Ramirez wanted Layton to grind out a few more and Layton refused to play ball. Worse, Layton might have rolled over on Ramirez—the kind of insult a hoodlum like Ramirez couldn't overlook.

When the telephone rang, I assumed it was McAvity. "Mr. Tony Leonard, please." The voice was female, very polite, and sonorous with the sound of old, old money.

"This is Tony Leonard."

"My name is Sylvia Gish." There was a pause and the flick of a cigarette lighter. "I may have some information that you can use. About Allan Layton."

"Information?" It wasn't the first time. If I had a dollar for every time someone has come up to me at a cocktail party or semiriotous gathering with "Have I got a story for you" hanging off their lips, I'd never need to write again. "Concerning what?"

"I don't care to say over the phone." She inhaled sharply, then blew smoke. "Shall we meet? I think you'll be very interested in this."

It was late—later than I liked to go out—but my intense curiosity was piqued. "All right. Where?"

She named a bar at the corner of Fifth and Sussex. "Do you know it?"

"Yes, I know it. How will I recognize you?"

The sound of smoke being exhaled. "You won't. I'll recognize you." Then I was listening to a lot of dial tone.

I WAS on my second gimlet when a woman slid onto the barstool next to mine. Her dark hair was caught up at the sides and held in place by a pillbox hat with a veil. She wore a black or navy blue suit—it was hard to tell in the dimness—and pale gray gloves. I watched as she fitted a cigarette into a long ebony holder. "You're looking well, Tony. That is what you're calling yourself these days?"

She was beautiful, her skin flawless and well-maintained, and artfully painted. "I'm sorry," I said, "I don't remember you."

She laughed, tilting her head back and exposing the graceful line of her throat. "You wouldn't. It was a long time ago, before the war. You were married to that English girl back then. What was her name? Alison?"

"Yes, Alison." It had been a long time since I'd heard that name.

"Whatever happened to her?" she asked. "To the two of you, I mean."

"She was at the cinema when the Luftwaffe paid a visit." It wasn't something I liked to talk about. "When the smoke cleared, there was nothing left but a pile of rubble. She was somewhere in the pile." I shook my head. "They never found her body."

We were both quiet for a moment.

"How did you find me?" I asked.

"When you... 'died' in Mexico—yes, I heard about it—they printed your death notice in the newspapers, and a picture. I suppose being married to Linton Stirling's daughter will do that to a man, make him vulgarly famous, I mean. And you are in the phone book."

"I haven't seen the obituaries lately," I said.

"I'm Sylvia Gish, like I said on the phone. We used to go around together, Alison and I." She drew on her cigarette. "We went to the same school. Of course, she was a scholarship student...." She waved a hand in the air. "But that's old news, and you came here to find out about Allan Layton." She signaled the bartender. "Will you have another? You're drinking gimlets, aren't you?"

"Yes, and thank you, but let me get this." I laid some money on the bar. The bartender was making a larger-than-regular fuss with the cocktail shaker. I waited while he decanted a cold stream of gin and Rose's into two glasses. Despite the bar's shoddy interior, the drinks were delicious and ice-cold, and I felt myself cheering up a little.

"I heard about what happened to you." She tasted her drink, then set it down. "I'm so sorry. I ran into Alison's sister Babs at some party or other—this was probably back in '45—and she said you'd gone missing in action." Her gaze roved over my face. "Then we heard you'd been...."

"Tortured," I supplied. "You can say it. I hardly even burst into tears anymore."

She took another sip of her drink, putting temporary silence between us. "You want to know about Allan Layton."

"I would like to, yes," I said. "But I already know the official biography."

"So you'd like the dirt." She raised a perfectly groomed eyebrow. "Well, here goes. Allan and I were briefly married a while ago. Back then, I was writing the gossip column for the Los Angeles *Bastion*. You might remember we were in direct competition with Hedda Hopper and Sheilah Graham, that bunch. Louella Parsons once threatened to scratch my eyes out during a party at Zanuck's house because she thought I'd poached one of her sources. That's where I met Allan. He was just starting out in those days, fresh from the country. He still had a trace of that Arkansas accent." She paused to take another sip of her drink, another drag on her cigarette. "He was standing by the piano all by himself, wearing his clothes like they hurt. I don't think he'd ever been in a tux before. He was... so beautiful." She sounded wistful. "The shine hadn't worn off him... hadn't been rubbed off. Everybody else was drinking cocktails, but he had a glass of ginger ale. He kept turning it around and around in his hands, gazing down into it." She shook her head. "I felt sorry for him."

"I can understand that. It must have been like swimming in a shark tank."

"I went over and struck up a conversation. We talked till three in the morning. He'd come from absolutely nothing. His family was so dirt poor he didn't even have shoes as a kid." She paused. "Did you know he had green eyes? Yes, it's true. With blonds you always expect blue, but his were green."

"I've met him a couple of times," I said. "He always struck me as a very nice man." And so beautiful he made nuns and hardened dowagers dampen their drawers.

"Oh, he was. But insecure. I suppose it's inevitable, coming from nothing like he did. Anyway, he was trying to get into the movies. It's why people come here, isn't it?"

"I guess so." I pushed my empty glass toward the bartender and nodded for another. "Or they like the climate."

"No, it wasn't the climate with him. Allan had big plans for himself. He told me all about them." She drained her glass and set it down. "He made it happen too."

"So you said he was very young when you first met him," I prompted. Her talk was interesting, but I didn't have time for discursive meandering.

"He was nineteen the first time. That was at Zanuck's party. We saw each other quite frequently, and a few years after that, we ran away to

Reno together to get married." She laughed. "We were like two naughty kids. It only lasted six months, but what the hell." She glanced at me. "He hadn't yet made it, so he was doing bit parts and supplementing his income whatever way he could. The Hollywood *grande dames* were already hiring him, sometimes for entire weekends at the beach cottage or wherever." She laughed. "I'm not surprised. He was—" She glanced around quickly. "*Amazing* in the sack. I mean, Jesus. He knew where everything was. They were mostly studio executives' wives, perennially bored, you know the sort. Allan gave them a little tumble."

It occurred to me what she was getting at. "He was…?"

"A prostitute, yes. Well, more or less. A high-priced rent boy, if you like. A gigolo." She grinned at what must have been my expression of disbelief. "Oh, don't be so parochial, Tony! It's been done, you know, and the poor boy had to make a living. Speaking of that…." She reached down between our two chairs and brought up a brown paper grocery sack. "I thought these might be useful to you."

Nestled inside were three reels of what I recognized as celluloid film. I took one out and tilted its label toward the available light: *Once, Twice, Three Times a Night*. "Oh."

"Too strong for your delicate constitution?" she asked, smirking.

"No, it's just…." It felt disrespectful, that's what I wanted to say. The man was dead.

"It was no big secret, Tony. Allan made smut films—just like every other Hollywood hopeful. I'm sure you already knew that." I wondered aloud how he got into making them for a sleaze like Vic Ramirez. "Vic? He carried a torch for Allan. First time he saw him. Vic's got an in with just about every movie producer and director in town. He promised Allan he'd get him into the movies. He'd be a big star."

It was the same old story. I'd heard it a dozen times before. "Allan believed him."

"Why wouldn't he? Vic was the go-to guy in those days. If you wanted it, chances were Vic had it or could get it for you." She lifted her glass and took a sip. "And he did get Allan into the movies. The man wasn't lying." She drew a slow, meditative breath and laid her glass down. "Vic and Allan were very good friends. That's the part most people don't know. Everyone assumes Vic had Allan under his thumb, but that's not true. Vic knew what Allan wanted and could get it for him."

"What did Allan want?"

"Besides the movies?" She shrugged. "Love. Companionship. The pleasures of the flesh. He once told me—this was after we'd both had a few—that he wanted to go away somewhere with a beautiful young man. To some holiday resort, perhaps in the South of France, and spend a week there, doing nothing but fucking. He couldn't, of course. Can you imagine the scandal?" She was quiet for a moment, gazing into the middle distance. "We were only married for six months, but I cared for him a great deal. I did what I could for him."

I wondered what she meant by this last. Did she mean that she fronted for him, helping to convince the industry and the popular press that he was absolutely on the straight and narrow? Or did she act as his procuress, finding suitable young men and screening them?

"He was such a very, very nice man, Tony." Her features trembled on the edge of some dark emotion, but she busied herself stubbing out her cigarette. "I hope the police find whoever killed him." She looked at me, her face twisted with anger. "I hope they burn the bastard."

"So do I." I took up the paper bag and rose to go. "Mrs. Gish, thank you."

"One more thing." She took out a compact and lipstick. "Allan has family—still living, I mean. Mostly back in Arkansas, but there are one or two relatives who live in California." She reapplied color to her lips in a series of short jabs. "He hadn't spoken to them in years. It could be they'd resent a stranger poking around in family business." She snapped the compact closed and gave me a raised-eyebrow look. "I'd be careful if I were you."

Chapter Sixteen

IT TOOK a considerable amount of digging and an uncomfortable afternoon spent under the gaze of a surly-looking clerk, but I found what I was looking for in the state records. Just outside Carmel, there were 14,000 acres of prime ranch land, perfect for raising livestock or—if you were of the moneyed upper class—a bigger-than-average hobby farm. The clerk reluctantly informed me that there were photographs of the property, but I preferred to see the place myself. I've always been the hands-on sort.

I drove up there one day around two, following the same route I had when I'd visited Ludlow Valley. I encountered little traffic on the way up and arrived sooner than I'd expected at the gates. I didn't see any intercom system, so I leaned on the horn until someone showed up to let me in.

He was tall and lean, heavily tanned, and stringy-looking, like a piece of meat left drying in the sun. He came and leaned on the car, peering in the open window at me like I'd landed from the moon. "Yes?"

"I was wondering if I might come in and have a look round," I said, heavy on the English accent.

He shook his head, then leaned lazily to one side and spat into the dust. "No, sir. This here is a private residence."

"Oh, that is unfortunate." I tried to look as crestfallen as possible. "You see, my name is Henry Lord. I'm a producer, and we're currently scouting locations. From what I've seen of this place, it looks absolutely ideal." That particular trick was so old it had a long white beard. I was briefly ashamed of myself.

He reached in and laid a hand on my arm. "A movie?" Obviously the gentleman didn't get out much.

"Yes." I pretended to rummage through a valise I'd laid on the seat beside me. "Let me see, I have it right here—"

"No need of that. I'll have George let you in." He waved to someone on the other side of the gates, which swung open to admit me. "Go on up to the main house. I'll meet you there."

A NARROW asphalt drive wound through a dense forest of maples and oaks and other trees I didn't particularly recognize. The main house was at the top, set against a backdrop of grassy enclosures and wide, rolling lawns. In construction it was vaguely semicircular, crouched around a swimming pool; the architecture was wholly modern, with a nod to traditional California design. It was a nice house, but nothing to wet your pants over.

The man I'd spoken to at the gate was waiting in the kitchen when I arrived. He introduced himself as Harold Layton, and we shook hands.

"No relative of the movie star, are you?" I asked. "Allan Layton?"

He'd been pouring coffee. His head jerked up, eyes blazing. He stared at me, his gaze tracking over my face, remembering me in case he needed to find me later. "Allan was my brother."

My stomach clenched. "I'm so sorry," I said. There really wasn't anything else to say. "He was a wonderful actor."

"This is his house." Harold passed me a cup of coffee with a hand that trembled. "Cream and sugar?"

"Black's fine."

We went through to a spacious living room decorated in the sunburned shades of the West, with enormous windows that looked out on a green expanse of pastureland and rolling hillsides. The furniture was grouped around a huge stone fireplace surmounted with a fine art print of Sitting Bull. *Pretty damn swanky*, I thought. Sitting Bull looked like he agreed with me. The room had none of the cluttery knickknacks and junk you usually see, but tasteful items of sculpture and folk art, which appeared to have been carefully chosen for both effect and their ability to fit into the color scheme. Several large, framed canvases displayed what I assumed was all the rage in the modern art world: circles and boxes, triangles and fields of blue or green. One was particularly weird, just two curves and a line. I'd seen it somewhere before. I was certain of it.

I SAT on a sofa that sank by a good three inches before it finally stopped. The cushions were large, luxurious, and could have easily smothered a lesser man. "So you live here, Mr. Layton?"

"I didn't used to. Took it over after Allan died." He drank some coffee and laid the cup noisily back into the saucer. "He loved this place. Used to hightail it out here whenever he had some time between pictures." He narrowed his eyes at me. "You knew Allan?"

"Yes," I lied. "Oh yes, knew him quite well. He was very well liked."

"Yeah." Layton's brother seemed to be a man of few words. "Come and see the rest." He led me down a spacious, light-filled hallway into a formal dining area. "Used to have dinner parties here. Sometimes for the whole weekend. People liked to come up from the city and stay over. Allan didn't mind." He pointed out several works of art on the walls. "Mr. Ramirez now, he liked pictures."

"Did you say Ramirez?" The artwork was, like the picture of Sitting Bull, the product of highly regarded artists who made highly expensive pictures. "Vic Ramirez?"

"Oh, you know Mr. Ramirez." His expression opened up a little. "Him and Allan were great friends. They went back a long ways. Vic gave Allan his start in the business—" He was interrupted by the shrilling of a telephone from elsewhere in the house. "I gotta get that. You go on, have a look around."

So Sylvia Gish was right: Allan and Vic were friends and quite possibly business partners. She'd had no reason to lie to me, but it was satisfying to have confirmation. If Layton and Ramirez had been partners, that might have given Ramirez motive to have Layton bumped off. From what I'd heard, Vic Ramirez harbored no special love for anyone or anything, and if Layton was beginning to balk at the seamy side of things, Vic would absolutely have him taken care of.

I HAD intended to drop in on Ed at the hospital, but what I'd learned from Sylvia Gish and Allan Layton's brother was burning a hole in me. So Layton wasn't Ramirez's victim—he was his friend and business partner. His brother said Layton and Ramirez went back a long way. It could be that Layton met him when he and Sylvia went to Reno for their quickie marriage. (I'd forgotten to ask her if she'd gone back there for a quickie divorce.)

McAvity was in his office, peering into a file folder. He looked up at me, grunted, and went back to the folder. "You're here again, Leonard."

"Vic Ramirez and Allan Layton were business partners," I said.

McAvity didn't even twitch. "Uh-huh."

"You knew?" I fumbled for a chair and sat.

"We suspected it might be the case. They seemed awful chummy when I saw them last March at a fundraiser." McAvity laid the folder aside. "That what you came to tell me?"

I conceded it was. "But if Layton and Ramirez were partners, and Layton didn't want to play anymore, maybe Ramirez had his boys do an ice pick job."

McAvity raised an eyebrow. "You trying to do my job for me, Leonard?"

"He met me at a bar. He said he had something to tell me, something to do with evidence in Janet's murder."

"Does it matter anymore? Old man Stirling had her knocked off and hired some shell-shocked goon to do it." He stuck a cigarette in his mouth and lit it. "And you already know the business with the high-heeled shoe. She even admitted it, when we questioned her." He shrugged, exhaling smoke. "The job's done. The case is filed. If any new leads surface—I'm not saying they will—then we'll deal with it."

"What if Janet had something to do with Vic Ramirez and the whole smut film racket?" I asked. When McAvity was finished laughing, I said, "She liked variety. It's not beyond possibility—"

"Leonard!" His voice snapped like sails in a high wind. "I got work to do. People like to see their taxes well spent, not pissed away on a murder investigation the DA's done with. Get out of here. Go home."

Layton had approached me particularly—in a bar. Somehow he'd known which bar. He knew I'd be drinking. How? We'd only met at Stirling's house, and he didn't know me from the King of Spades. How had he known to come looking for me in a bar? Where had Deborah met him? She fancied herself of the *bon ton*, but I doubted she had the kind of cachet to crash any of the really swanky Hollywood parties.

But Pepe had said Deborah and Layton were seeing each other, that Layton was her new "fancy man." Layton would hardly take up with a nobody—even a filthy-rich nobody—unless he had an angle. He was Hollywood royalty. He had an image to maintain. He wouldn't be interested in squiring a nobody around town. He and Deborah were friendly enough that she invited him to the house, so maybe they hadn't just met. Maybe they knew each other long before now and had just renewed their acquaintance. Maybe Deborah kept him around because, as Sylvia Gish had said, he was dynamite in bed.

I SPENT all day and into the evening trying to work on my novel, but felt too knotted up to get any writing done. It was about nine o'clock when I decided to go for a walk, maybe just wander around a bit. I needed to feel solid ground under my feet and breathe something besides cigarette smoke.

Layton, Deborah, Janet, Vic Ramirez. The names rang in my head, and I seemed to be tapping out their rhythm with the soles of my shoes. Layton.... Hollywood royalty, an icon, loved by everybody. Deborah.... Janet.... Vic Ramirez, hoodlum and gangster.

Maybe he had nothing to tell you. Maybe it was a setup.

The thought arrested me so powerfully that I stopped right where I was. Why would Layton want to talk to me?

He didn't. He was trying to find out how much you knew about Janet's murder. He was feeling you out.

There was a bench nearby, next to a bus stop. I sat and lit a cigarette. Layton had been awfully friendly to me almost as soon as we met. He'd ingratiated himself with Ed and me so smoothly that I hadn't even noticed. He was just a friendly guy, I told myself. Just a friendly guy who's decent enough to take a drink with you. What if Layton's baby-faced assassin character wasn't entirely fictional? He was able to make people trust him. Women, especially, would fall all over themselves for a taste of his golden beauty. Allan Layton was everybody's wet dream. Was he also a contract killer? The idea was ridiculous in the extreme, and he'd hardly jeopardize his career for the sake of one last hit. I tried to imagine Layton as a hit-man-for-hire. The idea was ridiculous, and then again it wasn't. It occupied that narrow line between reality and possibility, and really, wasn't anybody capable of murder if sufficiently pushed in that direction?

But Whitlaw had confessed. He was in police custody, awaiting trial. If Layton was mixed up in Janet's murder, it hardly mattered anymore.

I had a momentary flash of Ed, sitting up in his hospital bed, warning me: *Tony, stay out of it.* Did he know more than he was telling? Maybe he was right. Perhaps the time had come to let go of it. Janet was dead; her murderer was in custody; the case was over and done with. I needed to go home and get busy trying to finish my novel.

"Hello, Tony." The voice was warm, kindly, its vowels gently swollen with an accent both familiar and exotic. "I've been looking for you. I suppose I ought to have come to your home, but time is short and I have been very busy."

I raised my head. "Seeker."

"Yes. Did you think I had forgotten you?" He leaned down, like he intended to hug me, but instead he grabbed my arm with one hand and yanked me to my feet. His other hand held a silenced Luger. He wasn't shy about poking it into me. "So many people have warned you to stay away—the police, your lover—but you don't listen." A dark, late-model car was waiting at the curb, and he shoved me into the backseat. "Now you have to face the consequences. People always say that, but they seldom understand what it truly means." He got in beside me and shut the door. Two other men sat up front; I didn't recognize either of them. "Go," he said to the driver. "We'll take you for a little drive, Tony. Show you something of the countryside."

I expected they would head up into the Hollywood Hills, but they didn't. The driver turned the car toward downtown Los Angeles, crowded at this hour with traffic, the sidewalks clogged with pedestrians, people coming out of theaters and bars.

"If you're planning to kill me," I said, "shouldn't you do it somewhere else? There's way too many witnesses here."

"Shut up." One of the two up front said this, but I didn't know which one.

"Where are you taking me, anyway?" Might as well make conversation while I was on my way to hideous torture and eventual death.

"Shut up."

"You know, your conversation is very limited. I'd work on that if I were you."

Seeker's gun pressed into my ribs, hard enough to bruise. "Tony, you really should shut up. I cannot control these two." He nodded toward the front seat. "Given the right circumstances, they can be vicious."

Given the right circumstances, so can I, I wanted to say, but I didn't. The bon mots could wait till later, when all of us were in a better position to appreciate them.

We took the Boulevard heading south in the direction of Laguna Beach, and I was reminded of the impromptu picnic Ed and I had shared some months before, just after we'd met. I seriously doubted these men were taking me on a picnic. It was more likely they'd bring me to some isolated cove and drown me.

Eventually we came to a section of the beach known as Shaw's Cove, a sheltered inlet just off the highway. The driver pulled the car onto the shoulder and parked—illegally, probably—and we went down a short embankment to the sand. I thought about making a run for it for about ten seconds before I realized it was the worst idea I'd had in a long time. Running in sand is difficult at the best of times, and I was pretty sure my captors were armed. I wouldn't make it very far before I got a bullet in my back for my trouble. I thought of something Ed had said, the day he'd walked in on Seeker's visit, before Christmas: *I know who he is.* Curiously, he hadn't bothered to refute my saying that Seeker was FBI; nor did he agree that Seeker was part of law enforcement. He hadn't really said anything at all, actually—beyond telling me to stay away from Seeker.

We walked for some distance along the shore, sticking close to the surf for some reason I couldn't fathom. There were other people around—mostly snorkelers or casual bathers—but they ignored us. Eventually the sand gave way to a rocky promontory surmounted with a beach house equal in size and aspect to several others along the coast, but huddled closer to the cliff. As we got closer, I saw someone had cut a series of steps into the stone, a rather haphazard walkway ascending from the beach and moving in a meandering pattern upward. There were no handrails I could see, just the stairs, scaling the rock face. Anybody with the sheer bloody-mindedness to climb up there would be lucky to escape with his life.

I had the nasty, unshakeable feeling I was going to be compelled to climb up there. Any moment now, one of them would say—

"Start climbing, Leonard." When I didn't move, a gun barrel poked me in the back: Seeker. "Climb."

"If you think I'm going up there, you're completely mental," I said. From my vantage point, the stairs seemed to ascend infinitely, going on and on into darkness. "I won't be much good to you dead."

Seeker laughed. "What makes you think that? What we want, you have, and it doesn't really matter if you're alive or not. We can simply take it from you. But a friend of ours, he wants to see you. Says he met you once before and enjoyed your company." He shoved the gun in my side again. "I'll be right behind you. Get moving."

"I assume there's a front door," I said. "Why can't we go in that way?"

"The police are watching the house. They expect us to go that way." He poked me with the gun again. "Get moving."

I put my foot on the first step and reached for a handhold on the slippery rock. There wasn't one. I groped around and found a tiny niche, barely the width of my small fingernail, and used it to pull myself up. Everybody tells you not to look down. The key to climbing is don't look down. Apparently seeing the distance between yourself and the ground plants the idea in your mind that you're going to fall. In my case it didn't matter, since I'd already assumed gulls would very soon be picking my shattered remains off the rocks at the base of the cliff. I put my foot on the second stair and groped for another handhold that wasn't there. "Isn't there an easier way to do this? Couldn't we just drive up to his house?"

"And get arrested?" Seeker said. "Keep climbing."

I hugged the rocks, moving slowly and carefully upward, exquisitely careful with where I put my hands and feet. I'd trained for this sort of thing, but that was wartime and these were skills I'd no real need to use since. It wasn't a pleasant experience, that climb. It was more like inching up an endless ladder with half the rungs missing while wondering at which precise moment I'd slip and plunge to my death. Near the top, the stairs were wider and someone had carved actual handholds in the rocks on either side. I crawled the last three or four feet, then collapsed flat on my back on a broad, grassy spot that would be perfect for a picnic, if you fancied gazing into the abyss. My heart was pounding so hard it practically rattled my teeth, and my hands were slick with sweat.

"See?" Seeker hauled himself up until he was sitting beside me. "It's not so difficult. A little bit of exercise."

"You are a sadistic son of a bitch," I panted.

He stood and poked the tip of his shoe into my ribs. "Get going. He doesn't like to be kept waiting."

I struggled to my feet and took up my usual position in front of Seeker. It was as dark as a soda jerk's future, but I had no illusions. I knew if I tried to run, Seeker would shoot me, and I suspected he'd have no trouble hitting the target. The sound of the surf receded as we moved farther inland, away from the sea. A series of small lights had been strung between the trees, offering illumination as well as direction.

The beach house, Seeker assured me, was just a little farther. He led me through the trees and up to a broad, flat-roofed house built in the ultramodern style, with large windows and glass block panels set at either side of a wide rear door. It was the house I'd seen from the beach, below. With the Luger pressing firmly against my lower back, he shoved me ahead of him. "Knock on the door—two short and two long." And, when I didn't immediately comply, he said, "Do it." The Luger punched a fresh bruise into the flesh just above my kidneys.

I did as he asked, and we waited. After a moment or two, the door swung open, and a tall, fat man stood there, examining us with the keen eyes of a potato.

"Where's Luis?" Seeker pushed past the man at the door, dragging me after him. The inside of the house was furnished in the usual beach-cottage style, with low chairs and sofas set close to the floor and a stone fireplace, massive and grotesque. The large windows reached from floor to ceiling and in daylight must have provided a spectacular view. Just now they revealed the dark shapes of trees and the darker night sky beyond.

"Here you are at last." A man came toward us from the back of the house. He was young, slender, and looked deceptively fragile. I recognized him immediately—the festival-goer who'd given me the marigold, back in Ixtagapa at the Day of the Dead festival... the man who'd broken into and ransacked my house. He came toward me and took hold of both my hands, smiling as if we were long-lost brethren. "So good to see you again, amigo. You look very well, I must say—for a dead man."

Chapter Seventeen

"*LOS MUERTOS vivientes*," I murmured.

He laughed, like a man enjoying a private joke, and released my hands. "I believe it was the left arm," he said. "Closer to the heart, no?" He gestured that I should take off my shirt. "I'd hate to tear such fine silk, but I will if I have to." A gun appeared in his hand, a Luger like the one Seeker carried. What was it with thugs and German guns? "Take it off."

My heart pounded in my chest, and my face was suddenly suffused with heat. I unbuttoned my shirt and let it drop onto the floor behind me. "Shall I do the rest while I'm at it, or is that enough for now?" The first thing the Gestapo had done that day was strip me naked and leave me standing in the cold for what seemed like hours. Indoors, yes, but it was winter, and they stood me on a wet stone floor until I couldn't feel my legs. They hadn't even bothered questioning me. It was intended to humiliate me, to begin the long process of tearing me down, dismantling the human part of me. It worked to an astonishing degree.

"Just the shirt, Mr. Leonard."

I did as he said. The one Seeker had called Luis came to where I was and took hold of my left wrist. "You will please excuse me," he said. "It is my business." He turned my arm so the palm was facing outward and leaned in to peer at the small wound made by Papa Loi, the teethmarks. "Yes." He straightened and nodded. "*Exactamente como él dijo que sería.*" He said something to Seeker and the other man, a handful of Spanish. "*Escribe esto.* Write this down. Two curves and a line."

"I told you it was him," Seeker said. He smiled at me. "You have been very helpful to us, Mr. Leonard. I cannot express how much I appreciate it."

"Can I put my shirt back on?" I was polite merely out of habit. I was under no illusions they would let me go.

"Of course." Seeker bent and retrieved it from the floor, then handed it to me. "Quickly, now."

I buttoned my shirt and waited while they conferred among themselves in Spanish. Perhaps they were trying to decide what to do with me. "What does it mean?" I asked. "Two curves and a line. What is it?"

Seeker grinned, a flash of white teeth in his tanned face. "We are cultured gentlemen, every one of us." He waved a hand negligently in the direction of the other men. "We have an interest in American art. When a piece we like comes on the market, we buy it."

"You're art dealers." Said aloud, it was even more ridiculous. "You expect me to believe that."

Seeker moved to put his arm around my shoulders. "But only for certain types of art." He tugged me forward, walking me toward a large Everton Price abstract hanging on the opposite wall. It was about five feet high and perhaps twelve feet wide, an absolutely massive unframed canvas mounted on stretcher bars. It depicted two squares—one red and the other yellow—set against a smeared green background. In the top right-hand corner, three colored blobs fought amongst themselves, no doubt egged on by the two squares. "We have a friend who buys for us, mostly in South America, and ships the paintings here. In return, we are only too happy to select some other pieces and send them to him. It is a mutually agreeable situation."

"How does he know which paintings to send?" I had the ridiculous idea that I might save myself if I could keep him talking. "He would have to know your personal tastes, wouldn't he?"

Luis laughed. "In that, Señor Leonard, we are of startlingly similar tastes, so it is easy for him, and for us. We try to choose the work of unheralded artists when we can."

Of course. Customs officials wouldn't look twice at a piece done by an unknown artist, especially if it looked like something a child might do. "How magnanimous of you," I muttered.

Seeker gestured toward the Price painting. "In order to fully appreciate the work, one must examine it at close proximity." The arm around my shoulder moved, became an elbow in my back, and I was standing with my nose practically pressed against the canvas. It didn't look any better at this distance. "Our friend marks his choices, so we will know that the canvases he chooses to send are the correct ones." He leaned against me, the heat of him burning into my back, and suddenly he was whispering. "If you turn the canvas and examine the reverse side, you will see something to interest you."

I did as he said, but saw nothing of any particular import. The canvas appeared to have been expertly stretched over bars that were quite a bit wider than usual, creating a broad margin of canvas perhaps four or five inches wide. The whole of it was held in place with industrial staples. It wasn't a bad job. "I don't see anything."

Seeker's breath blew warm against the back of my neck. "You aren't really looking."

I was beginning to get irritated with this whole routine. If they'd brought me here to kill me, then why not go ahead and kill me? Was I supposed to be the evening's entertainment? Was that what this was all about? Maybe they'd humiliate me a bit, then drop me over the cliff, and some unsuspecting tourist would find my shattered carcass lying on the sand, with nothing to identify me except the strange marks on the inside of my arm: two curves and a line.

That's when I saw it. There, on the lower right-hand corner of the canvas, a crude representation in blurred pencil: two curves and a line. I suddenly knew why Seeker had sought me out in Mexico: because I could be useful to him.

THEY GAVE me a cigarette and a chair to sit on, while they bickered amongst themselves in rapid-fire Spanish. The night wore on, and at times I dozed—or thought I did, drifting for a while in some other reality. My mind chased itself in circles, trying to figure out what the scar on my arm had to do with imported artwork, but it was like trying to decipher something written in an unfamiliar language. At first I wondered whether the bite marks Papa Loi had left were accidental, or if he'd had his molars filed that way on purpose. Weren't there people in the world who did that? Strange tribes in their sheltered mountain enclaves, or the jungles of the Amazon—they did it, shaped their teeth deliberately so a bite would leave a reminder, an indelible mark. Wasn't it a rite of passage somewhere? Had he marked me as a message to others? Maybe Seeker had sought me out in Mexico as a wealthy American who'd be amenable to the transport of illegal substances. Maybe it helped that I was a drunk. I was less likely to ask questions that way. Apparently I made a remarkably good fall guy.

I drowsed in the chair, drifting, wondering idly when I'd last had a full night's sleep. Seeker and the others seemed to talk for a very long time, in Spanish too rapid for me to follow. Now and then an argument broke out, and the men around the table waved their arms and shouted; twice I thought they'd come to blows. I'd no doubt I was the subject of their disagreement. The fact that they were shouting didn't auger well for my future.

"Wake up." Someone kicked the bottom of my shoe, hard. The tremor traveled up my leg and into my pelvis.

"I am awake," I said. Apparently this wasn't good enough. Rough hands grabbed my arms and hauled me onto my feet. The two goons who'd forced me up the cliff, frog-marched me to the door and into the backseat of a car hidden by some bushes at the side of the house. "Where are we going?" I asked. I didn't have the energy to be flip with them, and if I tried to crack a joke, I was sure I'd break down crying.

Nobody answered me. The car pulled onto a secondary road that joined a state road and from there, the highway north. We drove for a long time, perhaps even as long as an hour, during which the silence in the car was absolute. Eventually we left the lights and civilization of LA behind in favor of the semiarid scrublands that ran beside the highway. An idea was growing in my head, the same idea everybody gets when they're sitting in the backseat: *What would happen if I jumped out?*

We were just then driving through a relatively uninhabited area, but I knew that wouldn't last. Before too much time had passed, we'd be into the smaller cities lying to the north of LA, the populated areas where concealment would be next to impossible. On impulse I asked, "Where are we going?" but nobody replied. They were probably heading toward the desert, where they'd take me out of the car, shoot me in the head, and drive off again. Death Valley, perhaps, if one preferred a poetic touch. The only trouble with the desert was its lack of concealment. Even if I were able to escape my captors by leaping from the car, there was nowhere to hide… no convenient stand of timber or roadside culvert where I could wait until they lost interest and drove away.

I didn't really think that would happen. People like Seeker and Luis—experienced people, men who'd killed a time or two before— weren't likely to drop me by the side of the road and simply drive off. They'd make sure to walk me far enough into the desert to prevent me from ever getting back. If this were summer, the heat would definitely finish me off before too long… but it was winter, so the odds that I would die that way were low. No, they would have to leave me somewhere far enough from civilization that I would never get back, and seal the deal with a bullet in my head.

"HEY LUIS." Seeker tapped the driver on the shoulder. "Pull over."

Luis half turned. "Now? We're in the middle of nowhere."

"I need to take a piss. Now pull over."

The car whined to a reluctant stop on the shoulder of the road. Seeker moved to get out. "You come with me." He gestured at me with the Luger in his hand. I wondered how he'd manage to piss, holding it. I fervently hoped he'd shoot his dick off. "In case you're wondering, it's loaded."

"I wasn't wondering."

We moved off into the sagebrush and creosote, perhaps ten feet from the road. An occasional car passed by, but that was about it. The sky was dark blue and full of stars, and I thought abstractly how it might be nice to spend a night out here with Ed, watching the sky until the sun came up.

Fat chance of that now.

Seeker was talented; he held the gun on me with one hand while undoing his pants with the other. "Too bad about Layton, huh?"

"What about him?"

"You were a friend of his." He pissed unashamedly and took his time shaking everything dry. "Close buddies, I heard."

"Not really. I met him once."

He closed his flies one-handed. "He is a magnetic creature. For many people, once is enough."

"There's something I don't understand," I said. "Why did you have to show Luis my arm? I don't have anything to do with—"

"You were an experiment," he said. "We considered expanding our trade route into other areas, places where tourists go when they want to relax and have a good time. There are many untapped markets... and your need to disappear provided a unique opportunity to test things, to see if we might export our product unmolested. Most Americans, they travel to Tijuana or Mexico City and no farther. You went all the way to Ixtagapa. In Ixtagapa, there are many people who have never tried our product."

"So he didn't really need to bite my arm." This annoyed me more than it should. "There are other ways to administer the drugs."

Seeker turned back toward the highway. "Of course. Marking you was a test signal, you might say. We sent you back with a small amount of cocaine concealed in the clothing I gave you. The marks allowed us to identify you to our friends back here."

It all fit together. "Was that why your... goons invaded my apartment? They were looking for cocaine?"

He tutted. "Don't call them goons. Luis's feelings will be hurt." He waved the Luger at me. "Come on. I'd rather not stand here all night."

"What?" I could see the car from where I was standing, the interior light on and the passenger side door open, spilling an uncertain illumination onto the empty ground. "We're going back to the car... aren't we?"

"If a tree falls in the desert...." Laughter. "Does anybody care?" The barrel of the Luger dug into my back. "Sorry about this, Tony. Start walking."

"I'm not in the mood for a stroll, actually... and it's cold out here." I wrapped my arms around my torso in a vain attempt to warm myself. Who knew the desert was so bloody cold at night?

"This is not a request, Señor Leonard." Seeker, standing behind me, grabbed a handful of my shirt and twisted it around his fist until the collar pulled tight against my throat. "I have no problem killing you. In fact, your death signals the conclusion of a certain piece of business you and I started in Mexico." He laughed almost noiselessly. "Linton Stirling requested that I assist you with your... transition." The Luger jabbed me in the kidneys. "From life to death, you understand. But I am a businessman. I saw an opportunity, and a way to signal to my associates that conditions were right to begin our new venture."

"So you double-crossed the old man."

I thought about the bizarre Price abstract with its wide folds of canvas and the strange markings, two curves and a line. "You're smuggling cocaine. In the paintings. That's why you mark them, to identify them to your Mexican suppliers."

"Not just Mexico. The whole of South America, and honestly, the very best product comes from Colombia, as I'm sure you know." He dug his fingertips into my shoulder. "The initial cocaine extract is very pure, very pure indeed. Undiluted, it can kill. It often does."

I stumbled over some hidden obstacle in the dark and nearly fell. Seeker grabbed my shirt and yanked me upright. "So you're using art to smuggle drugs. It's hardly original." The wide folds of canvas on the back of the Everton Price painting must have been purpose-made to conceal a shipment of cocaine. Hide one or two such altered artworks in a shipment and gamble on not getting caught. You receive the cocaine. Your South American partner receives cash—or heroin, or narcotics, or whatever it is he wants. It's so childishly simple that it borders on the absurd. "So what happened to Allan Layton?"

"He outlived his usefulness," Seeker said. "As you have also."

People say you relive your entire life in those last few seconds before you die. I didn't. I stood there and waited for him to shoot me. I wasn't disappointed.

The first one slammed into my left shoulder, driving me to my knees. The desert rose up toward me, pulling me down, and my body suddenly weighed a thousand pounds. I put my hands down to catch myself, and something punched a hole in the soft flesh of my side. My legs got tired. I lay down on the ground. *Now he'll shoot me in the head, and that's the end of that*, I thought. The stars were very bright above me, each one picked out of the coal-dark sky like an individual diamond. It would be daylight in a few hours, and elsewhere, people would be waking up, rousing themselves from the soft cocoon of sleep.

Footsteps crunched near my head, and I could smell sweat and gun grease. A form roughly the shape of a man loomed over me, blotting out the stars. "Say good night, Tony."

I couldn't resist. "Good night, Tony." A gunshot sounded close to my head, and the muzzle flash blinded me.

Good night, Tony.

Chapter Eighteen

THE SUN was trying to burn a hole in the top of my head. Clearly, it hated me and wanted me to suffer the torments of the damned. The palms of my hands were abraded and bleeding, and I'd scrubbed the knees out of my trousers, but I knew if I could only reach the highway (which was clearly a mirage), I could die in peace.

I stumbled up out of the sagebrush and creosote bushes, my clothes stuck to my body with blood. I knew by touch that the last bullet fired had ricocheted off a nearby rock, grazing my head. It was a bloody wound, but not deep or serious—it still throbbed like nobody's business. Another scar to add to my collection. The wound in my shoulder was remarkably shallow, a clean through-and-through hole approximately the size of a pencil eraser. It bled almost as much as the head wound. The slug in my side was the worst of the three, since it had entered the thick muscle covering the ribs and lodged deep in the tissues, affecting my gait considerably. I estimated it had taken me the rest of the night to drag myself to the highway, in the hope that I might flag down a passing car with sympathetic passengers who'd get me to a hospital. I was ferociously thirsty and sun-blind, moving on fear and instinct, and if I didn't get to the road, I knew I would probably die here. It wasn't an appealing thought.

I sat on the hard shoulder for a while, wishing I had a newspaper or a drink. I wanted to drink an ice-cold gimlet while sitting in the sun with Ed, maybe at some decadent Mexican resort… although the way I was going, I'd probably never get there. Some things in life you're better off not wanting in the first place.

I had nobody to blame for the way things had turned out, nobody but myself. If I'd kept to my own patch of grass and minded my own business… if I hadn't gone to Janet's guesthouse that night, if I hadn't found her bloodied, beaten corpse… if I had done a thousand things differently….

The sun rose while I sat there by the roadside, and the traffic picked up. Farm trucks passed by on their way to market, and sleek yellow school buses rushed toward their destinations. I waved at various automobiles as they went by, but failed to attract the attention of anyone. Doubtless they saw my torn and bloodied clothing and decided I was merely another drunk—a little out of his jurisdiction, it was true—looking for a free ride. I thought about trying to walk somewhere, perhaps to a service station or a store, but I discarded that idea quickly. Dragging myself to the road with bullet holes in me had been hellish enough, and I doubted I had the strength to stand, let alone walk. This wasn't doing my illness any good either. I'd end up in full flare—if I lived long enough.

It was beginning to get warm with the sun shining full on me, and I had nothing to drink. *Horst tells me you were licking moisture from the ceiling.* I knew my thirst would grow incrementally as time passed and the sun rose higher in the sky. At first it would seem bearable, and I would pretend the deprivation didn't bother me in the slightest, but my confidence wouldn't last. There would come a time when a drink of water seemed to be everything a man could want in the world, when my tongue would swell in my mouth and I'd contemplate slitting my own wrists because my blood was liquid and I could drink it. Men went off their heads that way, and some of them begged, promised anything, in exchange for a sip of water, or a sip of anything, really.

I wondered idly how much blood I'd lost. By that time I was lying on the ground, having exhausted my precarious strength and being unable to determine what I should do next. If I died, would someone come along and pick me up? Would they identify me by the cards in my wallet and send for my next of kin? Only I had no next of kin unless you counted Deborah, and I tried never to include my sister-in-law in anything if I could avoid it. I'd be taken to the city morgue and put into cold storage and eventually I'd have a no-frills funeral, courtesy of the taxpayers of California. *Thus passes Anthony Leonard, also known as A.J. Dunbar, also known as a drunken, silly bastard.* Self-pity, then, in the midst of everything—one vice I'd tried not to indulge. God knows I'd tried out all the others. But the sun was warm on my face and on my back, and perhaps it wouldn't hurt to lie down for a little while and rest.

"TONY." SOMEONE'S hand was on my back, gentle. Someone's voice was at my ear. "Tony, the ambulance is here. We're taking you to the hospital. Can you hear me?"

I knew that voice, or thought I did. I'd heard that voice before. "Who are you?" The sun was shining at his back, casting most of his face into shadow, but I knew him. I'd know that face anywhere. What I couldn't figure out was how he'd come to be here, now.

I must have mumbled something, because he said, "I didn't mean for it to take so long. I meant to be back before now. I'm sorry." He looked... what was the word? Contrite. It was an entirely new look for him.

"So who are you today?" I asked. "Bad guy or good guy?" I seemed to perceive things in an entirely new light, the entire world impossibly sharp around the edges. It was probably the blood loss.

The ambulance attendants lifted me into the vehicle, and he climbed in, sat beside me, and held my hand. "Rest now," he said. "You are safe. I'll explain it all to you, I promise."

I slept, and woke later in a clean white bed with a clean white bandage on my head and more clean white bandages on my hands. The wounds in my shoulder and my side throbbed with a catchy beat. You could almost dance to it.

Rafael Sequerra was asleep in a chair beside my bed, his tie loose and his shirtsleeves rolled up. He needed a shave.

"What the bloody hell is wrong with you?" I said. "You shot me."

He roused himself and rubbed his eyes. "I can explain about that." He did, but in such a rambling, roundabout fashion that it made very little sense.

"Let me see if I can skim the cream here," I said. "You really are an FBI agent masquerading as a drug dealer. You'd been put on to something that was stirring among Linton Stirling's bunch—"

"It was a cocktail party," he said. "At the Stirling house. It's amazing what people will say in front of the hired help. I make a very good waiter." He raised an eyebrow. "Your wife was there. She was complaining about you, saying how it was ridiculous for you to spend your time helping drunks when you ought to have been by her side. She wasn't wanting for company, though, if you catch my meaning." He rubbed his hands over his face and yawned. "There were two of them. Muscle Beach types, and practically cavemen, but she was having a good time."

"I'll bet." I tried to roll my eyes, but my head hurt too much.

"Problem was, they were known enforcers for the mob—at least, the branch of it that spilled over from Vegas. The mob's been digging itself in deeper out there." He shrugged. "Just ask Bugsy Siegel... he's dead. Bad example. So Janet's old man—who, you probably know, had investments in certain clandestine areas—decided to put the kibosh on things. She was making him look bad. Anybody who saw her that night would put two and two together and come to the conclusion that she was passing out party favors to the mob."

I eased myself up in the bed. "What about Donald Whitlaw?"

"The veteran?" He shook his head. "He wasn't even in the city when Janet died. I had a couple of our guys chase it down. Whitlaw confessed, but it was just hot air. He's what they call a 'wet brain' alcoholic, Wernicke-Korsakoff syndrome. The DA released him a couple days ago. I say 'released,' but what I mean is he was transported out of the state. He was responsible for killing those two men on Fromsett Street, though. They won't get a conviction. His lawyer will plead insanity." Seeker reached for his jacket, which he'd slung over a nearby chair, and fumbled in the pockets for his cigarettes.

"You can't smoke in here," I said. "Hospital rules."

He frowned, swore briefly in Spanish, and put the package away.

"So...." Something occurred to me. "If Whitlaw didn't kill Janet... who did?" The wound in my head throbbed in time to the beat of my heart. "And why the hell did you shoot me?"

He looked ashamed of himself—briefly. "The plan was to eliminate you, to take you out into the desert and leave your body for the vultures. I told them I would do it. If one of the others did it, you'd be dead for real." He looked away, seemingly unable to meet my gaze. "No way was I going to kill you. But it had to look genuine."

I remembered how the third bullet had ricocheted off a nearby rock, merely grazing me. He'd done it deliberately, fouled the shot on purpose to avoid hurting me. I was momentarily suffused with a wild, foolish gratitude that brought tears to my eyes.

"Which is why you are in the hospital being treated for superficial gunshot wounds and dehydration instead of... otherwise." He drew a deep breath and stood. "I found this card in your wallet." He passed me the small square of printed card that I could practically recite from memory. "They gave you some medicine for it." He studied me for a moment. "It's bad, isn't it? I mean, you can get really sick from it. It sounds pretty nasty."

"It is nasty," I said. "The medical boys call it systemic lupus erythematosus, or lupus. In the old days, they thought it caused lycanthropy and vampirism. If you had it, you were under a curse. The medicine helps, but it's not a cure. I'm not supposed to sit out in the sun."

He raised an eyebrow. "And you ran away to Mexico?"

"It made perfect sense at the time."

"Geez, I'm sorry," he said. "Now I feel *really* bad about shooting you."

I laughed, until it started to hurt. "Seeker, I'm glad you're one of the good guys."

I WAS sleeping off what felt like the worst hangover of my life when the door to my room creaked open and quiet footsteps crossed to the bed. A familiar voice spoke my name very softly, and I opened my eyes.

"Welcome back to the land of the living," Ed said.

I reached for him and pulled him down to me, and I held him for a long, long time. When I drew back, my face was wet, but he didn't say anything. He even pretended interest in his wristwatch while I wiped away the tears.

"What the hell were you thinking?" As nice as the embrace had been, he was as pissed off as I'd ever seen him. "I understand your interest in finding whoever killed Janet. I really do." He turned away, arms crossed over his chest. "And I understand you wanting to get to the bottom of this business with Allan Layton." He turned back to me. "What I don't understand is your headlong rush to get yourself killed. You're completely insensitive to your own safety. You take off on a whim, drive up north for hours to find some private hospital for drunks. You nearly get yourself killed out in the goddamn desert. You're out at all hours, roaming around the streets, alone and unarmed. Do you have a death wish, Tony? Is that it?"

I couldn't look at him, and then I did, and his face was red and wet, and his fists were clenched. He held himself rigid, his muscles clenched like he was warding off blows. He'd only just gotten out of the hospital himself, after that horrific attack. They'd beaten him unconscious. He'd nearly died, and all because he was working a case that wasn't even his to begin with, that had been ably handled by the police. He was working it because it was important to me. He'd nearly gotten himself killed, and it was all because of me.

"I'm sorry," I whispered. It wasn't nearly enough, and I knew it. "I found her. If I'd never seen her body, then maybe...." My chest was tight. "I had to find out who did it. I had to make some sense out of it."

"You were still married to her when...."

"She was an absolute bitch," I said. It didn't feel right, speaking ill of the dead, but it was the truth. "But she was still my wife. I had to find out."

He didn't say anything. He leaned down and kissed me. It was better than a drink of water.

TWO NIGHTS later I signed myself out of the hospital and went back to my house. I hadn't been away that long, but it felt like months had passed. I unlocked the front door, went in, and laid my bag down by the telephone table. Maybe it was the result of my injuries, or maybe it was something else, but I felt inestimably weary. Getting shot does that to you. I kicked my shoes off, left them by the front door, and went through to my bedroom on stocking feet. It wasn't a particularly warm night, but I wanted to open windows. I wanted to open a lot of windows. I wanted a drink.

At the hospital they'd discarded my torn, bloodied clothes and supplied me with some clean cast-offs from the lost-and-found room: a plaid shirt in worn, almost transparent flannel, and a pair of faded dungarees with the cuffs turned up. I resembled an extra from some film about the Dust Bowl. As soon as I could, I shucked the clothes and took a long, hot shower, letting the water wash away the residual dust and grime of the desert and the hospital smell of strong disinfectant. It felt good to shave in my own bathroom, in front of my own mirror, with the cool night breeze drifting through the open window.

I toweled myself dry and dressed in a pair of loose linen trousers and a polo shirt left over from the wardrobe Janet had selected for me shortly after our marriage. Then I went through to the living room, took the bottle of gin out of the liquor cabinet, and got the cocktail shaker down from the cupboard. The gin wasn't Tanqueray—I'd run out several days before—and there was no rosemary anywhere in sight, but I didn't care. I'd escaped almost certain death by the putative skin of my teeth, but mostly because Rafael Sequerra put himself in danger and came back for me. It was worth celebrating, as far as I was concerned.

I'd just decanted the first ice-cold gimlet into a martini glass when a light rapping sounded at my front door. It was Ed. He was smiling, and he had a bottle of Tanqueray. He came into my arms, mindful of my wounds and very gently.

"I was hoping you'd come by." I handed him the glass.

"Thanks." He took a sip and grunted softly in pleasure. "You mix a damn fine drink, Tony." He laid the glass down on the kitchen counter, took my face in his hands, and kissed me, long and hard and deep. He did it again, until my knees were weak and I'd forgotten all about the drink.

"Bedroom," I murmured. "Now." A plume of hot, demanding lust rose inside of me. I wanted him, and the darkness, and the naked sheets beneath our bodies for as long as it took to burn away bad memories.

I didn't bother to turn on the light. I grabbed the front of his shirt and pulled him toward me as I lay—very carefully—on the bed. My wounds gave an unpleasant twinge, but I didn't care. My knees spread, I held him on top of me, our bodies tangled in an aching knot of love and desire. His heart beat strongly against my chest, his skin warm through his clothes.

"Come here," I said.

"I am here." He nuzzled my neck, tongue leaving trails of heat on my skin.

"Closer. You're not close enough." I tugged at the hem of his shirt. "Too many clothes."

He sat up, his body crouched above mine, and pulled his shirt off over his head. The muscles of his chest and shoulders stood out in the faint ambient light from the window. He sat back on his heels, straddling me so our cocks rubbed together, and the sensation was more than I could bear, a pleasure so strong and cogent that I nearly came then and there.

I kissed him very tenderly but also with a great deal of heat, and his tongue slipped into my opened mouth, tasting me, warming the way for him. My lust had gathered in my belly, where it throbbed with an insistent, drumbeat pulse that made the muscles of my thighs shudder. He stripped me efficiently and in a concentrated silence, and now and then, his gaze would seek mine in the almost-darkness, trepidation in his blue eyes. He touched my scars reverently—the newer ones, the gunshot wounds, but also the older scars left there by the war—and kissed my shoulders gently.

"It's all right," I told him. "I won't break."

"I don't want to hurt you."

"You won't." And we kissed for what seemed like a long time until we were at that place where words vanish, were replaced with mere syllables of longing. The muscles of his back stretched and flexed under my hands, his strong, unbroken body moving over me, into me. His breath became ragged as we surged together over and over, and there was no sound in the room except the lush syncopation of flesh on flesh. Our faces were close together, and we held our mouths so we were touching but not kissing, breathing into each other. I was close... so close that I knew it would take next to nothing to tip me over the edge, but I didn't want to come, not yet. I wanted to watch him come instead.

He arched his back and groaned, shuddering as he spent himself inside me. His face went slack with the force of his completion, his arms trembling to hold himself up. He settled down on top of me, muscles twitching and juddering, panting hard against my shoulder. My swollen cock was trapped between our bodies, and I rolled my hips forward, rutting against him until the moving ridge of pleasure ploughed into me, pushing me over the edge.

Ed started to move away from me, and I stopped him. "No, stay there." I liked holding the weight of him on top of me as my body jerked and shuddered through the aftershocks, and tiny points of pleasure bloomed like pinpoint stars. I held on to him, my arms around him, our mated skins warm and lovely in the dark.

SPECIAL AGENT Rafael Sequerra's office was located on the fourteenth floor of the federal building in downtown Los Angeles. His single window faced south, but there was nothing of any importance to see except traffic and the faint outlines of buildings in the distance.

I found Seeker sitting behind his desk, frowning over an open file folder containing what looked like crime scene photographs. I knocked at his door and stepped into his office. "The girl told me to come in."

He glanced up, smiled, and came out from behind the desk. He was wearing a dark blue suit, with a blinding white shirt and a whimsical tie in a pattern of flowers over repeating stripes. His shoes were polished to a blinding sheen; he looked happy and relaxed. "Tony." He shook my hand, holding on for a long time, our palms pressed together. "You look great."

"Thank you."

He tilted his head and gazed at me, still smiling. "I think Ed Malory's been good for you."

"I think so too."

He offered me a chair and I took it; he went back behind his desk and sat. I didn't quite know how to say what I'd come to say, and every time I tried, my throat closed together and I couldn't speak. "Seeker.... Agent

Sequerra... you didn't have to come back for me. I know it. You probably compromised your investigation and put yourself in ten kinds of danger." I fumbled for a cigarette and lit it, just to give my hands something to do. "You saved my life, but I expect you already know that." I drew hard on the cigarette, then blew smoke. I couldn't think of anything else to say. When I raised my head to look at him, he was smiling. "Thank you."

He looked away, pretending interest in the folder in front of him. I got the feeling he wasn't thanked very often for the work he did—for the missing loved ones he found, for the murders he prevented, for the crime syndicates whose members he put behind bars.

We were quiet for a moment—perhaps neither of us knew what to say—and then someone tapped on the door, and a girl entered with a laden tray. "Agent Sequerra, your coffee." She was young and pretty, in a bottle-green suit and high-heeled pumps. The morning sun struck sparks off her auburn hair. She was the very model of a modern secretary, but then her gaze landed on Sequerra, and a certain tautness in her face fell away. She saw nothing but him, and the image of him filled her soft brown eyes. "If there's anything else at all, just say the word." She smiled at me, then slipped out the door.

"Lovely girl," I said. She was very much the type we saw during the war, the beautiful WACs and canteen girls who did the really important jobs and who managed to keep their heads through all sorts of horrendous circumstances.

"My secretary," Sequerra said.

"Your secretary is in love with you," I observed.

He actually blushed. "She is engaged to be married."

"That what she tells you?"

"You have probably deduced that I'm not the... marrying kind." His gaze shifted away from mine, a signal that this portion of our conversation was at an end. "And there are worse things in the world than loneliness." He pronounced the last word very quietly, and it was like a stab in the gut. I thought about saying something but knew anything I'd say would sound trite and condescending. He pretended busyness with some papers. "I meant also to tell you about Layton."

I took the cup of coffee Seeker passed me and nodded my thanks. "Allan Layton?"

He'd been working with Hank McAvity, he told me, and between them, they'd managed to piece together some things about Layton's involvement in the case. The way he said "the case" made me think there was more to this than Seeker was saying. "I would have called you down here in a day or so, to go over matters with you. Since you were still married to... the decedent at the time of her death, you should know the full details." I knew Layton and Ramirez were friends and business partners, that Layton had acted in blue films—or whatever they were calling them nowadays. I still had the smut films Layton's ex-wife had given me. I'd yet to look at them. I knew Layton and Ramirez had expanded their illegal empire, hiring others to make movies for them, people like Lydia Race, who'd needed a favor once and got it. She'd been paying for it till the day she died.

"Ramirez was responsible for the ice pick job on Layton," Seeker said. "His boys had their orders. Near as we can tell, they were following you because Ramirez figured you knew a lot more than you were telling. You've got a talent for sticking your nose in." He shrugged. "Anyway, Layton's business was on the rocks—"

"—which meant Ramirez's business was also on the rocks."

Seeker nodded. "Seems he'd been investing unwisely—Layton, I mean." He reached for the coffee pot and refilled both our cups. "And behind Ramirez's back. He'd started making his own films, directing them, producing them, whatever. It was a stupid thing to do. He knew what Ramirez was like. He figured he could undercut his partner and Ramirez wouldn't notice."

"Maybe it's true what they say about blonds," I muttered.

Seeker, cup to his lips, shook his head. "He wasn't dumb, just careless. He took too much for granted. Like I said, his business was on the skids, losing lots of money. He needed an investor, somebody with enough cash to drag him back into the black again. He was willing to do anything—or anyone—to get it."

I'd been just about to reply when the door opened and the pretty secretary ushered Hank McAvity into Seeker's office. He grunted a greeting, nodded brusquely at me, and sat. He had something to say, and he said it the way he usually did, with no unnecessary preamble. "You probably figured it out already"—I wasn't sure if he was talking to Sequerra alone or to the both of us—"Allan Layton was the man in the guesthouse the night Janet died."

My heartbeat thudded in my chest, paused, then walloped me in the ribs. The aberrant beat was almost painful; it scared me. "Did he kill her?"

McAvity nodded. "Yes. I'm sorry." He looked over at Seeker, who nodded almost imperceptibly. "Ice pick to the base of the skull. He was good at it. She wouldn't have felt a thing."

How ironic that Layton had died the same way. I didn't say this out loud. There wasn't any need to say it.

"He was... servicing her," Seeker said quietly, "in exchange for her investment in his businesses. We think she got tired of the arrangement, or perhaps tired of him. She closed up her bank book, wouldn't give him any more money."

"Layton took exception to it," McAvity said. "There was an altercation, during which he held her down and...." He shrugged. "But he didn't do that to her face. That was done postmortem, by someone who'd discovered the body and who had no real love for the decedent. It's violent and disturbing, but...." He lifted his shoulders again and let them drop. "Interference with a corpse probably isn't an indictable offense in this case. The DA isn't interested in pursuing it, so that's that."

I felt cold all over, even though it was warm in Seeker's office. "What about the postcards? I was getting postcards in the mail."

Seeker and McAvity exchanged a look. "There's no real solid evidence, but everything points to it being your sister-in-law," McAvity said.

Deborah.

"Maybe she was jealous," Seeker offered, "or this was another way to get back at her sister. I understand there was significant animosity between the two women."

"Yes. Deborah hated Janet." *You'd have to hate someone to beat their dead face to a pulp with a high-heeled shoe.*

"There's one more thing." McAvity reached into his pocket and brought out a small brown envelope, the kind the jeweler gives you back your rings in. "Personal effects." I reached out, and he dropped it into my palm. It was Janet's wedding ring, the one I'd given her. "We recovered that at the scene," McAvity said. "I'm sorry."

"So am I." I stood slowly. I felt like a tired old man. There were a hundred things I sensed I ought to say, but I couldn't say any of them. Whatever I said would sound like so much pointless noise. "Thank you." I shook their hands and turned to go. All I wanted just then was to go back to my place and close the door. All I wanted was to wake up and have the world be right for a change.

Epilogue

I WENT back to Janet's house a few days later. It was deserted; nobody was around. I half expected to see Deborah, but she'd gone away, leaving the servants to maintain the Stirling mansion in her absence. There was no sign of life behind its windows, and no one appeared to question me, to demand to know what I was doing there or why I'd come.

Deborah's things were just as she'd left them. There was a book on the bedside table, turned onto its open face; I closed it and set it back on the shelf. Of course, the bed wasn't the same bed in which Janet had died, and the clothes in the closet weren't Janet's clothes, no more than the liquor bottles lined up on the windowsill were waiting to make a toast to her return. She wouldn't be coming back. She was a page someone had already turned. She was gone forever.

I'd told Ed Malory I married Janet for her money, and in a way, it was true. But it wasn't just her money that drew me to her. I'd spent a year in solitary confinement, tortured to tell the Gestapo things I never knew to begin with. I was emptied of all human feeling, a hollow man looking out upon the world with eyes too long accustomed to the darkness. Janet was full of life, a lovely, laughing girl who didn't care what anybody thought or said, who looked forward eagerly to the next drink, the next party, the next exhilarating fuck in the dew-damp morning grass. She was my resurrection. Yes, I loved her.

I took the wedding ring—Janet's ring—out and laid it in the center of the table. Considering the shape and tenure of our marriage, I ought to have left it in the bed, but no matter. Nothing's permanent. It only ever seems that way. We are carried along on a current we can neither perceive nor affect, with no way of knowing where we'll end up.

I left the little cottage just the way I'd found it and pulled the door closed behind me when I left. I wanted to do something more for her, but I couldn't think of anything. I suppose one wants a certain deal of sentiment before indulging in such gestures, or some vestige of fellow-feeling. *We're practically family*, Deborah once said. *It's the least I could do.*

185

I never saw Deborah again. I never saw any of them again, except Pepe, who walked past me on a downtown sidewalk and turned to look back at me and nod. I never saw anyone again—except for Ed. I haven't found a way to say good-bye to him, not yet. If fate deigns to smile on me, I hope I never will.

J.S. COOK was born and raised on the island of Newfoundland. She holds a B.A. and an M.A. in English Language and Literature and a B.Ed in post-secondary education. She makes her home in St. John's, Newfoundland, with her husband Paul, and Lola, her spoiled rotten dogter.

J.S. Cook also writes as JoAnne Soper-Cook.

Twitter: https://twitter.com/jsopercook
Website: joannesopercook.net

Gangster Nino Moretti's world is a series of contrasts between extreme wealth and abject poverty, an unstable existence punctuated by booze and bullets. For Nino, the gangster lifestyle is even more dangerous because he is a finnochio—a gay man—in a position of absolute power at the head of his own criminal organization.

When Nino rescues beautiful mob accountant Stanley Zadwadzki from a violent assault at the hands of sadistic rival gangster Big Frank O'Hara, both Nino and Stanley become hunted men. Stanley places himself under Nino's protection as Nino's accountant and unofficial companion. As a warning, Frank murders Nino's office boy. In a quest for revenge, Nino tracks Frank to Little Italy, where the resulting confrontation forces him to shoot a bystander to protect Stanley. With a gang war looming, Nino must set aside his feelings and concentrate on asserting his superiority over Big Frank—or lose everything he holds most dear.

www.dreamspinnerpress.com

In the frigid winter of 1891, with the nation still reeling from the Barings bank crisis, Inspector Philemon Raft returns from an involuntary sabbatical, tasked with solving the kidnapping of highly placed peer Alice Dewberry. Thrust into a sordid underworld where the upper classes indulge in disreputable overseas investments designed to fatten their pocketbooks, Raft finds himself at loose ends without his companion, Constable Freddie Crook. Far from offering their help, the ton use every asset at their disposal to keep Raft from discovering the truth about hapless kidnap victim Alice Dewberry—who may not even exist.

Soon Raft discovers that his old nemesis, the workhouse master John Gallant, has returned to London. Gallant doesn't say what he wants—but he *knows* enough to ruin Raft's career and even his life. Raft tries to solve the case with his usual strange insight, but there are other, darker forces at work. This is a frightened London: the London of Whitechapel, of Jack the Ripper, the London of poverty, dirt and despair, where a right turn down the wrong alley could earn Raft a swift trip to the morgue.

www.dreamspinnerpress.com

When former Indiana farm boy William Henry Rider goes on a bank robbing spree in Benedict Fouts's corner of Depression Era Illinois, it's up to Ben to bring him in. But Rider is no ordinary criminal. Famed for robberies that happen in the blink of an eye, Rider becomes a folk hero who steals from the rich and burns the mortgage papers of poor farmers teetering on the edge of financial ruin.

Intrigued to learn that Fouts has been assigned to his case, Rider approaches him in a darkened movie house with a unique proposition: "We'll have ourselves a game of Cops and Robbers. I'll run, and you catch me. The clock starts right now, Ben."

Ben knows he's the only one who can stop the Bureau from murdering Rider, but he's soon struggling with another reason to chase the enigmatic fugitive.

www.dreamspinnerpress.com

In 1942, Pearl Harbor has been bombed and the war is very much in evidence, but it would seem to have little to do with Frank Boyle, a respected Bronx born insurance investigator. He's a man who can keep secrets, and no one suspects that his boyhood friend—local mob boss Nicky Brooks—is his lover. When Brooks accidentally kills Frank's younger brother in a shootout, Frank must choose between his affair with Nicky and revenge for his brother's life.

After Frank betrays Nicky, police detective Sam Lipinski, a Bronx native who has long carried a torch for Frank, makes a move against the mob and lands squarely in the way of Nicky's plans. Sam smuggles Frank out of New York to keep him safe, and sets him up him in a small northeastern city. But there, a messy insurance investigation involving the Roarkes, who may or may not have killed their own mother for the insurance payout, places him in danger again. Dodging bullets, shady characters, and fallout from the war, Sam and Frank will need far more than luck on their side if they're ever to see a loving future.

www.dreamspinnerpress.com

Jacob van Willingen arrives in a remote Romanian village aiming for a short visit. A member of the highly secretive Society for Psychical Research, Jacob has been charged with exterminating Caleb Donnithorn—but the society's intelligence about the reclusive nobleman is less than complete. As he studies his target, Van Willingen is drawn to Donnithorn, enthralled with the nobleman's alluring brides, three of society's most luminous geniuses gathered from the corners of Europe to create a fantastical machine: a resurrection engine that can capture a human soul at the moment of death.

Caleb Donnithorn represents everything that is evil in the world, but there is more to him than is initially apparent. What he knows about van Willingen is a truth so shocking it will shake the young scholar's world to its very foundations. Cast out from his friends and his beloved Society of Psychical Research, Jacob van Willingen will jettison everything he holds dear to remain with one whose love commands the highest price of all.

www.dreamspinnerpress.com

The Second World War touches Newfoundland in unprecedented ways, throwing spies and patriots together inside Jack Stolyes's Heartache Café.

Heartache Café

American expatriate Jack Stoyles embarks on a self-imposed exile to St. John's, Newfoundland. With good reason, Jack calls his place "Heartache Café." He's content—until Samual Halim walks into his life.

When a constable goes missing, Jack finds himself caught between a manipulative woman, a corrupt cop, and a sabotaged work site.

Valley of the Dead

When Egyptian diplomat Samuel Halim enters Jack's Heartache Café, Jack's life changes forever. Then Sam disappears along with the code key to decipher a Nazi radio command that will set Rommel's troops in motion, leaving Jack with nothing but a fragmented phone call.

In the teeming heat of Cairo—a city rife with romance, secrets, sex, and danger, where no one is who he seems and violent death waits around every shadowed corner—it's up to Jack to find the new love of his life and deliver the code that will change the course of history. But as Sam's secrets come to light, there's more at stake than the tenuous relationship forming between the two men.

www.dreamspinnerpress.com

The year is 1934, and disgraced federal agent Nathan Devereaux is escorting convicted felon John Banks to visit his dying mother. Banks is despondent, miserably ill with a heavy cold, and unenthusiastic about traveling by plane. It isn't a responsibility Devereaux wants, but something about the prisoner's plight resonates with him.

Devereaux charters a plane to Wisconsin, hoping to get there before Banks's mother breathes her last. But a routine journey swiftly turns into a sojourn in hell when a violent winter storm forces the plane miles off course, and Banks's seemingly bad cold turns out to be diphtheria.

Stranded many miles from the destination, Devereaux must find a way to save Banks's life without compromising the mission. Like Banks, Devereaux has secrets of his own, and the scope and purpose of his mission don't quite square with the stories he tells. Making matters worse, he is the only one standing between Banks and certain death, but even a federal agent can do only so much—especially an agent with blood on his hands.

www.dreamspinnerpress.com

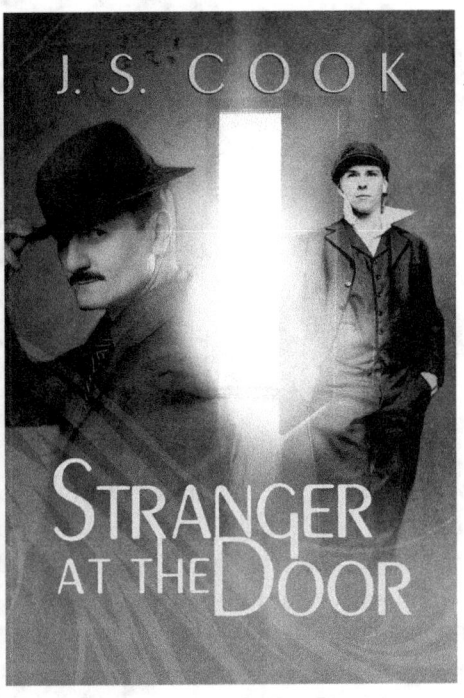

www.dreamspinnerpress.com

JoAnne Soper-Cook

The Eye of Heaven

When Dante di Salvatore, former prostitute and adopted son of one of Florence's reigning nobles, is bitten by the ancient vampire goddess Lillith, his mortal life is over. Once enslaved by the vampire queen's malign influence, Dante allies himself with Rouen, a young man of dazzling beauty and great influence who is enamored with Dante. But they cannot truly be together unless Dante changes Rouen into a vampire, and for Rouen, accepting the dark gift may ultimately cost him his immortal soul. Soon the great city of Florence will be taken to account for her sins as the streets are scourged of everything the fanatical preacher Serenola deems unnatural.

But many silent, mostly unseen creatures of the night are coming together from the disparate corners of the earth to do battle one last time against Serenola, evil disguised as good. What Dante does not realize is that he, above all others, holds the key to not only his own salvation, but the preservation of all of vampire kind—and perhaps even the human race.

www.dreamspinnerpress.com

Veteran police chief Eli Gallagher doesn't ask for much, but he does insist that his officers uphold the "serve" part of "serve and protect." Conscientious young Deputy Stan Leach takes Eli's motto to heart, maintaining a high standard of personal accountability.

When Eli's long-distance boyfriend, Gilbert Nees, telephones from Philadelphia, Eli thinks he intends to further cement their relationship. Unfortunately, Gilbert's news is anything but good. But Eli doesn't have time to wallow, because a violent act results in murder in the small town of Morristown, Mississippi.

But as Eli and Stan uncover evidence, their personal lives begin to unravel. Stan, working closely with Chief Gallagher, grows increasingly attached to Eli and learns what it really means to be an advocate of justice.

www.dreamspinnerpress.com

FOR **MORE** OF THE **BEST GAY ROMANCE**

DREAMSPINNER PRESS
dreamspinnerpress.com

www.ingramcontent.com/pod-product-compliance
Lightning Source LLC
Chambersburg PA
CBHW070122260626
47160CB00004B/1587